Those Who Come the Last

by
Nicki Huntsman Smith

NHS Marketing, LLC

A Shadow

by Henry Wadsworth Longfellow

by Henry Wadsworth Longfellow
I said unto myself, if I were dead,
What would befall these children? What would be
Their fate, who now are looking up to me
For help and furtherance? Their lives, I said,
Would be a volume wherein I have read
But the first chapters, and no longer see
To read the rest of their dear history,
So full of beauty and so full of dread.
Be comforted; the world is very old,
And generations pass, as they have passed,
A troop of shadows moving with the sun.
Thousands of times has the old tale been told;
The world belongs to those who come the last,
They will find hope and strength as we have done.

Prologue

Not for the first time during the past few days, Ray tried to open his eyelids only to discover a lack of bodily cooperation. His fingers felt wooden against his face, but he finally managed to quell the eyelid mutiny and rubbed them open. The light filtering in through a tent flap carried the golden quality of late afternoon sunshine. He wondered if Lizzy had captured him again and dosed him with midazolam. This mental fog felt different, though, not like the tranquilizing effect of midazolam nor the mood-elevating ketamine.

How long had he been out? Where was he? Then a more urgent question: were the children safe?

He sat up too quickly, making his head swim. Waiting for the dizziness to pass, he assessed himself and his surroundings. He was nestled in a sleeping bag of excellent quality; the North Face logo embroidered on the side confirmed it. He could see his breath, which meant it was cold outside, but he felt warm and comfortable inside the bag. The Klymit tent, also top-notch, was the type nature enthusiasts carried on their backs when they scaled mountains. Not that he personally would know anything about that kind of adventuring, but he recognized good brands when he saw them.

He rubbed his eyes again, grasping for memories prior to blacking out: the children running toward the giant Ponderosa pine; him heading in the opposite direction to lure Lizzy away; a sudden slamming sensation in his chest that knocked him to the ground; pain so intense it couldn't be registered on any known scale; weakness so disabling he could barely lift a hand to write the warehouse security code on Serena Jo's notepad.

Her beautiful eyes had filled with sadness as they gazed down at him. The painful pounding in his chest——his excruciating heartbeat——had thumped slower and slower and slower. His final thought had been: Lizzy killed me.

Then blackness.

He remembered being certain he was dying.

With the same wooden fingers, he reached inside his shirt, wincing in anticipation of the injury he would discover there. Had Serena Jo sewn him up? Was she giving him antibiotics to stave off the inevitable infection? His fingertips encountered nothing unusual, just the skin of his chest and a smattering of hair. No gaping hole nor injury of any kind.

How was that possible?

"You're wondering how you could have been shot in the chest and survived with no aftereffects. It's a valid question."

The woman who spoke stood in the tent's opening. Because of her small stature, she didn't have to stoop much. If Serena Jo were a foot shorter and twenty years older, she'd look just like that.

"Close your mouth or you'll draw flies," the woman said, not unkindly.

She stepped inside, squatted beside him, and pressed a protein bar into his hand. "You'll need your strength back now that you've returned to the land of the living." The voice was low, like that of a cigarette smoker but without the gravelly quality. Ropy muscles visible beneath the fitted tee indicated more than a nodding acquaintance with fitness. The tanned, lined face spoke of a life lived outdoors squinting at the sun.

"Are you Serena Jo's mother?" he managed, his voice a croaking frog.

"That I am," the woman replied. "I'm Hannah." The small hand she extended was veined but otherwise youthful for a woman in her ... fifties? Sixties? There was strength in her handshake. "And who are you?"

"I'm Ray. What happened? Are the children all right? And Serena Jo?"

"First things first. How do you feel? Any pain?"

Ray shook his head. "No, which makes no sense. I remember getting shot in the chest. How long have I been unconscious? The wound has healed, so I must have been unconscious for weeks."

The woman's smile was that of a mischievous child, and her laughter sounded like baritone wind chimes on a blustery day. "Forty-eight hours. And you weren't unconscious. You were dead."

Chapter 1

Fergus

"Escape isn't likely. This cell is quite secure. Ray saw to it," Fergus said.

Serena Jo ignored him, continuing to scrutinize every inch of the space where the two had been confined an hour ago.

He sighed. "You really should sit. You'll lose more blood if you keep pacing like a lion in the zoo."

The woman spun to face him. She was almost a foot taller than him, which presented opportunities for covert glances at the full bosom. Those opportunities weren't acted upon, though. He saw her now not as a desirable woman to be wooed and courted, but as a protective mama bear. Her progeny were two of the most precocious children Fergus had ever encountered. A more evolved man might be able to reconcile the two——desirable woman and mama bear——but he couldn't. He would ponder that self-revelation at a later date, assuming they somehow escaped Lizzy's former prison.

"You don't know them like I do," she said. Pain hovered around the edge of her voice, but Fergus knew the stoic Serena Jo would never succumb to anything so trifling as a through-and-through gunshot wound. Thankfully, it hadn't struck an artery in her thigh.

"Who? The Murdocks?"

"Yes. They're the scourge of Appalachia. They don't even have a holler to call their own. Their junk cars and gap-toothed offspring took over the little town of Idlewild like … like … philistine kudzu."

Fergus laughed. "That's the first time I've ever heard those two words used together. Willadean didn't get her writing chops from you, did she?"

"Clearly not," Serena Jo huffed, sitting on the narrow bunk bed. She glanced down at the gray blanket, still neatly tucked around the edges and corners. "So that woman lived in here?"

Fergus nodded. He'd lost no sleep over the death of Lizzy. "For eight months, according to Ray."

"She was sneaking out through that small opening? It doesn't seem possible." She stared at the hatch in the mesh fence through which Ray, the former government warehouse administrator, would pass Lizzy food, water, and other necessities. In this place, she'd lived like an inmate in an upscale federal prison.

"It's called hypermobility. She was able to pop her shoulders out of their sockets and wriggle through. Ray said she'd been filing her fingernails down to a long point to manage the thumbscrews on the other side."

Serena Jo arched an eyebrow. "Clever."

"Indeed. But as far as I know, neither of us were gifted with the hypermobility genetic mutation."

"There must be some other way out of here."

"Perhaps, but first you need to rest. That wound is still seeping. We need to change the bandage again."

The Murdocks had tossed a first-aid kit into the cell before re-securing the steel mesh to the cinder block walls using a motorized screwdriver and construction screws. There wasn't a pointy fingernail in the world that could budge them.

"At least there aren't security cameras in here," Fergus continued as he tended to her injury.

A soft hiss escaped her lips. "Our people will come looking for me," she said between clenched teeth.

"Yes, at some point. But these thugs are quite safe here. It would be like the siege of a medieval castle, but their castle is supplied with everything its residents need to live for decades."

"Don't underestimate the Whitakers."

"No worries there. But don't underestimate this facility nor the cretins who have captured us."

"They won't stay here for long. These guys are grunts. They're here on a reconnaissance mission for their leader."

"I thought the toothless man with the fast reflexes was the leader?"

"No, that's Gavyn. He's the nephew. I have no idea who the others are."

"The nephew of whom?"

"Silas Murdock, the patriarch of their clan."

"A clan that can't claim a holler doesn't sound like much of a clan."

"It is if the clan runs all the local crime business. Before the pandemic, I mean. Nothing good has come from that family for generations. They wanted no part of Roosevelt's New Deal back in the Depression. Lots of Appalachian folks viewed the federal work programs as government handouts. They allowed their children to literally starve to death rather than take government jobs. That so-called pride prevented their families from thriving through honest work, so they eventually turned to dishonest work. The modern Murdocks operated one of the largest meth operations in Tennessee. They also dabbled in auto theft, prostitution, and of course moonshine. But everyone does that."

"There's no stigma attached to the production of illegal alcohol?"

"Not in these parts. Their corn whiskey is actually the most impressive thing about the Murdocks. Whitakers have been bartering our Old Smoky for their White Lightning for a hundred years. It's the only business that takes place between the two families, and only because of the moonshine pact during Prohibition. Not even the occasional murder of family members on both sides and the subsequent revenge affected that pact. We take our moonshine seriously in these parts."

"Fascinating," Fergus replied. He found something else fascinating: as Serena Jo talked about local lore and family history, a Southern accent crept in. While away at university, she must have worked hard to lose that accent, along with other tell-tale indications of an uncultured, rural upbringing.

There's a reason folks don't leave the holler.

The meaning behind Skeeter's cryptic words had been divulged at least. Whitaker holler residents were aware of their genetic gifts to a point, even if they didn't fully understand them. He wondered now which of Skeeter's abilities had been transferred to his offspring. Unlike her father, Serena Jo felt pain, but did the magic gene mitigate it?

Fergus hoped so. He had a feeling the Murdocks' intentions toward their captive were far from painless or honorable.

"We need to find a way out," she said, apropos of his thoughts just then. "I can survive rape and beatings, but if they take me back to Idlewild, Silas will use me as leverage. That's what I would do," she added with no trace of anger. She might have been a plumber recommending copper pipe over PVC.

"Leverage for what?"

"Leverage to steal the fruits of our collective, generational labor: our land, our farms, our livestock, even our heritage. Other than the occasional moonshine barter, Whitakers have nothing to do with Murdocks. They're not worthy of our notice. I know that sounds elitist, but it's an Appalachian thing. A hierarchy has existed for as long as both clans have lived here."

"I've heard of these anthropological circumstances before. This Whitaker-Murdock business, is it similar to the Hatfields and McCoys of yore?"

Her laugh was bitter and short-lived. "Our feud makes the famous one look like a community theater production."

It was Fergus's turn to laugh. "Nice simile. Maybe Willadean did get some of her writing talent from her mama. Promise you'll sit still for a bit so that wound stops bleeding. We'll put our heads together. Surely two intelligent people like us can figure a way out of this."

She nodded. "I'll make an assets and liabilities list." She withdrew a small spiral notepad from her jeans pocket and flipped through the well-worn pages toward the back, pausing on one containing a bloody smudge and hen-scratched numbers. She glanced up at Fergus with a guarded expression, then moved on to a blank page.

Imprinting that bloody smudge and writing those numbers were Ray's final acts before he died. Fergus could have used his new friend's help right then. Nobody on the planet possessed more knowledge of the warehouse than Ray.

It was a damn shame Lizzy had killed him.

Chapter 2

Ray

"What do you mean, I was dead?" Ray said to the small woman squatting beside him inside the tent. She looked kind yet mysterious, and somehow otherworldly, like a benevolent stranger in a fantasy novel. He wondered if her ears were pointed beneath the silver-streaked flaxen hair.

"Wasn't I clear?" came the pert reply. "Dead means dead, as in no longer alive."

"So I actually died for a few seconds? Did you do CPR?"

"You died for more than a few seconds. And no, I did not perform CPR. At least not in the traditional sense." There was that mischievous grin again. She looked less like Serena Jo when she grinned like that and more like an elf.

"Then what happened?" he said, trying to scramble out of the sleeping bag. It suddenly felt like a down-filled casket.

Hannah didn't answer right away. Instead, she helped with the bag's zipper so he could free himself.

"It's complicated," she said finally. "Perhaps you should just accept that you're healthy and be grateful for it. We have our work cut out for us. You're the one from the storage complex, right?"

"How did you know that?"

"I've been watching the goings-on around here. From a distance," she added.

"Aren't you from the village? I met Serena Jo's father, but I didn't see you there."

"That's because I don't live there. Never have. But I always kept tabs on my family. Even more so lately. There are far fewer people in the world these days, but they're more dangerous than ever."

"I'm completely confused," Ray said.

"Sadly, you'll probably remain in that state for the foreseeable future. As I said, we have our work cut out for us. My daughter and the red-haired man have been taken prisoner by the Murdocks. They're inside your warehouse. I intend to get my daughter out of there." The tone in the low voice shouldn't have sounded menacing coming from such a harmless looking individual. But it did.

"Who are the Murdocks?"

"They're cockroaches in human form. Now, see if you can stand. Sometimes the legs are a bit wobbly *after*."

If he hadn't been so distressed by thoughts of Serena Jo in the hands of human cockroaches, he would have pressed the issue of his miraculous recovery. Instead, he stood awkwardly in the confined space. His legs didn't feel wobbly at all.

"I feel great," he said in amazement. He knew that would likely change when he left the tent. In preparation for the inevitable agoraphobia tsunami, he took several cleansing breaths as he reached for the flap.

"Glad to hear it." She looked at him quizzically. "Why are you breathing like that?"

"It's a coping technique. Agoraphobia," he replied. Then he stepped outside. Instead of the usual crush of anxiety, he felt invigorated. Fresh mountain air filled his lungs, driving out the stench of his own body odor. The expanse of blue sky didn't overwhelm him like it usually did. Instead, it seemed to welcome him to the Great Outdoors. *Well, hello there, Ray! Glad you could finally make it!*

"Any anxiety now?" Hannah said.

"I feel fantastic. It's crazy. I've never been able to manage this without drugs, life-threatening distractions, or a hell of a lot of cleansing breaths."

"Interesting. Perhaps being dead gave you a new lease on life."

"I think I was just *mostly dead*," he said with a manic giggle. "I've never felt this happy being outside before. I think I could scale a mountain or surf the giant waves off Kauai!"

"Let's dial it down a notch, big guy," Hannah said with an indulgent smile. "Euphoria also happens sometimes, too. You'll level out soon, though. In the meantime, let's get the gear packed up and head out. We'll strategize while we walk. I want that warehouse of yours in my crosshairs before noon."

As they walked, Ray noticed a number of small details. "My clothes are clean. Did you run them to the laundromat before raising me from the dead?" He grinned.

"For someone whose pants reeked of days-old urine, you're a bit cocky. But yes, I washed them. And I put them back on you, including your underwear. I got tired of holding my nose."

Blood rushed to his cheeks, but the embarrassment only lasted a moment. He felt too damn good to be mortified about having a stranger change his underwear. "I was held captive by a serial killer named Lizzy for a couple of days. She dosed me with drugs to keep me manageable. I guess the old bladder had a mind of its own. Then, miraculously, your daughter rescued me and took me to the village. I met her father there. Your husband? Ex-husband?"

"We were never married," she said lightly. "Then what happened?"

Ray stumbled across a vine but caught himself before he fell. He remembered what Lizzy had said about walking in the forest: *try to lift your feet rather than shuffling like a hobo.* Interesting that he remembered such minor details after being dead. He smiled to himself.

"Earth to Ray," Hannah said sternly.

"Sorry. Skeeter and I took the two boys, Cricket and Harlan ... oh, that would be your grandson ..."

She nodded, gesturing for him to continue.

"We needed the boys to direct us to Lizzy's house. I managed to get Willadean out of there. She and Fergus, the red-haired man, had also been captured by Lizzy and were being held in a house. Much nicer than the one she chained me up in."

"This Lizzy got around."

"As I was trying to get the children home, I got shot. Your daughter found me. I gave her the code to the warehouse. That's all I remember. I wish I knew what happened to the kids. And to Lizzy."

Hannah moved through the forest like the point man on a black ops mission. "The Lizzy woman is dead. Euel killed her——Skeeter is what you call him. The children are fine. But as I mentioned, the red-haired man and my daughter are now the captives of the Murdocks inside your warehouse. That's why I need your help."

"So you didn't resuscitate me just to be nice?" Another giggle escaped him.

"I hope this manic phase passes soon," she muttered.

"Okay, sorry. I can't help that I feel better than I've ever felt in my life. And I'm more than happy to help. Even though I haven't known Fergus long, I consider him a friend. We had an instant connection. Even more so with your daughter. Do you know that you created the most beautiful creature on the planet?"

"Oh, you have it bad, don't you? I suppose that could prove useful. You'll be as motivated as me to get her out of there. So, tell me about this place of yours. I've studied it from the outside, of course, but have no idea about the interior. And more importantly, besides the main rolling metal door, what other ways are there of getting inside?"

"There are additional doors, but none we could use. I welded them closed the first month I was there. Some of the TV networks were still broadcasting then, and I watched the riots and looting. It was terrifying. The government had placed the second largest Strategic National Stockpile in the nation, whose contents were worth half a billion dollars, in a low-profile, low-traffic setting."

"An interesting decision on their part. Please continue."

"When I saw all the violence and craziness happening in the world, I secured the place as if it contained all the gold of Fort Knox. But what it actually contains is more valuable than gold these days. I thought I could use its contents to help the survivors once things settled down. And things did settle down, but not in the way I'd hoped. People just died. Nobody came knocking on my door, other than Fergus. He happened to pick the one door that wasn't welded shut. It weighs more than a ton, by the way. Nobody's getting in there without the security code or a bulldozer."

"We can't go through that door anyway because the Murdocks will post a guard there," Hannah replied promptly. She seemed to process the details almost faster than he could relay them.

"There are two other options for gaining entry: the rooftop hatch and the HVAC ductwork."

"Tell me about them both." Gone was the mischievous grin, replaced by the stern facade of a leader preparing for battle.

The notion of going into battle took the edge off Ray's euphoria. He began to describe the layout of the warehouse in tedious detail. By the time they arrived at the edge of the forest surrounding the self-storage complex, his giddiness had vanished completely.

"We'll stay here for a while," Hannah said, shrugging out of her backpack. "I know it's chilly, but we can't have a fire. We'll wait until the witching hour to make our move."

She'd opted for the HVAC ductwork as their point of entry since the Murdocks might be using the rooftop for surveillance. They might even now have rifles sighted along the tree line where he and Hannah crouched. *It's what I would do,* she'd said.

"When is the witching hour?" he whispered. Hannah had mentioned that the Murdocks could have sentries positioned in the forest, so stealth was critical.

After witnessing her daughter being taken captive, she'd returned to the only person who could help gain access to the facility. The one who was still recovering from being dead. He shook his head in bemusement every time he thought about it. Did the woman have mental problems? Was she delusional? She had certainly done something to aid in his fast recovery. Or perhaps more time had passed than the forty-eight hours she claimed; that would explain why he couldn't feel any evidence of an injury. Or maybe the wound hadn't been as bad as he'd thought. His memory of that excruciating heartbeat was already fading.

"Between 3 and 4 a.m.," Hannah said, interrupting his thoughts. "That's the time of night when most people are likely to be asleep and when tired watch guards struggle to stay awake."

"Makes sense. So we have a long wait."

"Yes. And we need to be a bit less conspicuous," she said, eyeing him critically. "Wriggle inside these bushes as best you can."

"But they're covered in thorns."

"That's why no one will look for us there. Come on. Don't be a sissy."

A few minutes and a dozen scrapes later, they were camouflaged within some underbrush. Hannah settled into a resting squat. It looked like an odd position to a lifelong desk jockey like him, but it made sense when he thought about it. The cold earth wasn't soaking into her backside, but rather into the rubber lug soles of her boots. From that squat, she could spring into action faster than if she were sitting.

She saw him studying her. "Outside of yoga classes, Westerners lost this archetypal posture long ago, along with others. Squatting is perceived as undignified in this part of the world, yet it's actually an incredibly healthy way to rest. And also to relieve oneself more naturally," she added with a wink. "If those joints don't regularly stretch past ninety degrees, the body says, *So I don't need to produce synovial fluid in there. Gotcha.* Synovial fluid is the lubricant that provides nutrition to the cartilage, and if you don't use it, you lose it. That's one of the reasons why babies are so bendy. Their synovial fluid hasn't dried up like it has in older people who haven't maintained a healthy musculoskeletal system."

"You're an interesting lady," Ray said, momentarily captivated by the mother of the woman he was currently crushing hard for.

"I've been around the block a few times," she said, reaching into her pack to retrieve more of the protein bars, a pair of infrared field glasses, and a handgun. The MK 23's silencer came next.

"I can see that." Ray was familiar with the handgun's history. Navy SEALS carried the .45 caliber weapon for their personal-use firearm. "I assume you're ex-military?"

"No, but I can see how you might think that. I've had an unusual life, Ray, and I know how to handle myself around dangerous types. Dangerous types are something I happen to be an expert on."

"Really? How so?"

Instead of answering, she placed a finger against her lips, then deftly attached the suppressor to its weapon. She stretched out on the forest floor and wriggled back halfway through the thorny vines. Maybe it was because of her small size, but the briars didn't seem to snatch at her like they did him. Only her lower half was visible now as she lay flat on the ground.

The next moment he watched her body jerk twice and heard the sharp *pop-pop* of what sounded like a cap pistol. She began squirming backward a few seconds later, autumnal leaves entwined now in the silver-blond hair. The grin was back. She looked more than ever like some fae woodland creature.

"Got him," she said.

"Was it a bear?" he said, remembering his recent brush with one while chained inside a disintegrating cabin.

"Not a bear. A man."

"What? You just killed someone?"

"Yep. It was Eli. No loss there."

"You knew him?"

The small woman shrugged, then placed the weapon on top of her pack while tearing open a protein bar with her teeth. "I'm starving. You should eat, too. They don't taste great, but they contain three hundred calories and forty carbs. You need to fuel up for tonight."

He reached for the package wordlessly. Hannah had just killed a man and the next moment was gobbling food with no qualms. What did that say about her?

"You're wondering how I can be so callous."

He nodded, chewing on stale peanuts, waxy chocolate, and protein paste.

"Let me ask you something. If a scorpion were crawling along the floor toward your toddler, would you hesitate before crushing it under our shoe?"

"Of course not. But a scorpion isn't a human being."

"No. Scorpions are actually superior creatures to the Murdocks."

"You called them cockroaches in human form. Why?"

"Because they're the lowest of the low. They have no sense of honor or integrity, they breed like malevolent rabbits, and everything they touch turns to shit."

"Those are strong words. You must have some history with them."

"You could say that." She stood, brushing crumbs from her thigh and picked up the field glasses. An arboreal arrow-window presented an opportunity to keep tabs on the warehouse while hidden in the brush. "Nothing happening," she said, lowering the binoculars. "I need to know exactly what items you have in that warehouse. What all was compiled at the Strategic National Stockpile in Trenton, Tennessee?"

He pushed aside his concerns about the woman and recited from the mental spreadsheets he could still effortlessly summon.

Hannah frowned when he finished. "This is not good news. Actually, it's the worst news possible. The Murdocks won't give all that up without a fight, especially the drugs. And they will use my daughter as leverage to ensure the Whitakers don't fight. They believe no one knows that Serena Jo has been captured. In actuality, the one person who will unleash hell is a mere two hundred yards away from them."

"There's just the two of us, Hannah. How many Murdocks did you see go into the warehouse?"

"Six, but one of them was Eli, so that leaves five. Gavyn is heading up their group, which is good news. He's fast as a racer snake, but none too bright. I can handle him. Actually, I can handle all of them, but I need your help with the layout of the place. Otherwise, I'd do this myself and not risk an innocent life."

"So Eli wasn't innocent?"

Hannah gave him a thoughtful look. "You need to grasp what we're up against. And you need to know that I'm not the one to be worried about."

"It's not that I'm worried. It's just that I value human life. That's why I couldn't bring myself to … eliminate … Lizzy when I had the chance. She was a psychopathic serial killer, but who was I to decide she didn't have the right to live?"

"Who else is there to do it, then? Do you believe there's a god in heaven who points a finger from the clouds and zaps everyone who needs zapping?"

Ray laughed. "No. I'm not religious. The no-killing-humans thing is just personal ethics."

"Good for you. And I don't say that sarcastically. I'm glad that there are people like you. But I'm also glad there are people like me who don't mind getting their hands dirty while taking out the garbage."

A disturbing notion occurred to him. "You're a mercenary. Or maybe some kind of vigilante."

"I'm not fond of either of those words. I do what needs to be done, quietly, and without a lot of pearl-clutching or hand-wringing afterward."

"So tell me why Eli needed to be killed."

"Because he was a Murdock."

Ray sighed. "That's not a compelling argument. You can't tell me there's not one Murdock worthy of life."

"No I can't tell you that, because I know exactly one. You're looking at her."

"Oh," was all he could manage for a few moments while his mind reeled. "So these are your people?"

She frowned, turned her head, and spat on the ground. "No, they're not my people. I left Idlewild when I was seventeen and went over to Whitaker holler. Whitakers are the sworn enemy of the Murdocks. I stayed with Euel Whitaker long enough to get pregnant and have a child. I left the child with him because the last thing I wanted was to be tied down to a man or a place. But before any of that happened, I was forced to live in the hell hole of Idlewild, parenting myself when my drug-addict mother was too stoned to function, while barely being tolerated by a sociopathic father."

"Is Idlewild the Murdocks' holler?"

She snorted, giving him a scathing look. "No. The Murdocks don't have a holler. They took over Idlewild back when it was just a gas station, a Piggly Wiggly, and a stoplight at the intersection of Main and FM26. Think of the Murdocks as a rural crime syndicate. Their specialty during the last decade was methamphetamine. They're so ruthless, even the state police left them alone out of fear of retaliation. The Murdocks' other specialty was going after the children of anyone who crossed them."

"You paint a disturbing picture."

"It gets worse. Once I got my period, the only reason I wasn't raped by all the men over the age of twelve was because of the sociopathic father I mentioned. Silas Murdock is the clan's patriarch and also the devil incarnate, if you believe in that sort of thing. Disallowing the ritualistic rape was the only kindness he ever showed me. His minions do his bidding without hesitation. I didn't know Eli personally, but I know his father. Wyatt is Silas's most trusted lieutenant. You don't get to be a lieutenant if you have an ounce of compassion. You earn it by proving you can be more ruthless and savage than the next person."

"I see."

Her head tilted to one side. "I doubt that. But you will in the days to come. What we have to do tonight will spark the smoldering powder keg of hostility between the two clans. We'll be invoking open warfare. It can't be helped, though. We're getting my daughter out of there."

Ray pondered everything she'd said, letting the grisly details of her story soak in. "How many Murdocks are there in Idlewild?"

"Last time I checked, at least a hundred men and sixty women, not counting the breeders."

"Breeders?" he said. His stomach pitched suddenly, as if standing on a tempest-tossed boat.

"Yep. And it's as bad as it sounds. Some of the women are allowed to become soldiers if they're strong and tough enough. Back when there was heroin, the rest were kept strung-out so they wouldn't run away. These days there's no heroin, but there's nowhere for them to run to anyway. The men keep the breeders knocked up, creating new Murdock cockroaches to replace the ones who die off."

"Jesus."

"Told you they were bad. Do you see now why I didn't bat an eyelash when I squashed one just now?"

He nodded, swallowing hard. "So the Whitakers ... your daughter ... they know what's going on in Idlewild?"

"They know the Murdocks are the scourge of Appalachia, but they've never understood the depths of their depravity. I could never bring myself to tell Euel everything. And I didn't stay in the holler once Serena Jo was born. I knew I was leaving her in good hands. I also knew if Silas guessed she was mine, got on me by a Whitaker, there would be hell to pay."

"Surely you came to visit her and the grandchildren."

"I did, but not in the way you might think. I watched them grow up from afar. I'd check on them every now and then between projects, but I did it covertly. I'm good at covert," she smiled. "It was best for everyone that way."

Ray expected to see the pointed chin quiver or perhaps a sudden misty quality that would further enhance those captivating eyes. But neither happened. Hannah seemed content with her life choices and her place in the world. And while he couldn't grasp how a person could abandon her baby, it seemed somehow normal for Hannah to have done so. Not every woman who gives birth is meant to be a mother.

"I know what you're thinking, but Euel was by far a better mother than I ever would have been. He's very maternal."

"How did you know that's what I was thinking?"

She smiled. "It's written all over your face. You don't play much poker, do you, Ray?"

"I hate that game. Maybe it's because I never win. Something's bothering me, though. Something about the numbers. My government clearance allowed me access to the actual mortality rate of the pandemic—well over fifty percent, they said. Of course, it ended up being much higher than that. So how could so many Whitakers and so many Murdocks have survived?"

"That's the billion dollar question, isn't it? Think in terms of genetics rather than viruses or bacteria. I won't say more, though, because then you'd think I was crazier than you already do."

"Genetic engineering? That doesn't seem possible. We don't have that level of technology."

She gave him a wink instead of an answer.

Even though hours had passed since he'd awoken, Hannah's company had made the day pass quickly. Through the opening in the brush, he could see that the sun was a finger's width away from dipping behind the mountains.

"Now would be a good time for a power nap," she said. "You go first. I'll keep an eye on your warehouse."

Ray didn't think he'd be able to sleep, but once his head touched the ground, he was out within seconds.

When he awoke, full darkness was upon them.

Hannah's low voice came from a few feet away. "It's go-time, Ray. Put on your big boy panties."

Chapter 3

Willadean

"Pops, you know this isn't like her," Willa said to her grandfather. He'd been assigned babysitting duty for the night. She hated that word. Babies needed babysitting. Not two people who would be turning thirteen in a year.

"Don't you think I know that? Ain't nothing to be done until morning. Your mama can take care of herself."

"True. Mama's a badass."

Pops merely arched a silver eyebrow in response. He let her get away with the occasional naughty word, as long as it wasn't one of the really bad ones.

"If she's not home by morning, are we sending out a team?" By "team" she meant three or four Scouts. The highly trained members of that group resided at the top of Whitaker holler's hierarchy. She'd set her sights on becoming one as soon she met the minimum age requirement of sixteen. Four more years seemed like a lifetime from now.

"Reckon so. But I got a feeling she'll be home before then."

"Is it one of *those* feelings?" she said.

Pops merely lowered the one eyebrow, then raised the other. His eyebrow control always impressed her.

"Okay, don't tell me," she said.

"Hadn't planned to."

She was about to spout off with some tart retort when her gaze fell on his bandaged hand and its missing fingers. Lizzy had been a psychopathic serial killer before Pops put her down like a rabid dog, but "witch" worked just as well. Her grandfather was a fast healer, like most folks in the holler, but he couldn't grow back the fingers Lizzy had chopped off. He hadn't complained about those missing fingers even once.

"I'll cut you some slack because of your injuries."

"I appreciate that, Your Highness."

"At least don't make us go to bed at the usual time. I won't be able to sleep knowing Mama is out there in the woods, maybe in trouble. I wish she'd taken one of the Scouts instead of just Mister Fergus. He wasn't coming back with her, so she's all by herself."

"I know, but there was no changing her mind about it. She doesn't want anyone to know about that warehouse."

"But why? Mister Ray has candy and Pop-Tarts in there."

"'Cause there's a lotta other stuff in there too that woulda caused problems. Folks are doing just fine without candy and Pop-Tarts and such. Things are good here in the holler, and I say if it ain't broke, don't fix it."

"Ugh, cliché, Pops. So she wanted to keep it a secret, just like some of the stuff we brought in the U-Haul?"

"That's right."

Willa pondered the fairness of that decision. To the untrained observer, Serena Jo made decisions based entirely on what was best for the residents of Whitaker holler. But through careful observation these last two years, Willa learned that Mama not only loved to control every element of her world, she loved to control all the human beings within her orbit.

"Doesn't seem fair," Willa said. "Shouldn't folks get to vote on the warehouse business? Mister Ray gifted it to everyone, not just her."

Pops snorted. "What gave you the impression your Mama is runnin' a democracy?"

"As for the U-Haul, she brought all the stuff inside it. So that's different. But the treasure in Mister Ray's warehouse doesn't belong to her."

"We ain't gonna discuss this further. And if you're smart, which you are, you won't be bothering your mama about it neither. Now you two get on into bed." He gestured to Harlan who was standing in the darkened bedroom's doorway.

Willa frowned at her grandfather, which had no discernible effect other than a level-eyed stare, then spun on her bare heels, creating an invisible cyclone of annoyance scented by freshly washed pajamas. Even the nighttime enjoyment of laundry day felt disappointing at the moment. Normally, she loved lying in bed, breathing in the aroma of soapwort and cedar, but tonight she was too worried about——and irritated by——Mama.

Once she and Harlan were situated in two of the three beds which took up most of the room, she waited to see if Pops would fall asleep at the kitchen table. Sure enough, within a few minutes, gentle snores penetrated the bedroom's gloom. Old people could fall asleep mid-sentence. Pops claimed 'easy-sleeping' as his super power, which Willa found hilarious. Tonight, she was too distracted by the day's events to be amused.

"You gonna try to do your thing?" she whispered to her brother. She could barely make out his signed response in the dark:

Yes.

"I guess I'll just lay here awake all night while you go off on one of your little dream adventures." She didn't bother softening the jealous tone. She was still angry that Harlan had never mentioned his ability to astral travel, and even angrier that the talent had been denied her.

Harlan gave an odd little snort of laughter. Except for talking to Mister Fergus right after Cricket got shot by the witch, it was the only sound he ever made. He preferred to communicate his thoughts through sign language and drawings.

His fingers flew in the darkness, illuminated by a shaft of moonlight: *You have plenty of stuff you can do, Willa. Don't be jealous of this. Now be quiet and let me go to sleep. I don't even know if I can make it happen, but I aim to try.*

"Fine," she huffed.

Chapter 4

Harlan

When he awoke in the astral plane, Harlan couldn't tell where he was. A week ago, that might have worried him. But ever since Mister Fergus had explained how to always find his way back home, he was no longer concerned. Which was good, since he really needed to focus on finding Mama instead of worrying about getting lost and waking up somewhere other than in his own bed.

Mama's beacon wasn't as strong as Willa's, though. Yes, he could sense her when she was nearby in both the real world and the astral plane, but she didn't broadcast a glowing Batman-type signal in the night sky like Willa did. Willa would love the Batman metaphor. If he remembered it later, he would tell her about it. A huge weight had been lifted now that he could talk about his astral adventures. Maybe in the future, he would be more open about some of the other contents of his War Chest of Oddities.

Or maybe he wouldn't.

He frowned with his imagined face, buffeted by the chilly night air, and concentrated.

Ahhh ... there she was. Mama's beacon pinged softly at the edge of his inner compass. He pictured himself as the floating arrow on that compass now, made a note of the northwesterly direction of the ping, and altered course slightly to the left. Once he had done so, her signal began to grow stronger with every night-gray valley and starlit hill he soared above.

Time meant nothing in the astral plane. He might have been flying for minutes or hours. Suddenly, an opening in the thick forest canopy appeared. Nestled within it lay a sea of building-shaped shadows surrounded by street-shaped black voids.

Was this the source of the candy and Pop-Tarts?

The Shift confirmed.

He should probably begin thinking of the Shift in different terms now that he knew her name. Mister Fergus hadn't said much about Amelia after she'd helped him direct his enhanced langthal to heal Cricket's gunshot wound, and maybe that was for the best. It seemed more appropriate to attribute the Shift to a supernatural source rather than just a special human being living in Florida. The Shift always gave smart advice, whereas humans often made mistakes.

Harlan knew Mama was in that big building just beneath him, along with Mister Fergus. Both beacons pinged now. He didn't have to wait long for Mister Fergus to notice him.

Hello, Harlan. I hoped you might show up.

Hi, Mister Fergus. Is everything okay?

Definitely not. Ever hear of the Murdocks?

Yes. Whitakers trade moonshine with them every year.

That's what your mother just informed me. It seems they're not the nicest people. Five of them have captured us and are holding us in a cage inside a warehouse.

Oh no! You were just in the witch's cage not very long ago. You are having bad luck with cages.

(smiling) It would seem so. At any rate, you need to let your grandfather know what's happened. We need a rescue operation. I'll convey the details to you so the Scouts can plan it.

Is Mama okay?

Mister Fergus didn't answer immediately. Harlan's imagined stomach did a flip flop. Finally, a reply arrived.

She is okay, but she was shot in the leg. It is not a mortal injury, and I can confirm that it hasn't slowed her down in the least.

I wish I could talk to her, but her voice doesn't appear in my head like yours does.

Right, so you will just have to trust me for now. Our situation is rather dire, so I need you to return to your bed and let your grandfather know right away. I would contact him directly, but we haven't established a reliable telepathic pathway yet. His thoughts aren't coming through at the moment.

He's asleep. Maybe that has something to do with it.

Yes. Wait a minute, Harlan. Something is happening here ...

What? Is Mama still okay?

Seconds or hours passed before Mister Fergus finally responded.

I hear noises down the corridor. And gunfire. I think someone is using a silencer. I'm not sure what's happening, Harlan, but I need to concentrate. Go on back to the holler and tell your grandfather that our location is in the complex of the self-storage buildings near Tremont. He'll know where it is from your mother's maps. Tell him there are five armed Murdocks in the building.

Mister Ferguss please keep Mama safe!

Your Mama is quite capable of taking care of herself, but of course I'll do anything in my power to protect her. Goodbye for now.

The connection ended. Harlan found himself still hovering above the building. What was going on inside? A third signal pinged now, a new one that somehow felt familiar. He tried to reach out to it ... to zero in on it ... but a wall slammed down in his head.

That had never happened before. It almost felt as if someone ... perhaps a woman ... had closed her mind to him.

The Shift confirmed.

Harlan nodded his imagined head. Okay, he thought, time to go home and sound the alarm.

Chapter 5

Fergus

"What do you think is happening?" Serena Jo whispered, her hands pressed against the steel mesh wall of their prison cell.

Overhead lights illuminated nothing out of the ordinary down either direction of the cavernous corridor. But their range of vision was limited. Interspersed with the *pop-pop* sounds of suppressed gunfire, the occasional – and much louder – *BANG BANG BANGs* of a non-suppressed weapon echoed from the direction of Ray's sleeping quarters.

"I think we may be getting rescued," Fergus said. "Although I don't know how anyone from the village would have realized we were in trouble. At least not yet."

"You think my people are here? That seems unlikely. I gave orders when we left not to expect me for up to a day."

"Who else could it be? Besides the Murdocks of Idlewild, is there another warring clan you've yet to tell me about? The Hornswogglers of Padooka County?"

She flashed him a scathing look and stepped away from the mesh. "Whoever it is, get ready."

"Way ahead of you." He sat on the bunk bed and reached for one of his Doc Martens. After a precise squeeze, a blade sprung from below the leather toe-bed.

"You are so not a college professor," she said with a glance in his direction.

"Your daughter says the same thing."

"Why didn't you use that before they locked us in here?"

"An opportunity didn't present itself. As with baking the perfect soufflé or shepherding a woman toward a mind-blowing orgasm, timing is critical."

The noise of gunfire stopped suddenly, replaced by unnerving quiet.

What was happening out there? Who had prevailed? If not the Murdocks, would the victors prove even worse? Fergus understood the immeasurable value of the warehouse's contents. He had been hoping that information wouldn't become common knowledge.

The sound of footsteps squeaked from the end of the corridor; rubber-soled shoes produced an oddly familiar noise. Fergus recognized it now. He'd heard that exact squeak a few days earlier in this very building.

He was wondering whether one of the Murdocks had perhaps stolen a pair of Ray's shoes when Ray himself appeared on the other side of the steel mesh. He wore a huge grin. Dead men didn't grin like that.

Before Fergus could react, a second person appeared beside him. Fergus's inner radar blared like a tornado siren. The small woman standing beside a very much alive Ray smiled as well, gazing at Serena Jo. Other than the height difference, their physical similarities were unmistakable.

"Hello, my dear. I'm so glad to finally see you again in person. The last time we were together, I cradled you in my arms. You're even lovelier close up than you are from a distance. More importantly, I'm so proud of how you're running the holler. No man could do a better job."

Serena Jo's open, silent mouth conveyed her shock.

"What happened out there, Ray?" Fergus asked. "You can tell me how it is that you're alive later. Have the Murdocks been managed? There are six in total."

The small woman answered before Ray could. "There are six bodies now. You must be Fergus. I'm Hannah, Serena Jo's mother. She and I will have much to work through in the coming days. But for now, Ray, why don't you get started on those screws."

"Yes, ma'am," Ray said, still grinning like an idiot.

The loud whirring of the electric screwdriver prohibited conversation until the job was complete. Within moments, the prison wall clanged to the concrete floor.

Now that Fergus could clearly see both Ray and Hannah, he found himself at a loss for words. Thankfully, Serena Jo wasn't.

"You were dead the last time I saw you," she said to Ray. "Explain yourself. Then we'll move on to you." She gave Hannah a flinty look.

Hannah's bow managed to be indulgent and mocking at the same time.

"According to Hannah, I was dead. She performed some kind of resuscitation on me. The last thing I remember was lying on the ground looking up at you, Serena Jo. When I awoke afterward, Hannah had dragged me into a tent, nursed me back to life, and cleaned me up. Even washed my underwear." Ray winced at the embarrassing blunder. "Obviously, I wasn't really dead, but I can't explain it. Look," he added, unbuttoning the top of his shirt to reveal a chest conspicuously absent of bullet wounds.

Fergus hadn't been present at Ray's death, but there was no reason to doubt Serena Jo's depiction of events, nor her assertion that Ray was truly dead when she'd left him in the woods.

With narrowed eyes, Fergus studied the woman standing beside Ray. Hannah returned his scrutiny.

"This makes no sense," Serena Jo said with a frown. She opened Ray's shirt further, running her fingers over his chest. His face turned red, but he didn't stop her.

"I know, but I'm happy to be alive and kicking," Ray said. "I could use a drink. Who's with me?"

"Make mine a double," Fergus said, stepping out into the corridor. "After that, we'll dispose of the bodies. I'm thinking your refrigerated area will do nicely until we get all this sorted out."

"Wait a minute," Serena Jo said. "We need to consider that the Murdocks have already sent a second team. They're despicable, but they're not stupid."

"Exactly, my dear," Hannah replied. "Let's take that bottle with us, boys. Ray, before we leave, we'll use your welder to reinforce the roof hatch and the rolling door from inside. Then we'll exit the same way we entered."

"What way was that?" Serena Jo stopped in the middle of the corridor with her hands on her hips.

"Through the HVAC system," Hanna replied. "You're tall but slender, so it won't be a problem for you. Ray barely managed. His broad shoulders wedged in the ductwork a couple of times. The little guy here should be fine."

Hannah gave Fergus a playful punch to the shoulder. When her fist connected, he felt a strong bio-electrical current, confirming his suspicions.

Hannah belonged in *Cthor-Vangt*. Nobody but residents, either full-time or part-time like himself, emitted that level of voltage. Yet he had never made her acquaintance in all his years below or above the earth's surface.

Fergus said, "I'll ignore that remark because I find you intriguing. I can't wait to enjoy an enlightening, perhaps slightly inebriated, conversation with you."

"I wish I had a dollar for every time I've heard that. Let's split into two teams and round up the deadwood," Hannah said, gently guiding Serena Jo by the elbow.

When Fergus and Ray arrived at the first body, Fergus wasn't surprised to see a dime-sized hole in the center of its forehead. The second body lay near Ray's sleeping quarters in the same state. When they began dragging the third body in the direction of the refrigerated area, Fergus said in a low voice, "Did you actually kill any of them, or did Hannah do all this?"

"All my shots went wide. Hannah is incredible. I figured she was Special Forces, but she denied it. I think she's some kind of mercenary. She told me she's not afraid to get her hands dirty, which I interpreted to mean she eliminates bad guys. I guess that could be considered noble."

"Depends on who gets to decide who the bad guys are."

"True. But I trust her, instinctively, like I did you."

"Hmmm."

Moments later, with the task of body disposal complete, the four gathered again near the rolling door entrance. Serena Jo started to speak, but Hannah interrupted.

"The short-term goal is to get out safely before Murdock reinforcements arrive. We'll take as much as we can of whatever we don't want them to have——weapons, pharmaceuticals, etc. The long-term goal is to make it difficult if not impossible for them to break in."

"What about securing the HVAC exit?" Ray asked.

"Leave that to me."

In another half-hour they were ready to leave. Ray produced additional backpacks in which to carry dozens of boxes of ammunition, life-saving medicine that didn't require refrigeration, and narcotics for pain management. He also stashed a few bags of Jolly Ranchers in his pack for the kids. Pushing those heavy bundles through the ductwork took longer than Hannah liked. By the time the four popped out into the chilly pre-dawn air, she'd become almost testy.

"Once the Murdocks figure out that they can't get in through any of the doors, they'll find this." Ray gestured to the silver umbilical-like tunnel connecting the large HVAC unit to the back of the building.

"Replace the panel first, Ray," Hannah said. "Use the power tool to make those screws even harder to remove. But I promise, the Murdocks won't notice it." She unzipped her backpack and withdrew what looked like a folded square of stiff plastic wrap. "It took me months after infiltrating a company called Hyperstealth to get my hands on this gem."

"What's Hyperstealth?" Serena Jo demanded.

"A biotech firm in Canada. Have you seen the Harry Potter movies? This stuff is like an invisibility cloak. When I saw the news story about it a few years ago, I knew I had to acquire some. Just watch."

She unfolded the material and wrapped it around the steel box at the corner of the building. The HVAC unit disappeared. In its place, a plain section of the building appeared.

"That's amazing!" Ray said.

"Yes. I had to sleep with one of the developers to get it. Small price to pay, though." Hannah chuckled.

"Depends on how ugly the developer was," Fergus said.

"I've had worse. Ray, add a few screws to hold the film in place. Hurry, please. We've taken too long already."

Fergus edged up next to her and whispered, "Is the enemy showing up on your *scythen*?"

"You're an odd little fellow, aren't you?"

"Indeed. Well ...?"

"I have no idea what you're talking about."

"Sure you don't."

Hannah stared for seconds longer than was comfortable, then raised her voice so the others could hear. "Let's move out, folks."

"We'll finish this later," Fergus whispered.

Hannah laughed. Fergus found it absolutely captivating.

During the hike back to the village, Serena Jo responded to the whistled signals from Scouts hidden in the forest. Fergus never even saw them. Were all mountain people this competent in the woods? Were the Whitakers better at stealth than the Murdocks? Or was it a skill unique to the Scouts? Fergus barely even noticed the journey, being otherwise distracted by the new addition to their group.

Hannah led them through the woods with the skill of a trained wilderness guide. And while Fergus knew Serena Jo could feel pain, it wasn't slowing her down now.

With the arrival of Hannah, the jigsaw pieces of the family's genetic puzzle fell into place. No wonder Serena Jo and her children were so exceptional; Skeeter and Hannah contributed talents from two diverse yet equally remarkable bloodlines.

A final whistled tune as they entered the outskirts of the village assured their safety. The sun's rays peeked over the roofs of the ramshackle houses, illuminating a small group of villagers heading toward them. Fergus zeroed in on Skeeter's expression. What was the status of his relationship with Hannah? Had they remained in contact over the years? Had there been another lover after Hannah, or was she the reason Skeeter still wore a gold band on his left ring finger?

Fergus had the answer the next moment, as Skeeter fell at the feet of the small woman.

"I thought you were dead," he whispered.

"Euel, you should know me better than that," Hannah replied, squatting beside him on the hard-packed dirt. She took his face in her hands and kissed him squarely on the mouth.

"There were times I knew you were nearby," he said, even softer now. Fergus had to move close to hear.

"Yes. Often. You've done a perfect job of raising our daughter and the grandkids. We'll talk more later. Just the two of us. For now," she said, standing and raising her voice, "we need to strategize." She nodded to Serena Jo, who was observing the display with a baleful expression.

Hannah's nod offered a silent acknowledgement of Serena Jo's authority within the village.

"Scouts, meet at the kitchen house in thirty minutes," Serena Jo said to the growing crowd. "We've got trouble with the Murdocks."

At the mention of the notorious surname, calls of "lowlifes," "hooligans," "criminals," and a few others Fergus had never heard before circulated among the assemblage. There was no shortage of colorful and creative epithets in Appalachia.

Skeeter watched Hannah's backside as she followed her daughter home. Not surprisingly, Willadean and Harlan stood on the porch, identical mouths open in surprise at the sight before them. Perhaps on some level the two realized who approached them, even if they had never met their grandmother in person. Fergus would love to be a fly on Serena Jo's wall during the next few moments, but instead, he gave Skeeter an affectionate pat.

Skeeter didn't notice the pat. He stared now at Ray with narrowed eyes. "How in the heck are you standing there, young man? I heard you was dead." Skeeter seemed to have gathered his wits.

"The news of my death was greatly exaggerated," Ray said. "If you want more details, you'll have to ask Hannah."

"Ray, I think the three of us could use some of that bourbon you brought."

"I thought you was dead, Mister Ray!" a small dark-haired boy hollered from the porch of a ramshackle structure.

"Hi, Cricket! So did a lot of folks."

As the three walked past Cricket, a man appeared in the doorway to his cabin.

Skeeter said in a low voice, "That's his daddy, Ezra. 'Bout as worthless as they come. Half the time he ain't even home at night when the boy goes to bed."

"What a shame. Isn't he too young to be left alone overnight?" Ray asked.

Skeeter snorted. "Young-uns in the holler grow up fast. 'Specially these days. Anyways, we're close by. I check in on him a lot."

Fergus slowed, glancing back at Cricket's father. He'd only seen the man on a couple of occasions during his time in the village, and had never spoken directly to him. Ezra looked like a grown-up version of his son, but without the easy grin and open demeanor. Without a word, the man turned and disappeared inside the ramshackle house.

Chapter 6

Ray

It wasn't easy parsing the human cacophony which came from all directions. Especially since all he could focus on was Serena Jo leading the discussion from the center of the large room. The dining tables had been cleared to make room for the gathering. Male and female villagers ranging in age from sixteen to sixty sat on benches, stood in small groups, or leaned cross-armed against perimeter walls. The diversity ended at their facial expressions: they all shared the same look of barely restrained excitement.

According to Skeeter, the Whitakers had been itching to take on the Murdocks for decades. Now it seemed the opportunity had finally arrived.

They were going to war.

While the notion of bloodshed prompted anxiety in Ray, he realized that countless opportunities to impress Serena Jo would present themselves in the days to come. And more than anything Ray had ever wanted before, he wanted to spend the rest of his time on earth with Serena Jo and her family.

"Why wait?" a stony-faced man said from a corner. The deep voice silenced the clamor like a rumble of thunder rolling over an outdoor picnic. "Let's go now. We can be in Idlewild in a day and have the Murdock clan in the ground before dark."

"That kind of thinking will get people killed, Trevor," Serena Jo replied. "It's tempting to rush this, to ride in like Lee at Chancellorsville and be done with it in one fell swoop. But we don't want this to turn into a Gettysburg. The situation calls for a clear-thinking, calculated response."

Appalachians knew their Civil War history better than the average American. And of course Serena Jo would understand the effectiveness of such an analogy.

"They kidnapped and shot our leader. That's not something we can let slide," Trevor replied.

"I don't intend to. But we will do this the smart way, which is almost never the fast way. Your son made the Scouts three months ago." She acknowledged the handsome boy standing beside his father. "Do you really want to see him die too young because we weren't patient and methodical?"

She had chosen her argument wisely. It's one thing to sacrifice yourself to a cause, but quite another to bury your child. Nobody took issue.

Serena Jo continued, "Before we make a move, we need to know what we're up against. The way we find out is to send in a spy ... a mole, actually. The mole will infiltrate the Murdock's clan and report back."

"Who's dumb enough to try to infiltrate them sonsofbitches?" a wiry youth with a bobbing Adam's apple asked.

He couldn't have been more than eighteen. Like everyone in the room, he'd won a place in the elite Scouts. This boy, who probably hadn't lost his virginity yet, could well lose his life in the inevitable violence that would play out over the next few weeks.

"That would be me," said Hannah from a distant corner. Ray hadn't noticed her.

I'm good at covert ...

"No offense, ma'am, but you're no spring chicken, and I don't know you. Just because you're Serena Jo's mama doesn't mean we trust you," Trevor said.

Hannah moved to her daughter's side. "Understandable. I'm sure I'd feel the same way if I were in your situation. Euel can vouch for me, though." She indicated Skeeter, whose gaze remained focused on her like a tractor beam. He gave a measured nod.

"I'm not going alone, though. I'll need a volunteer to accompany me. Someone the Murdocks don't know. Someone I can trust and who can think on his feet. What do you say, Ray?"

Ray exchanged a surprised look with Fergus, who sat on a nearby bench.

Fergus stood quickly. "Hannah, Ray is no spy, nor is he a warrior. I'll volunteer."

"The Murdocks may have seen your comings and goings within the holler," she said with a dismissive wave.

"So what if they've seen me?" Fergus continued. "I can say I'm a defector, unhappy with the insufficient number of eligible women in the village."

"What a minute," Ray said, intensely aware of Serena Jo's eyes upon him. "I'm happy to go. I just don't know how much help I'll be. Covert may be your thing, Hannah, but it's not mine."

"Covert isn't required. Quite the opposite, actually. You'll stumble into Idlewild as noisily and clumsily as possible. You're a distraction. I'll be conducting surveillance nearby. They'll never see me."

Several low vocalizations and a sudden stirring within the gathering indicated disapproval.

"We don't know this guy, either. I'm getting mighty uncomfortable with this, ma'am." Trevor spoke directly to Serena Jo, ignoring Hannah and Ray. "Sending folks we don't know into enemy territory? That doesn't seem like a *smart way* to do things."

Serena Jo's eyes narrowed at the subtle mockery. "You make a valid point. Why don't you go with them?"

"I'd be proud to go, but on my terms. Not with two strangers."

Ray felt the insult behind the word. Anyone not born in the holler would probably be a stranger forever.

"Besides, the Murdocks know me all too well," Trevor continued. "They'd shoot me on sight."

Serena Jo graced him with a rare smile. "Not if they believe you're defecting. That can be your cover story."

"Why would they believe that?"

"If Hannah is right and the Murdocks are aware of our activities, they may also be aware of the dynamics here in the village. It's no secret that you and a few others have questioned my authority." She raised a hand, silencing an objection that didn't come. "I don't blame you. If our situations were reversed, I'd probably resist as well. And if there ever comes a time when someone can run things better than me, I'll step aside. But we all know that time hasn't come yet."

Ray watched the man, studying the crags etched into weathered skin, the thick calluses on the hand that rubbed a dark beard. He saw the moment when Trevor made his decision.

"It's not a bad plan. If I'm persuasive enough, Silas will jump at the opportunity to have me."

"You got that right," Hannah said. "Silas is proud, but not too proud to turn down one of the elite Whitaker Scouts."

Trevor didn't respond to the compliment. Instead, he performed a visual assessment of Serena Jo's mother, from the silver-blond hair to the waterproof mountain boots. Ray was already aware of Hannah's top-notch gear, but it seemed Trevor recognized quality when he saw. A few uncomfortable moments passed. "I want a private meeting with these two folks before we head out," Trevor said finally.

"Done," Serena Jo replied. "I'll attend as well."

"Nope. Just the three of us."

Golden eyes narrowed at the defiance. Eventually, she gave a brisk nod. "Very well. I want you all to head out at first light. Dismissed, everyone," she added, then strode out the door.

As the group dispersed, Fergus latched onto Ray's elbow and guided him to one of the outside tables where they could have a moment alone.

"Are you sure about this, Ray?" Fergus said, his voice pitched low. His warm breath created clouds of steam in the chilly air. "You don't have to put yourself in danger just to win over your dream woman. There are other ways to do it. Besides, I think she fancies you already."

Ray's pulse quickened, whether from the upcoming dangerous mission or the notion that Serena Jo "fancied" him, he didn't know. Probably both.

"I trust Hannah," he said. "If she thought I'd be in danger, I doubt she would have included me. She knows the Murdocks better than anyone."

"How so?" Fergus said. Sudden keen interest made his blue eyes sparkle.

"She's the daughter of Silas, their leader. She doesn't want people to know that, though."

"I daresay she doesn't. Does Serena Jo know? Or Skeeter?"

"She didn't say. Let's keep it between us, okay?"

"Very well. But I'm not comfortable with this, Ray. You're trusting a stranger much too quickly."

"I trusted you right away, and that turned out fine." Ray gave the small man a pat on the back as Hannah and Trevor emerged from the building.

"Private meeting at Trevor's house, Ray," Hannah called. "We're going to work out the particulars. Your little friend isn't invited. Sorry, Fergus."

The grin she flashed was disarming, but Ray noticed Fergus's instant tension.

"You're not too fond of Hannah, are you?" Ray whispered, shrugging into his coat. All the other gear he'd brought was now stowed in Skeeter's cabin. He would decide what to take on the mission based on Hannah's advice.

Fergus did have a point; he already trusted Hannah completely. But why shouldn't he?

"It's not that I don't like her. She's rather captivating, actually, but in a completely different way than her daughter. I suspect there's a lot about Hannah we don't know. That's all."

Fergus seemed to be holding something back, but there wasn't time to press the issue. Hannah and Trevor were waiting for him on the hard-packed dirt that served as Main Street.

"Duly noted. I'll see you later."

✳✳✳

Once Ray caught up to Trevor and Hannah, they walked briskly past the houses, most in some state of disrepair, toward the outskirts of the village. Ray had noticed before that the dwellings appeared especially primitive for the 21st century. One would expect that in rural Tennessee, but most of these structures had been built decades ago ... possibly Depression-era. Perhaps even earlier.

"Trevor, I'm curious about your village," Ray said. "Please don't take this the wrong way, but it looks like it's from another time. No modern plumbing and rudimentary electrical capabilities. Not that those things matter now, anyway. I'm just interested in its history."

"'Cuz you want to be a part of its future?" Trevor asked. Ray felt a wave of relief when the man gave him a wink. "You're right, though. Folks around here don't take kindly to change. We don't see anything wrong with doing things the way they've always been done, even when some newfangled way comes along to make them easier."

"So it was a conscious decision to let technological advancements pass you by?"

"You could say that. We're proud folks. More than a little stubborn, too. And technology costs money ... money that could buy a new hunting rifle or a pair of shoes for the kids."

Ray nodded. "And as things turned out, you're well-positioned in this new world." Ray's long-held 'hillbilly' prejudices had begun to fade even before this revelation.

"Here we are," he said as they reached a small, immaculate house. Tenacious flakes of white paint still clung to a few nooks and crannies, but mostly the weathered boards had reverted to their original pigment-free state.

Despite its humble appearance, Ray soon discovered a tidy, cozy interior. The cast-iron stove, seemingly a staple with mountain folk, provided adequate heat to warm the space; Trevor must have started a fire in its belly before the meeting.

Ray flashed on his recent experience in a mountain cabin with a cheerful fire and a maniacally grinning Lizzy. He trembled.

"You folks care for some tea?" Trevor said, gesturing toward the dented kettle placed on the stove's surface. "It'll warm you right up," he added to Ray, mistaking the shudder.

"Fennel?" Hannah said, noting twined bunches of feathery plants hanging from the rafters.

"Yep," Trevor said. "Good for digestion, and the licorice flavor is tasty. I'm partial to chamomile, but I'm out. Gotta trade for some as soon as I can catch my breath. We've been busy these last few weeks with all the goings-on."

"I'd love some tea. Ray, you'll have a cup too."

He chafed at the commandeering of his personal tea decision, but let it slide. Clearly, Hannah's natural instinct was to take charge, even in mundane situations.

"Have a seat, folks. Won't take but a minute to boil the water."

Ray and Hannah positioned themselves on the only two chairs beside the 50s era aluminum table. The padded seats had been mended with duct tape, but the table's Formica surface gleamed.

Trevor placed two delicate china teacups on the table, then balanced tarnished metal strainers filled with seeds on their rims. When he poured the hot water into the cups, the licorice aroma permeated the air. Ray breathed in the pleasant scent.

"I think this is my first fennel tea. It smells wonderful. Thank you, Trevor."

"I'd offer sugar, but I've been out for the last couple of years," he said with another wink. "I have plenty of honey, though, if you like yours sweet. My boy does."

Ray remembered the good-looking young man standing next to his father at the meeting. "What's your son's name? He must be impressive to have made the Scouts at such a young age."

"Brock. He's a good boy, but a bit too big for his britches lately. Comes with the age, I suppose."

"Exactly," Hannah said with a nod of approval. "He made the Scouts at what, sixteen? That's remarkable. He must be quite proficient."

"That he is, ma'am," Trevor replied, pulling up a wooden stool and joining them at the table.

"You know, we haven't officially been introduced until we've shaken." Hannah thrust out her small, capable hand.

Trevor took it into his much larger hand, then raised an eyebrow. "You got a nice firm grip, ma'am. I like that."

She released his hand after a few seconds. Then she placed her elbows on the kitchen table and focused her full attention on the man. Ray did the same but studied him more discreetly.

The beard showed signs of having been neatly trimmed, unlike many in the village. Ray's own facial hair would require much longer than the week it had been given to equal the length and fullness of Trevor's. The brown eyes seemed guarded, but the gaze was steady. Based on the crows' feet, he was probably close to Ray's age — early forties, give or take. Living a primitive lifestyle in nature, exposed to the elements, must surely expedite aging, though. Perhaps he was younger. Ray pondered Trevor's relationship with Serena Jo until Hannah interrupted his thoughts.

"So is there a Missus Trevor?" Hannah said, with a glance at the teacups.

"No ma'am. She died in childbirth. It's just been me and Brock since."

"I see. You seem like a capable man, Trevor. I'm curious about you acquiescing to the leadership of a woman after the pandemic. I'm familiar with the region and its traditions. You're okay with my daughter calling the shots?"

Ray stifled a chuckle. Some folks might find Hannah's bluntness off-putting, but he enjoyed it. As a textbook introvert who despised small talk, he welcomed her candor.

Trevor took his time responding. He seemed to be considering just how honestly to answer.

"To be honest, I wasn't okay with her calling the shots at first. It isn't easy taking orders from a female. But she knows what she's doing. When she came back to the holler after being gone all those years, folks didn't take to her right away. She's a bit hard around the edges, if you don't mind my saying. But she brought a truckload of useful supplies, and she's been generous with them. She has our best interests in mind. She likes being in charge, but so does every man I ever worked for. Can't hold that against her."

Hannah nodded, satisfied. "Not everyone is meant to be a leader. There's no shame in that."

"Don't feel ashamed. That doesn't mean I'm gonna blindly follow someone, though. That's why we're here. Gotta get to know people before I expose my back to them."

"I understand. For the record, I agree," Hannah said.

"So tell me about yourself. If you're leading this mission, I need to get a feel for you. And you," Trevor added with a glance toward Ray. "Then we'll talk logistics and strategy."

Ray hated that he was surprised by the man's use of the words. He really needed to work harder on preconceived notions of intellect.

For the next few minutes, Hannah relayed a near-exact version of the personal history she'd shared with Ray. Despite Trevor's attempt at stoicism, Ray could tell the man was as shocked by the ongoing events in Idlewild as he himself had been.

"I had no idea things were that bad there."

"Most people don't."

"I guess I shouldn't be surprised. If what you're telling me is the truth ..."

"It is."

"Then it sounds like we need to do more than just a little reconnoitering. Maybe we need to be thinking along the lines of assassination. Cut off the snake's head and the body dies with it."

Hannah gave a bitter laugh, "I've considered that. Silas is my father, after all, and I hate him more than any stranger ever could."

Trevor nodded. "But ..."

"It wouldn't work. Silas is still officially in charge of Idlewild, but he's old. His eyesight and hearing are going, and even if his brain still functions, he no longer exudes strength. He no longer dominates with his mere presence, and his days are numbered. Somebody will step in when he — or she — thinks they have enough supporters to pull off a coup d'etat. I think I know of two people who fit that bill," she added.

"So, what are their names?" Trevor pressed.

Hannah took a sip of her tea, locked eyes with both Trevor and then Ray, and said, "The first is Wyatt, currently Silas's right-hand man."

"I know him. He's a sonofabitch, pardon my language. Who's the other?"

Hannah sighed heavily. "Piper, my twin sister."

Chapter 7

Willadean

"I have a lot of questions, Mama," Willadean said as she slipped out of her day clothes and into new pajamas. She'd finally outgrown her old ones, and they would be passed down to a smaller girl in the village. Nothing went to waste in Whitaker holler, especially clothing. Mama had loaded up that U-Haul with a variety of shirts and jeans and coats that would see Willadean and Harlan through adolescence. After the store-bought clothes were worn out or outgrown, she and her brother would be forced to wear homespun. Some of the folks in the village already did.

Thankfully, Willa was too skilled with a rifle to be relegated to the spinning and sewing committee.

"Questions about what?" Serena Jo filled the wash basin with steaming water from the kettle. She'd removed her filthy clothes already and slipped into a threadbare, long-sleeved nightgown, tucked up around her thighs now so she could access her leg injury.

"Oooh, I want to see," Willa said, distracted by the excitement of a bullet wound. Mama seemed fine, so Willa wasn't worried about infection. Besides, if it came to that, Mama had stashed a small bottle of amoxicillin under the cabin's floorboard for easy access; the rest of the antibiotics remained in the locked U-Haul. The strong medicine was reserved for dire situations when death was imminent, and not for patients who were old or who lacked skills that benefited the community.

In other words, as Mama had explained a while back, it was a form of community-based Darwinism. Survival of the fittest, but also survival of the most valuable people, the ones whose talents helped everyone else survive. Some might consider that cold-blooded, but it made sense to Willa.

"It was a through-and-through?" Willa asked, her nose inches from the dime-shaped, still-oozing hole.

Mama hissed as she dabbed at the wound with a clean rag. "Yes. I'll need your help with the wound on the back of my leg."

"You got lucky."

"I suppose. I'm sure there's a lesson in there somewhere, but right now this hurts too much to figure it out. Here, get the backside."

"Maybe everything doesn't need to have a lesson," Willa said, peeling off the blood-soaked bandage.

"I beg to differ. Lessons can be found everywhere, if one only takes the time to look."

"Hmmph," Willa replied. She gazed at the injury. "Dang, Mama. You could drive an 18-wheeler through this. The butterfly strip is holding up, though." Serena Jo hissed again when Willa wiped with the rag. "There's no red streak or other signs of infection."

"I didn't expect any. I would have felt a fever coming on by now. Good thing us Whitakers are fast healers." She twisted in the chair to give Willa a kiss on the forehead.

Willa thought of these sudden affectionate outbursts as Gratitude Kisses. Mama gave them when she was feeling especially thankful, like when Harlan fell out of a tree in the spring and only broke his pinky finger instead of his neck. Harlan got several Gratitude Kisses that day.

Harlan appeared at the bedroom doorway then and pointed to the front door. The next moment, three slow knocks and three fast ones echoed through the cabin.

"Come in, Cricket," Willa yelled, glancing at her brother with narrowed eyes. In addition to his astral travels, it seemed Harlan was also developing psychic abilities. Later, when they were alone, she would grill him about how he knew someone was coming to their house at bedtime.

The door swung open, revealing a sleepy-eyed Cricket in mid-yawn. Her best friend had outgrown his pajamas long ago, but he still wore them. It was either that or sleep naked. Cricket's father didn't bother with providing for his son beyond the resources all villagers enjoyed as a community. When he was older, Willa knew she'd have to have a Come-to-Jesus meeting with Cricket about the sorry crap-sack he had for a father. Until then, they had all agreed to say nothing. The last thing Cricket needed was something else to make him feel inferior.

"I can't sleep," Cricket said, stepping inside. "Papa's gone off into the woods again, and I got to thinkin' about the bad dream I had the night before."

"You can bunk with Harlan," Mama said, tugging her nightgown back down. She'd noticed Cricket's sudden blush when he saw her bare legs. Willa spotted it, too, and rolled her eyes. Cricket's obsession with Mama was becoming tiresome.

Harlan steered his friend into the darkened bedroom. Willa exchanged a disgusted head shake with Mama that said *Cricket's daddy is a piece of work* before following the boys to bed.

Under normal conditions, she would give Cricket a hard time about his personal hygiene as it applied to her brother's bedsheets, but she decided to forgo it tonight. Cricket seemed more than just sleepy. He seemed *morose*, a word she had learned from context clues in the book she was currently reading. She intended to use it regularly, both in her head and in conversations, until it sprang naturally to her mind. That's why she possessed such an impressive lexicon for a twelve-year-old. She worked at it every day.

"What do you think your daddy does in the woods?" Willa said, crawling into bed. She would skip her nightly journaling since Cricket was sleeping over. He'd want to ask her a million questions about what she was writing.

"I reckon he does some drinkin'," Cricket whispered.

"He does that already. Why does he have to go into the woods to do it?"

"Maybe he does worse drinkin' in the woods than he does at home. Maybe he don't want nobody to see."

Staring up at the shadowy rafters, Willa pondered two notions: shame and self-destructive behavior. She'd experienced shame before, and it wasn't pleasant. The only self-destructive behavior she could be accused of was indulging her curiosity. It seemed harmless enough on the 'de-structive behavior' scale, though she had lived through a few dangerous episodes as a direct result of her obsession with needing to know stuff.

She felt a sudden wash of empathy for Cricket, and even for his father. As the daughter of the indomitable Serena Jo, Willa resided on a lofty pedestal in terms of the village hierarchy. Poor Cricket and his dad scrambled about on the bottom of the barrel.

That must feel awful.

"You know it's a disease, right?" she whispered.

Cricket sighed loudly in the dark. "Yes, I know that. But sometimes when he comes home, he seems ... I don't know ... better, somehow. Like he got rid of some kind of poison while he was out there. I know that sounds crazy."

"Well, maybe he did. Maybe just being able to do the thing in private that he's embarrassed to do in public is liberating."

"I guess. I don't know, Willa. I just wish he wouldn't go off all the time. I worry about him. There's bad things in the woods."

"True, but your daddy is good with his rifle. Try not to fret about him."

Cricket was silent for a few moments. Willa thought he was about to respond when her friend's high-pitched snores came from Harlan's bed.

She could barely make out her brother's open eyes in the gloom. He stared up at the rafters just like she'd been doing.

She wondered what he was thinking about.

Chapter 8

Harlan

Slipping into an astral adventure was becoming easier every night. It used to be that Harlan had to wait and see if they would happen. Now if he concentrated right before he dozed off, they usually did. After listening to Cricket's snores for at least half an hour, Harlan closed his eyes, then woke up an unknown amount of time later soaring over the forest. He made a mental note of a few landmarks to get his bearings, then let the mysterious otherworldly forces — those that seemed to be in charge in the astral plane — guide him.

He noticed movement to the northeast, then dipped his imagined wings to the right. Moments later he discovered the source of the activity. Lots of predators roamed the woods at night, and smart folks didn't wander there alone. Cricket's daddy did, and on a regular basis. Was he overconfident, or did he just not care what happened to him? He should think about Cricket before putting himself in danger. Maybe Willa was right, though. Maybe the urge to drink moonshine without being embarrassed was just too strong to fight.

Harlan decided he would never try moonshine. It smelled disgusting, plus it seemed nothing good ever came from drinking it. People acted silly when they drank it. He was thankful Mama didn't care for the stuff. She was too smart.

He'd let his mind wander while flying, so refocused on events below. Sure enough, the source of the movement coming from the woods revealed itself as Ezra, Cricket's daddy. He charged through the vines and brush and boulders like he wasn't drunk. He didn't stumble at all, which seemed pretty impressive to Harlan.

Where was he going in such a hurry? Harlan figured Ezra traveled just far enough into the forest to get away from prying eyes. Based on the landmarks, he'd hiked miles from the village.

Harlan slowed now, keeping pace with the man below. He wondered if Ezra could sense that someone – or someTHING – flew overhead. Just then, the man tipped his head back and looked up at the starry sky. Harlan held his imagined breath.

After a few moments — or at least what felt like a few moments — Ezra focused again on the game trail in front of him, then took off. Harlan considered turning around and going home when he saw movement twenty yards or so in front of Ezra.

Please don't let it be a bear! Harlan thought. He would hate to be the one to tell Cricket that his daddy had been mauled ... or worse. A shadowy figure appeared in the distance, heading toward Ezra as quickly as Ezra approached. It moved like a human, not a bear, and it looked small in comparison to Ezra's bulky frame. The way it maneuvered through the thick brush reminded Harlan of Mama. No, that wasn't quite right. It reminded him of Mama's mama, the grandmother he had just met for the first time. The two figures came together on the trail. Harlan concentrated on decreasing altitude so he could get close enough to hear their conversation. It made no sense that Hannah would be meeting Ezra in the woods, miles from the village. She was supposed to be planning some kind of covert mission with Mister Ray and Mister Trevor.

When Harlan hovered lower, the small figure glanced up at the night sky, just as Ezra had done. Ezra hadn't stared directly at him, though. Her face was shrouded in a hoodie, making identification impossible. Harlan felt an itching sensation around the place where his brain would be if he were actually flying in his real body. He promptly imagined a brick wall around his skull. That's what The Shift told him to do, and The Shift — the voice in his head that was always right about everything — sensed danger. Time to head home, Harlan, *the Shift said.* Now!

Harlan reacted and skyrocketed toward home. He didn't wake up right away, though. Instead, he allowed himself to slip into a regular run-of-the-mill dream like everyone else had. It was a good one, too, filled with lots of puppies and mountains of candy.

Chapter 9

Fergus

Fergus had set his internal alarm clock to 5 a.m. He wanted to see his friend and the other two members of the covert mission before they headed northeast to Idlewild. Only fifteen miles separated the Whitaker's territory from that of the Murdocks, but it comprised some of the most hostile and rugged terrain found in the Smoky Mountains.

When he arose in the chilly cabin, he was alone. Ray had spent the night at Trevor's, and Skeeter was mysteriously absent. Fergus suspected the old coot and Hannah had planned some 'alone time.' His *scythen* had been picking up on subtle sexual communications between the two.

A change in the weather overnight would make the trio's journey to Idlewild even more arduous; the first snow of winter had begun falling. Dime-sized snowflakes swirled from the heavens, landing on the shoulders of the heavy winter coat gifted him by Skeeter. Fergus was thankful for it, too. His Army jacket provided a secondary layer beneath the patched parka hanging to his knees.

Nothing was thrown out in the holler, even before the plague. Fergus found that refreshing. Modern people immersed themselves in too much *stuff*, replacing old stuff with new stuff when the previous stuff was still perfectly fine. Growing up in the Old Country, Fergus understood subsistence, so the Whitakers' thrifty, resourceful lifestyle resonated on a deeply personal level.

Sporadic porch lamps flickered to life as early risers began their day. As he navigated the dirt road, he nodded to passersby and received an occasional "Morning, Fergus," in return. Skeeter said people in the village had taken to him quickly. That was no accident. Fergus had set his *scythen* to charm mode when he arrived. Sustaining the output didn't take much effort, though; he'd always been a people person, which served him well in his current line of work as a *Cthor* field anthropologist and DNA recruiter.

As he raised his hand to knock on Trevor's front door, it opened. A pleasant aroma of licorice floated out on a draft of warm air.

"We're still waiting on Hannah," Ray said, standing in the doorway. "Thought you might be her."

"I see you're loaded up," Fergus said, noting the gear stacked in the background. "I won't ask you about the mission details, but I hope they're considering your inexperience. I still don't see the need for you to go."

Trevor's face appeared behind Ray. Aloof brown eyes scanned Fergus. Fergus's *scythen* drew a complete blank with the stoic Scout. No inadvertent sender, that one.

"They understand my limitations," Ray replied with a self-deprecating grin. "I have other skills, though, so don't worry about me."

"I'll make sure we bring him back in one piece, little man." Hannah's voice came from behind, and Fergus whirled to face her.

What was it about this woman that made his hackles rise?

"See that you do," Fergus snapped.

Hannah laughed, then maneuvered around him. "We ready, boys?" she said, shutting the door in his face.

"Hmmph," Fergus muttered, turning to go.

He noticed two glowing lanterns hanging from the kitchen house, and his stomach rumbled. Perhaps he could finagle a day-old corn muffin from one of the cooks. Afterward, he'd seek out Serena Jo and uncover any contingency plans she had formulated in case her mother's mission failed.

"You realize he's undertaking this dangerous excursion just to impress you," Fergus said, sitting across the table from Serena Jo. Those words amounted to one of the worst offenses a male could commit against another male: going behind a friend's back to tell the girl he likes how he feels about her. Somehow, he knew Ray would forgive him, though. If Serena Jo's feelings inclined along the same lines, that knowledge would speed up the getting-together process ... if there was any hope of that happening in the first place. Politically, having a boyfriend from outside the holler would be a bad move for Serena Jo, but Fergus suspected she would do whatever she wanted then shape the narrative and opinions in her favor.

The snow had tapered off, and weak sunshine filtered through the cabin windows, highlighting a few strands of silver in Serena Jo's blond hair. She would age well, like her mother.

Fergus narrowed his eyes at the thought of the exasperating older woman.

"I figured it was something like that," Serena Jo replied, taking a sip of her beloved coffee. She must hold him in high esteem since she'd offered him a cup as well.

"And you don't have qualms that he's unqualified for the job?"

"A few. But I trust Trevor."

"Not your mother?"

"I don't know her. My father trusts her, though. That's good enough for me, I suppose."

"You *suppose*?" Fergus said, indignation getting the best of him.

Serena Jo almost smiled. "I'm trying to decide what you're so angry about. I've never seen you act this way. Did she get under your skin?"

"Yes," Fergus replied, "and I can't explain precisely why. It's not just that. I'm also worried about my friend. He's one of the finest people I've encountered in all my travels. I'd hate to see something bad happen to him."

"Interesting. You haven't known him long, yet you made this determination?"

"Yes. You know how your father gets feelings about people and events? I do, too, and my judgments are rarely wrong."

Serena Jo graced him with a rare smile. "I understand. I like Ray, too, instinctively, but also I like him because of the short time we spent together. He made an impression on me." She reached out and patted Fergus's arm. "Ray will be fine. As much as we don't trust Hannah, I do trust Ray's intellect."

"That's true. He's brilliant, you know."

Serena Jo nodded, then glanced behind him. "Good morning, Harlan. Actually, it's almost afternoon. You slept very late. Cricket and Willa have been up for quite a while. They're outside, probably at the kitchen house."

Fergus turned to see the boy rubbing his eyes and yawning. The twins would grow up to be beautiful, as most folks these days were. Fergus wondered suddenly if he would be around to witness it.

Harlan began signing. Serena Jo frowned as she read his fingers.

"What's happening?" Fergus asked.

"Harlan said he had another of his special dreams. He saw Ezra, Cricket's father, in the forest, meeting someone who looked like Hannah." She turned back to the boy. "I'm sorry, Harlan, but that doesn't make sense. Your grandmother was here in the village last night. Why would she travel into the woods to meet up with Ezra?" Serena Jo stood and walked toward her son. Fergus could sense the boy's agitation.

"Maybe it makes more sense than you realize," Fergus mused.

Harlan's fingers became a blur of motion.

"He's saying the woman might have been someone else, but he definitely saw Ezra and he didn't seem drunk. I'm not sure Harlan is qualified to know that, especially from a dream."

Fergus began to feel disquieted. Why would someone who reminded Harlan of his grandmother be meeting secretly with Cricket's father in the woods, far from the village? The obvious answer triggered internal alarm bells.

"Harlan, maybe it wasn't one of those special dreams. Maybe it was just a regular dream. Isn't that possible?" Serena Jo said.

The blond head shook vigorously.

"You're absolutely sure?"

A vigorous head nod.

Fergus said, "He has been right about other things he saw during his astral travels."

"Now he's saying he had to leave quickly. The Shift told him to get out of there. I have no idea what that means."

"I do," Fergus said. "We need to get to the bottom of this clandestine meeting. You'll have to trust me."

"No, I don't."

Fergus sighed. Now he'd have to break a promise——and so soon after committing a man-code offense. Was there no end to his treachery? "Serena Jo, Hannah's father is Silas Murdock. She likely has other kinfolk living there as well. I'd hoped she had told you. Perhaps that's why Harlan believed he was seeing his grandmother during his dream."

"Oh, dear."

"Exactly," Fergus replied. "If Ezra is a mole, the Murdocks already know what we've been up to and that a spy mission into their territory is currently underway."

"They'll be expecting our people."

"Yes."

Damn it. Ray could be walking into a trap.

"I'll send a team," Serena Jo said grimly. "Maybe they can catch up to them." She frowned. "But with Trevor and Hannah, I doubt it. They've got a six-hour head start."

Chapter 10

Idlewild

"Step aside," snapped a small woman with silver-blond hair. A man lounging on a wooden porch jumped up as if a sudden fire blazed beneath his butt.

"I think he's still asleep," the man said, scurrying out of the way.

"How would you know? You're out here, and he's twenty feet away behind a closed door, probably wallowing in those smelly bed sheets. I hope that lice-riddled slut isn't in there with him," the woman said more to herself than to the guard.

"He's alone," the man replied, lowering his voice now. "I don't think he can do much with Tandy anymore, if you catch my meaning."

The woman spun to face him. "You are not allowed to make disparaging comments about Silas. That is the prerogative of exactly one person in this town, and you're looking at her. Is that clear?"

"Yes, Piper. I mean, yes ma'am," the man said, his Adam's apple bobbing.

The woman smiled, then whispered, "Keep me apprised of all the comings and goings, and there will be a place for you." Any eavesdroppers would not have heard. And there were always eavesdroppers in Idlewild.

The Murdock clan's leadership had been in flux for the last year. Silas would celebrate his 85th birthday this Christmas, and some wondered if he'd be alive to drink the traditional White Lightning toast. They further speculated that his demise might come soon, and not because of the cancer currently eating him alive. Someone might wish to expedite his death and take control of Idlewild.

Silas still officially held the reins of power, but Piper and Wyatt had been running most of the day-to-day operations since summer. More recently, Silas had been abdicating even major decisions to first Piper and then Wyatt, and then back to Piper. The resulting clashes between his daughter and his first lieutenant seemed to amuse him, distracting from whatever pain the cancer inflicted on his shriveled body.

Everyone knew what was happening, and most folks weren't ready to pledge their support for either of the two would-be leaders until a clear winner emerged. If they jumped the gun and backed the wrong horse, they might pay a deadly price.

Piper stepped into the darkened bedroom. She sniffed at the stench—— cancer-rot coupled with unwashed bed sheets. "Good morn-ing, Silas," she said.

"Tandy don't seem to mind the smell," croaked the figure in the bed. He had interpreted her sniff. It was entirely possible he kept the bedding filthy on purpose, just to fuck with people.

"Tandy is a brainless vagina, nothing more." Piper struck a match and lit a nearby candle. The kerosene had run out months ago.

"She's a brainless vagina with a mouth that can suck a tennis ball through a garden hose," Silas replied with a raspy cackle that ended in a coughing fit.

Piper moved beside the bed, waiting for the spasm to pass. After Silas hawked up a wad of gray phlegm and spat it into a Mason jar on a bedside table, his watery eyes focused on his daughter. The eyes used to be brown, but cataracts had turned them into eerie whitewashed orbs. Nobody knew exactly how blind Silas was now, not even his daughter.

"Can we talk about more pressing matters than your concubine?" Piper asked.

"You sure do like them big words, don't you, bitch?"

Piper took no offense; her father had called her that since puberty. One might even consider it a term of endearment, since most women in Idlewild were called worse.

But no one besides her father was allowed to use that word. Not to her.

"I met with Ezra a few hours ago. We have trouble."

"Do tell." His voice sounded powerful now. He couldn't maintain it for long, but some vestiges of strength remained in the desiccated body, a testimony to the old bastard's tenacity.

"The Whitakers are sending a three-man team to infiltrate Idlewild. Or I should say a two-man, one-woman team."

Silas picked up on an undercurrent. "Who?"

"Trevor, one of their best Scouts, some new guy we don't know, and ... *her*. She's back."

"Fuck."

"Yeah. At least we've been tipped off. We'll be ready for them."

"What else?"

"Ezra wasn't included in the meeting, so we don't know the particulars. He believes the new guy is from around here, but he's not one of us."

By that, she meant the Mountain People, which included anyone born in Appalachia and raised within a social framework unique to the region, the protocols of which were instinctively understood by those immersed in it from birth. 'Us' included the Whitakers as well as the Murdocks, despite their inherent animosity, along with a half-dozen Tennessee and Kentucky clans who didn't survive the pandemic.

"Why are they sending spies?" Silas said, his voice returning to the raspy, weak version. That transition was happening more quickly these days.

"Ezra thinks it has something to do with the recon mission we sent to that storage complex."

"They still haven't come back?" he mused. "Maybe they're not going to. Maybe they found something valuable there and the Whitakers killed 'em."

"That's a possibility. Euel sent out some Scouts to look for his daughter, who hadn't returned when she was supposed to. Ezra didn't know where she'd gotten off to, but the red-haired man named Fergus was with her. Then the Scouts returned with him, Serena Jo, and the other man, whose name is Ray. And Hannah."

"Hmmm," Silas said, his milky eyes staring up at the rafters.

Piper waited. Silas was a lot of things, mostly bad, but he was almost as intelligent as herself, which made him the second smartest person she knew. Perhaps the third, if she factored Hannah into the equation.

The old man was analyzing what she'd told him. He would remember every word of the information because he retained everything. His eidetic or *photographic* memory wasn't shared with his daughters. Piper would have known if her estranged sister had the ability because they used to be close, as most twins are. But that was a lifetime ago, and Piper had experienced enough hardship and pain to develop a simmering resentment toward the sister who abandoned her.

Finally, Piper spoke impatiently. "We have two options——first, send teams to intercept the spies and bring them here for interrogation."

"And the second option?" Silas said, a smile pulling up one corner of his nearly toothless mouth.

"I can tell by your tone you already know."

"You're a smart little bitch, but you ain't as smart as your pa." He paused, stroking his chin. "Maybe Wyatt is the man for the job of leading this clan after all."

The woman moved so fast that even if Silas was able to see clearly, she still would have been a blur. She pressed a blade against his scrawny throat.

"Keep it up, old man, and I'll put you out of your misery right now."

The cackling fit that followed seemed to give him a boost of energy.

"That's why I keep you around, Piper. Every now and then you do me proud."

"Thanks," she replied. "Anyway, the second option is to let them come and see what they do next. Obviously, they'll have a plan to infiltrate us. I think we could obtain more information by observing their strategy than by torturing them. People will say whatever they think you want to hear when you're holding a knife to their cock or their nipples."

"True 'nuff. That's the way to go."

"Wyatt won't think so. He'll want to go charging into the woods."

"You're the one that got the intel, so you get to make the decision."

She nodded, then turned to leave.

The milky orbs followed her progress until she was gone.

Chapter 11

Willadean

"What do you mean, you can't tell me?" Willa kept her voice low since they sat in the kitchen house, where a few late-risers still remained, chatting about the weather and other boring stuff. Nobody outside of their three-person pack needed to know their business. Especially grownups. And Willa got the sense the news her brother withheld was big.

Cricket munched on the extra corn muffin he'd finagled from the cooks, probably donated because they felt sorry for him. Having a drunk for a father scored him a few perks. Ordinarily, Willa and the boys would eat at the picnic tables outside, but a cold front had put the kibosh to that. None of the early morning snow had stuck to the ground, but it was still colder than a witch's tit. She allowed herself the mental cliché because she found it both amusing and perplexing. She figured a witch would run hot, not cold.

After a moment, Harlan signed: *She made me swear a blood oath.*

"Bull crap. Mama has never been involved in a blood oath. She doesn't even know about them."

Harlan nodded vigorously. *Yes, she does!*

"Well, who told her about them, huh? Not me."

Harlan shrugged. *I don't know how she knew, but she did it correctly, so there's no way I can break it.*

Cricket observed the conversation with interest, clearly relieved not to be the focus of Willa's ire.

"Fine. But if I guess it, you're obligated to confirm. That's the loophole in a blood oath," Willa said.

Harlan narrowed his eyes and didn't respond. Every now and then, he glanced apprehensively at Cricket.

Willa read those glances as a clue and switched to their special twin-sign language, which Cricket couldn't follow. He'd only mastered the regular version, like Mama.

She signed: *Does this have to do with Cricket?*

Harlan nodded slowly. *Sort of.*

Willa picked up on the implication. *His daddy, right? This is about Ezra? What's that drunken fool done now?*

I told you, I can't tell.

She shot him her most intimidating look, which had no impact. That happened more often these days.

Switching gears now, she contemplated recent events, mining for tidbits that might pertain to Ezra. Fact one: Cricket's father had been MIA last night. Fact two: He'd returned this morning just as the three were heading to the kitchen house for breakfast. Fact three: When they'd passed him on the road, he looked tired but otherwise normal. Fact four: His usual shifty-eyed expression looked shiftier than usual. Fact five, and it was significant: Willa hadn't caught a whiff of moonshine when he walked by. Cricket's father had smelled like dirty laundry and body odor, but not alcohol. And folks who'd been drinking Old Smokey always reeked of it the next morning. Even Pops.

She twin-signed: *He was in the woods last night, but he wasn't getting drunk.*

Harlan gave her a hint of a nod.

Did you see him on one of your astral adventures?

Another nod.

If Ezra hadn't been drinking, what other mischief could he have been up to in the woods in the middle of the night? Decent folks were home sleeping then. The notion of *decent folks* triggered an image of what *indecent* folks might be doing in secrecy. Willa was old enough and had read enough books to know what grownups did under the sheets. And apparently, doing it with someone besides your spouse could make it even more exciting.

Was he hooking up with one of the married ladies?

Harlan snorted. It *was nothing like that …*

Willa picked up on the undercurrent. *Did he meet up with someone?*

Harlan's nod was more vigorous now.

Damn it, Harlan, just tell me.

Nope.

She gritted her teeth and concentrated. What other details about Ezra had she tucked away in her brain? He was a terrible father, even when he was home. He didn't beat Cricket, but he neglected him. If not for the kindness of the other villagers, Cricket would have perished in the aftermath of the pandemic. Ezra was lazy and barely contributed to their community.

But he did have a knack for beekeeping. It was his saving grace. Ezra didn't even need to smoke the hives before handling them. He was a kind of bee whisperer. Was it truly a skill or a talent, akin to shooting straight or field-dressing a bear? Yes, because honey was liquid gold in this part of the world, especially now. Honey provided sweetness in place of sugar, which had run out long ago. Honey had been used as a natural antibiotic for thousands of years. Just like the Mountain People, the ancient Egyptians used it in poultice form for wounds. And perhaps the most important feature of honey: It never spoils. Archeologists had dug up clay pots containing three-thousand-year-old honey that was still fit to eat. Ezra's ability with the bees was perhaps the reason he hadn't been ousted from Whitaker holler a long time ago.

All this data flashed through her brain in about five seconds, but it hadn't told her a damn thing about what the man had been doing in the woods at night, nor who he might have been meeting. Suddenly, a clue popped into her head. Why would a Whitaker need to meet someone secretly?

Because that person wasn't a Whitaker and was most likely from an enemy camp. And the only enemy camp she knew about was the Murdocks.

Bingo.

Ezra was meeting someone from Idlewild? You have to tell me if I'm right!

Harlan shrugged. *We think so. We're not sure who it was.*

Who else knows about this besides Mama?

Mister Fergus was there when I told her about the dream.

Hmmmm, Willa thought. Perhaps she could pry information from her former teacher. But before she went that route, she set her sights on Cricket, who was currently licking vestiges of cornbread and honey from his grungy fingers.

"Cricket, why did your daddy go off last night?"

"I reckon he wanted to do some private drinkin'."

"When we saw him a little while ago, he didn't smell like moonshine."

"He ain't been smelling like moonshine lately. Maybe he's giving it up!" Cricket said, excitement turning up the corners of his sticky lips.

Willa was entering thorny territory, so she chose her words carefully. "How many times a week would you say your daddy goes into the woods at night?"

"I reckon at least once a week. Sometimes twice. I don't always come to your house, though. Sometimes I stay home. I'm not a baby, you know. Not usually."

"Is it a regular day of the week? Or does something happen just before he goes off at night? I mean, like, something important?"

"It used to be pretty much every Friday. I know that 'cuz you and Harlan go over to your Pops' place on Fridays and I'm usually home twiddling my thumbs. But lately, it seems like it's … what's the word?"

"Random?"

"Yes, that. I ain't sure what you're getting at, Willa."

"When did he leave yesterday? What had happened just before he left for the woods?"

Cricket scrunched up his face in concentration. Willa used to think of it as the 'dumb scrunch,' but these days Cricket was exhibiting signs of higher intelligence. The 'dumb scrunch' sometimes precipitated interesting information.

"The Scouts had their meetin'."

Double bingo. She twin-signed: *What if Ezra is a spy? A mole for the Murdocks? What if he's been tipping them off to all the goings-on here in the holler?*

That would make him a bad guy, Willa, and I don't want Cricket's daddy to be a bad guy. Harlan looked distraught.

I don't either, but think about it. Cricket would be better off without him if he ends up getting banished.

Harlan glanced over again at their friend, worry and affection evident on his face. He turned back. *Think about it, Willa. What do you suppose will happen to Ezra if Mama finds out he's a spy? You think she'd just pack his bags and send him on his way?*

Damn. Harlan was right. She shook her head. No. *She'd put him in the ground.*

Chapter 12

Ray

"We still have miles to go before Idlewild," Ray said. "Why are we separating now?"

"Because something tells me we need to," Hannah replied. Her usual easy smile was gone.

The three would-be spies stood in a section of the forest Ray had never been in before. The snowfall had stopped, but the woods looked frigid and uninviting. Most of the leaves from the deciduous trees lay on the forest floor, looking less vibrant in their scarlet and gold than they had when clinging to the limbs. Autumn had come and gone too quickly, allowing winter to bully her way into the Smoky Mountains earlier than anyone would have preferred.

Especially those who had to camp out under the stars at night.

"That's not helpful. *Something tells you*? What, some kind of a gut instinct?" he said, contemplating the rest of the journey spent in Trevor's company without Hannah.

"You could call it that. You two just continue on with the plan as we discussed. The only difference is I'm separating from you now instead of later."

Ray struggled with unknowns. He always had. So when the specific plan of their dangerous mission changed suddenly, a familiar gnawing sensation blossomed in the pit of his stomach. After being shot, his usual anxiety at being outside had vanished under Hannah's care. But a few of his other neuroses still resided in the dark recesses of his psyche.

Hannah sensed his unease and squeezed his shoulder. It was a gesture meant to pacify him. For some reason it did. Something about the woman gave him comfort. Perhaps that was one of the reasons he didn't want to part ways with her so soon.

He glanced at Trevor, whose stoic face revealed nothing, then turned back to Hannah in time to receive a peck on the cheek. The next moment, she disappeared into the forest before Ray had a chance to question her further.

"How does she do that?" he asked, trying to keep his annoyance at bay. "She's like a tiny Sasquatch."

Trevor chuckled. "It's our way. Kids in these parts grow up knowing how to be quiet and stealthy in the woods. If they don't, they're likely to get smacked upside the head when they scare off the ten-point buck their daddy was drawing a bead on."

"So it's obvious I'm a city boy?"

"You could say that. Come on. I'd like to cover a few more miles before we set up camp for the night."

Trevor remained silent the rest of the day. Ray tried to engage him once, but the Scout merely placed his index finger against his lips and continued striding silently through the forest. Apparently, there was to be no chatting during the hike. Ray was fine with that, since he wasn't much on small talk anyway, but he'd hoped to get a better feel for his partner in crime prior to their arrival in Idlewild.

Finally, when it seemed like they had walked so far that Ray half-expected to see the Atlantic Ocean just past the next hillock, the sun slipped behind the mountaintops. The sudden half-light triggered an eerie, howling cacophony not too far away.

"The coyotes say it's time for humans to hunker down." Trevor said. The deep voice sounded like a natural part of the forest's ambient noise, blending seamlessly with the coos of a mourning dove and the tranquil bubbling of a nearby stream. "We can get some sleep, then arrive at Idlewild in the morning. That'll be better than showing up there at night."

"I agree with the coyotes," Ray said. He was tired, but the arduous hike hadn't exhausted him. Maybe he wasn't as much of a city boy as Trevor believed.

"No fire tonight, and I'll take the first watch," Trevor said, shrugging off his pack.

"If you insist, but I don't mind. Honestly, I feel pretty good."

Trevor just smiled and unrolled his sleeping bag, which looked as if it had served several generations of Whitakers. Ray was thankful for the Marmot ultralight sleeping bag he'd brought from the warehouse, rated to a chilly twenty degrees. It felt like they might come close to that tonight.

His Casio told him it was already hovering just above freezing.

"That's a fancy watch you got there," Trevor said.

Ray shrugged. "The G-Shock was one of the last items I bought before things went south. I figured, why the hell not? I'd had my eye on it for a while, and a tactical watch seemed like a useful item to have in an uncertain world. I bought plenty of extra batteries to go with it. A watch with a dead battery isn't much good."

"So you saw it coming? I reckon working for the government gave you access to information that wasn't shared with the rest of us."

There was no denying it. As head of one of the nation's five Strategic National Stockpiles, he'd received classified information that gave him an enormous advantage over most of the population. Many of the items he'd need to live comfortably were already stockpiled in the warehouse, and he'd been able to purchase whatever wasn't. During those days, he barely slept. The mental and physical spreadsheets demanded constant updating as random items popped into his head. Itemizing, cataloging, and purchasing everything one might need during the course of a lifetime might have been overwhelming for some. But Ray, a glorified bean-counter, had been up to the challenge.

"Yes," Ray replied. There was no point in hedging the issue. "I had a level-2 security clearance. We were told the mortality rate was around fifty percent, even though the CDC publicly claimed it was much lower. They did that to keep people from panicking. But anyone paying attention knew it was vastly higher than even the fifty percent they claimed to us insiders. On a personal level, I figured there were only two ways it could go: I'd die or I'd live. If I lived, I wanted to be ready for a life without restaurants, Netflix, and a dentist around the corner."

"Pretty smart. Mighta been good to tell others, though, so they could do the same."

Ray experienced a familiar twinge of guilt. Of course he'd contemplated doing just that, but if the world didn't end, his job would have. He was about to say as much, when Trevor held up a calloused hand.

"Look, I'm not judging you. I understand about security clearances. Besides, folks here in the holler read the writing on the wall, too. Our people weren't dying off like so many others, and we took our own measures. Even before Serena Jo showed up with that U-Haul, we limited access to our village and bought all the kerosene and seeds and other necessities we could afford. Not everyone had a Citi card, but those who had credit maxed it out. We all pitched in as best we could. And we were ready when it came."

Ray nodded. "Your people seem to have flourished."

"We're doing okay," Trevor said, smiling. "You really lived inside a building the last two years? Never went outside?"

To someone like Trevor, the notion was unfathomable. But to a person with agoraphobia, it hadn't been so bad. Or so Ray thought——until he met Serena Jo.

"I went up to the roof to fly my drones. That allowed me to feel like I was getting out into the world."

Trevor nodded. "Makes sense. Still, your drones can't smell the fragrance of the sweet pinesap flower that lingers like French perfume above the leaf litter. They can't stroke the lamb's ear plant, which feels like petting a kitten. Those things have to be experienced in person, not through a camera lens."

Ray blinked, at a loss for words.

Trevor noticed. "You thought I was just a dumb hillbilly, right?"

"Not dumb," Ray replied. "I hadn't pegged you as poetic, though."

"Mountain People are used to bigotry. Outsiders see a few missing teeth or hear a double negative and make their judgments. That's human nature."

"And it's a damn shame. I've had my eyes opened recently, I assure you."

Trevor pointed at a nearby hemlock. "I'll be up there for the first watch. If anyone comes snooping or a predator decides he's got a hankering for human meat, they'll be focused on you, not on the person watching from ten feet above."

"In other words, I'm bait."

"Just for the first four hours, then I'll be the bait."

"Fair enough," Ray said with a smile. Something had shifted in the dynamic between them. It felt good.

He was about to say as much, when a sharp explosion echoed through the forest, and a nickel-sized hole appeared in Trevor's forehead. Before Ray had a chance to react, a voice came from behind.

"Don't move a muscle, city boy, or the next one will come through the back of your head."

Ray obeyed. Miserably, he watched blood ooze from Trevor's head. The brown eyes remained open. The formerly stoic expression had shifted to one of surprise.

Fury exploded in Ray's belly. His hand twitched. He was thinking about the gun in his backpack and the hunting knife in his front pocket.

"You won't get another warning," the voice drawled. It sounded bored, as if the speaker had more pressing matters than dealing with an incompetent fool in the woods.

***

Ray thought the night would never end. They took no breaks to rest, and only twice he'd been given a drink of water from a dubious metal canteen. The water tasted muddy, as if collected from a rain puddle instead of a mountain stream. He hoped he wouldn't have to deal with a bout of dysentery in addition to being a captive of murderous thugs.

The fury had subsided, replaced with cold resolve. He would stay alive, no matter what. Not just to avenge Trevor's death, but to help in the inevitable battle. He knew he was in the company of the Murdocks because the small group's leader answered to the name of Wyatt. According to Hannah, Wyatt was the right-hand man of the clan's leader. Full-blown war between the two factions might have been averted before, but the assassination of a Whitaker Scout rendered it a foregone conclusion. Ray intended to play a crucial role.

During the hours-long forced march, Ray contemplated the situation. Had this group——composed of three men and a scar-faced woman——known of the Whitaker's spy mission? Or had they just gotten lucky and stumbled upon Ray and Trevor?

Ray soon had his answer.

"Piper's gonna be pissed," the woman said. Her voice was raspy, that of a lifelong smoker. "She wanted to let these assholes just waltz into town."

"Who gives a fuck if she is? Wyatt's gonna be the one running the show. Ain't that right, Wyatt?" someone said. Ray glanced behind him at the man who'd spoken, taking in the tobacco-stained beard.

"What the fuck you lookin' at, numbnuts? Eyes forward, you pansy asshole."

Ray turned back in time to see the man leading the group give him an appraising glance. Ray realized Wyatt was watching his reaction to the insults. Smart. You can learn a lot about a person that way. Then he winked at Ray and grinned. No missing teeth in that smile.

Ray maintained a bland expression, focusing on his boots as he navigated the forest's natural obstacles: woody vines, large rocks hidden within a carpet of dead leaves, and occasional animal scat. Ray was no hunter, so had no idea what type of animals were responsible for the random piles. But a mound they passed seemed especially fresh.

As if reading his thoughts, Wyatt said, "Mountain lions are making a comeback in these parts. Folks say you never know you're being stalked by one until you're dead. They always come from behind. I wonder how painful it would be to get eaten by a big cat like that." His voice was surprisingly high-pitched, yet melodic and pleasant. With a voice like that, Wyatt might have been a motivational speaker or a televangelist.

But Ray knew better. The man was a two-bit thug, the lieutenant of a four-bit thug in a backwater burg of rural Tennessee. A couple of big fish in a small pond before the world ended. Now their importance — their corruption — had mushroomed as a direct result of the reduced population. There weren't many people left these days, and that made the Murdocks more dangerously consequential than ever.

The woman gave a throaty chuckle. "I can think of worse ways to go," she said, evoking laughter from her male companions.

Ray thought about her scars, then remembered what Hannah had said about the Idlewild women: *Silas Murdock is the clan's patriarch and also the devil incarnate, if you believe in that sort of thing ... Some of the women become soldiers for the clan if they're strong and tough enough ... The rest are fed heroin or meth to keep them from running away, and then they're regularly knocked up, creating new Murdock cockroaches to replace the ones that die off.*

He shuddered. Not from fear, but from a profound sense of loathing. The old Ray might have been terrified right now. But Ray 2.0 banished thoughts of his own torture or demise to a rarely used mental compartment, then continued to monitor the ongoing conversation. He hoped to glean some useful information.

"What do you reckon Silas is gonna give you for getting one of their Scouts?" the third man said. This one walked ahead, beside Wyatt. Was that significant? Probably. No doubt an unspoken hierarchy existed within the Murdock clan, just like any East Coast crime syndicate. Ray studied him from behind. The man was taller than average, well over six feet, with a narrow waist and broad shoulders. His shaved head swiveled constantly, looking for potential danger. He moved differently than Wyatt, less like a woodsman and more like a soldier.

"Tandy!" the other two replied in unison.

Wyatt glanced back with a smile.

"Levi, you know there ain't no better prize than that little filly," said the man from behind. "Seriously, though, maybe Myra's right. I hope Piper ain't too pissed. She said we was supposed to let them assholes walk right into town. You made the right call by going after 'em. Look what we got to show for it! A dead Scout and a pansy-ass we can pump for information."

Despite his bravado, the bearded man was clearly worried about Hannah's sister. If Piper was anything like Hannah, the concern was justified.

"It was a calculated risk, and it paid off," Wyatt replied. "When we get there, nobody say a word until I've talked to Silas. Understood?" Menace shifted the voice into a lower pitch.

Ray wondered, though, if someone like Wyatt was actually more lethal when smiling and commenting on the weather.

"Yes, sir," all three replied.

Wyatt's shift in demeanor put a damper on the conversation. The group trudged wordlessly through the woods. Everyone but Ray seemed adept at avoiding the vines. Twice he tripped and fell, evoking derisive snorts from the two behind him.

When he stumbled a third time, he turned to offer a snarky preemptive. But the scarred woman and the bearded man had disappeared. No mountain lion could have taken two adults out that quickly and quietly.

Hope surged through him. He kept walking, making more noise than ever in an attempt to disguise the fact that two people were missing. And also to give cover to whatever Hannah may be planning next.

Ray saw the exact moment when Wyatt realized something was amiss. Levi's reaction came a half second later.

Perhaps the calisthenics in the warehouse were paying off; Ray's reaction time wasn't far behind that of his captors. He threw himself into the nearby brush and scrambled as far into the tangled darkness as he could before gunfire exploded all around him.

He kept crawling. Starlight didn't penetrate this far off the game trail, but he retained his sense of direction and continued heading west. When he realized he was making enough noise to summon all the mountain lions and Murdocks in the vicinity, he stopped. Regulating his breathing, he crawled into a mound of thorny branches similar to the one he and Hannah had hidden in near the warehouse.

Occasional shots echoed farther to the east, answered by gunfire not so far away. He had identified the cap-gun sound of Hannah's silenced MK23, but she'd switched to one of Skeeter's Mossberg rifles. He recognized its report.

Minutes passed in silence now. The sound of his heart pounding in his ears almost covered the crunch of dead leaves on the other side of his thorny hiding place.

"You can come out, Ray. They're hightailing it back to Idlewild." Hannah's voice was pitched low but sounded otherwise normal. She wasn't even winded.

He scrambled out just as she slid a lethal-looking knife from a calf sheath. Moonlight glinted on the blade.

"Follow me," she said, heading in the direction of the game trail.

He knew better than to let her get out of sight and jogged to catch up.

"Thanks. I guess I owe you one," he said. She didn't respond.

He remembered Trevor at that moment.

"Are we going back to retrieve his body?" he whispered.

"Trevor? No. Waste of time and energy."

"Oh. I assumed ... never mind."

"We have another task to perform before we return to the village."

"I'm glad to hear we're abandoning the mission. I think they were expecting us."

"They were."

"How do you know?"

"I just do."

"One of these days you'll have to explain these gut instincts of yours."

"No, I won't," she said. "We're here," she added, stopping at a giant poplar with a trunk circumference the size of a large tractor tire. At its base slumped the scar-faced woman, Myra.

Her eyelids flew open at the sight of them.

Hannah yanked off the bandana gag.

Myra promptly spat. Hannah wiped it off her cheek with a gloved hand as if she were brushing away a splatter of mud.

"You know how this is going to end, Myra," Hannah said. "The question is, do you want to go the easy way or the hard way?"

"I know who you are," Myra said. "I heard about you. At first, I thought you were Piper, but there's no way she coulda gotten here so fast. You're the sister."

"I can't deny it. Now, tell me how they knew about us."

"Fuck you."

Hannah reached out to the woman's foot, quickly removed her boot, and then her sock. Ray began to get a sickening feeling in his stomach.

Myra's big toe provided little resistance to Hannah's knife.

"You can cut off all my toes, I don't care. I been through worse than that. Nothing you do will make me talk."

Her scarred face seemed to confirm the truth of her words.

Hannah nodded. She'd been squatting on the ground, her face level with Myra's. Wearing a thoughtful expression now, she rocked back on her heels and studied the disfigured face.

"Clearly, they put you through hell. Let me guess: rape, beatings, time spent in the shed?"

Myra narrowed her pale eyes but said nothing.

"Why remain loyal to people who did horrible things to you?"

"They're my people."

Hannah gave a derisive snort. "That may be the stupidest thing I've ever heard."

"What would you know about loyalty? You left years ago. Who runs away from a father and a sister ... a sister who probably needed her help? You must be a special kind of bitch to abandon your family."

Hannah arched an eyebrow. "I'm definitely a special kind of bitch. Escaping an abusive situation isn't abandonment, though. It's self-preservation."

"Call it whatever you want. You walked away from your kin."

Something changed in Hannah's demeanor; it was subtle, but Ray noticed.

Myra had hit a nerve. Ray suspected it had nothing to do with running away from a psychopathic father and everything to do with deserting a sister. A special bond existed between twins, stronger than average sibling ties.

"I did what was necessary for my survival," Hannah said, her words clipped. "Now, back to you, Myra. What would you consider the optimal outcome for your current situation?"

Myra gave a raspy chuckle. "You drop dead of a stroke and your stick-up-his-ass boyfriend breaks his neck tripping over a vine."

Hannah snorted. "Bonus points for creativity. Like I said, you know you're not going to leave these woods. So how painful do you want your death to be?"

"Uh, Hannah, can we have a word?" Ray said. He would not mutely stand by during another murder.

Hannah swiveled to face him. The expression she wore was a new one. Ray's bowels turned to ice water. The whimsical woodland fairy creature was gone, replaced by someone who could slither into a darkened bedroom and slit a man's throat while his wife snored beside him. He knew Hannah was a mercenary of some type, and perhaps a torturer and assassin as well. How many people had she murdered while "taking out the garbage"?

She murmured, "No, we cannot have a word, Ray. Silence is your only recourse at the moment."

He dry-swallowed, then nodded.

"I'm feeling magnanimous, Myra. I've decided to let you live, but under a set of rather unpleasant circumstances. First, I'm going to cut out your eyeballs so you can't see to find your way out of the forest. Then I'll sever your achilles tendons so you can't walk out of the forest. After that, I'll shoot your kneecaps and cut off your hands so you can't crawl out of the forest. Finally, I'll slice off your tongue so no one can hear your screams. There will be no chance of rescue or escape. Who would want to live so horribly disabled anyway? Or, I will kill you quickly and painlessly if you tell me what I want to know. Your choice."

Myra began to talk.

She told them Piper had been meeting an informant in the woods between Idlewild and Whitaker holler for months and that the informant's name was Ezra. Ray remembered him as Cricket's worthless daddy. Piper had recruited Ezra at last year's moonshine barter, and he'd been feeding her information about the Whitakers for months. Recently, he reported activity surrounding a commercial storage complex. The Murdocks sent a reconnaissance team there, but they hadn't yet returned.

"That's because I killed them. All of them. Eli, too."

Myra's eyes grew large. "You killed Wyatt's son? You're gonna pay for that."

"I doubt it," Hannah said, then made a sweeping motion with the knife.

Ray closed his eyes as a macabre second mouth appeared under Myra's chin.

When he opened them again, Hannah stood inches away from him. For such a small person, her presence seemed to fill the forest. She didn't say anything, but rather studied him in silence, waiting for his reaction. Ray knew his life depended on what he said next.

And he didn't care.

"I realize you think you had to do it, Hannah. But I'm not going to lie. It makes me sick. It's one thing to kill a person who's attacking you or hurting someone else. But murdering a human being in cold blood makes me look at you differently."

One corner of her mouth turned up, and the normal twinkle returned to her eyes. Killer Hannah had vanished.

"Then it's a good thing I don't need your admiration, isn't it?"

Ray knew at that moment that if he'd sugarcoated his feelings in order to placate her, he'd probably be dead now. The right course of action had been the honest one, which, in Ray's experience, was almost always the case.

Almost always.

"Why not just let her go?"

"You tell me," she said, then took off.

He followed.

"You think she would have gone back to Idlewild and told them everything she knew."

"Yes."

"But what did she know that would have been so damaging? War between the clans is inevitable, right?"

"Yes. What else?"

"You told her you killed their reconnaissance team, including Wyatt's son. That might not have been the best move." The words were out before he could stop them. Ray held his breath, thinking of Myra's throat and the inky blood pooling on the forest floor.

Thankfully, Hannah snorted. "You're right. My ego got the best of me. I'm not perfect. What else?"

He pondered the question. "They already know about you, so it can't be that. Ezra told Piper you'd returned."

"Correct. But perhaps they don't yet know about my particular skill set."

"True."

"What else?" Hannah nudged.

Ray thought back to one of their first conversations. "You were killing another cockroach."

"Winner, winner, chicken dinner."

"Hannah, humans aren't cockroaches. There must be a few worthy Murdocks in Idlewild."

She stopped in her tracks and did the head swivel thing again. He winced in anticipation.

"Your world view is desperately, laughably narrow, Ray. You spent most of your adult life behind a computer screen, receiving a steady paycheck, driving a late model car, living in a nice house, following the law. You've never starved, truly struggled, or been tortured. I bet you've never encountered anyone who was evil on a *genetic* level. So you must take my word for this because I have experienced all those things and more. Everyone who survived the apocalypse — the good ones — will be safer in their beds at night when every last Murdock is dead."

"But you're one of them." He knew he was pushing his luck. "Actually, so are your daughter and your grandchildren."

"They're only half Murdock, and they were never exposed to Silas. Nature, nurture ..." She gave a dismissive shoulder shrug.

"What about you? Expanding on your Murdock eradication theory, you shouldn't be allowed to live either."

Hannah gave him a thoughtful look. "Maybe you have a point."

Chapter 13

Fergus

"Mama's a chimera," Willadean was saying.

Fergus had just caught Willa and Harlan lurking in the crawl space beneath Serena Jo's cabin; the tip of Harlan's boot sticking out from under the house telegraphed their location. They'd been eavesdropping, of course, listening to Hannah and Ray report to Mama about the failed mission. Fergus had been denied access to the debriefing, much to his annoyance.

"You know ... front of a lion, back of a dragon. Generally speaking, she's serious trouble coming or going," Willadean continued. "She'll open a big can of whoop-ass on the Murdocks for killing a Scout. I hate to think what she's gonna do to Cricket's daddy."

"I know what a chimera is, young lady," Fergus replied. He herded them away from the cabin and a few yards into the forest. He didn't want anyone to know he was interrogating children. "They killed Trevor? That's the worst possible news."

"Exactly," Willadean replied. "You don't take out one of our top tier people without serious consequences." The magnitude of her own words finally seemed to catch up to her. "That was Brock's daddy."

Harlan nodded silently. The golden eyes glittered with unshed tears. Willadean, on the other hand, was nowhere in the vicinity of crying. She seemed dangerously close to sprinting away and singlehandedly launching a tiny terrorist attack on Idlewild.

"What else did you hear?" Fergus prompted, ignoring her sudden ferocity. The child would likely grow up to be more dangerous than a mere chimera.

"There's going to be a war. Hannah, my grandmother, killed some of the Murdocks at Ray's warehouse. You were there for that?"

Fergus nodded.

"One of the guys she killed was the son of Wyatt, a top dog. But the Murdocks don't know any of that yet."

"That's good." Fergus said. He knew, though, that it was only a matter of time before vengeance would be demanded from both sides.

"Here's the problem, the way I see it. Hannah says there are only half as many Whitakers as there are Murdock cockroaches. That's what she calls them." Willadean grinned. At that moment, she looked more like her grandmother than her mother.

Fergus didn't much care for the resemblance.

"We only have about a hundred Whitakers, and that includes the cooks and the field workers and the kids. So our odds aren't good, but I figure each of our Scouts should count for two or three Murdocks. Don't you agree?"

"I do," he replied, even though he wasn't at all convinced of the superiority of the Whitakers. He knew exactly what type of humans populated the planet now, and the Murdocks could well be as inherently talented with firearms, murder, and warfare as some of those he'd encountered during his recent travels. And they might have taken additional brutish survivors into their fold.

Willadean nodded, relief visible on her face. "Hannah also killed two of the Murdocks who murdered Brock's daddy, but two more got away. They're probably back in Idlewild telling everybody what happened. So we need to get ready fast."

"Did you overhear what your mother plans to do about Ezra?"

"Yes," she whispered. The blond pigtails swung left and then right as the child scanned the perimeter. Few people were out so early on such a chilly morning, and none within earshot. "First, they're going to apprehend and secure him, quietly. Then Mama is going to tell Brock about his daddy. Then she's gonna have a talk with Cricket about *his* daddy. Poor kid. He'll probably come live with us, even though there's not enough room for the little weirdo. After that, she'll call a meeting. It'll be a straight majority vote between banishment and the death penalty. But we all know how that's gonna go. Mama doesn't tolerate traitors. She'll want to put him in the ground."

***

Fergus had no intention of standing idly by while a war between groups of precious survivors, many of whom were exceptionally gifted people, continued to brew. Why the *Cthor* had genetically engineered monstrosities like the Murdocks, he had no idea. After listening to Hannah's description of events in Idlewild, he'd been nauseated. The *Cthor* might have done it on purpose, or more likely, the Murdocks' malignity was an unfortunate side effect of DNA dabbling performed millennia ago.

Something else was beginning to come into focus, too. For quite some time, Fergus had known that a disproportionate percentage of twins had survived the orchestrated plague. They seemed to be everywhere these days, and he thought he might now understand why. Something Willa had said triggered the internal revelation.

Mama's a damn chimera.

Perhaps the *Cthor* had been trying to manipulate the way the human genome managed multiple embryos in utero. Perhaps their goal had been to create a superior being by combining two embryos during the gestation period. Sometimes it doesn't work, and the mother gives birth to normal twins. Other times, an embryo dies and is absorbed by its sibling, who is then born with two complete sets of DNA.

Otherwise known as a human chimera.

These rare humans had been known to scientists for some time, but perhaps the truly special ones had never adequately been studied before the world ended. Perhaps the truly special ones survived the deadly, *genetic* disease that killed all the average people. And perhaps those truly special ones now populated the world as savants, geniuses, and psychopaths. Everyone walking around these days with seeming superpowers may have started out as two fetuses. Take it a step further in the case of Willadean and Harlan: maybe there had been four embryos sharing their mother's womb.

The theory was fascinating. What's better than one human with one genome? Two genomes occupying one body. Or four occupying two bodies. Double the intellect, double the mechanical skills, double the creative potential.

Double the capacity for evil.

Fergus was no molecular geneticist and had no idea if his theory was sound, but it made sense even if he didn't have the science quite right. And the knowledge filled him with apprehension. The Whitakers, with half the numbers, would not survive a war with the Murdocks.

But there *was* something he could do to increase their odds.

He ran the children off, then headed toward the abandoned school house. Nobody was getting any learning done with their world in flux. The building was cold, but it was empty and quiet. After closing his eyes and clearing his mind, he sent his *scythen* west.

It took a while before snatches of random thoughts began filtering in.

Glad we got that second greenhouse built. We're going to need a lot more food after that big group showed up from Nebraska.

Steven thinks he's the boss of everyone. Somebody ought to take him down a few notches.

Dad is probably going to fight me on this since I'm only seventeen, but I'm not waiting any longer. I think I'll propose tonight.

Dani doesn't realize she wants to be a mother. Or maybe she has a mental roadblock about ankle-biters. I just need to give her more time.

That last one made Fergus smile. The honest, open, and kind Sam would of course be an inadvertent sender. Profoundly good people tended to be.

Hello, who is this?

Uh oh. Fergus hadn't been trying to connect with an ordinary person. He'd hoped his *scythen* would be intercepted by a *Cthor-Vangt* missionary in the vicinity of Liberty, Kansas. His plan had been to use that missionary to get a message to someone who could help the Whitakers.

Instead, an unknown neophyte picked up his signal.

My name is Fergus. With whom do I have the pleasure of chatting?

Oh, hello Fergus. This is Maddie. I thought you died in the Hays battle. Are you communicating with me from the afterlife?

No, no. I'm not sure that's even possible.

That's what you think! He could sense her smile.

I see you're honing your scythen. *I didn't know you were aware of it.*

Yes, that bullet to my noggin helped shake loose quite a bit of weirdness. I don't understand it all yet, but I'm working on it.

Indeed! Well, you can be of enormous help to me then. I'm in the Smoky Mountains at the moment, and I need to get a message to Dani and Sam. They're still in Liberty?

Oh, yes. Of course everyone loves Sam, and people are more used to Dani these days.

Excellent. Here's what I need you to tell them …

Chapter 14

Idlewild

"You fucked up in a big way, Wyatt." Piper didn't bother hiding her pleasure.

Silas sat on his front porch, dressed for the chilly day. His cadaverous frame was covered in winter hunting attire; he had left the threadbare wool blanket inside, the one that was usually draped around his bony shoulders. A blanket-wrapped leader did not exude strength.

Wyatt struck a casual pose, leaning on the quaint streetlamp in Silas's neglected front yard. Of course the electrical lamp no longer worked. One of Silas's wives had it installed at some point to add 'ambience' to their property. Silas didn't give a rat's ass about ambience, but it had shut the woman up for a couple of weeks. Then the plague had shut her up forever.

"What do you have to say, Wyatt?" Silas said with a snicker.

"I disagree," Wyatt replied. "Levi got one of their best Scouts. That's not what I'd call a fuck-up."

Silas grunted in agreement. The white-washed eyeballs glided back and forth between his daughter, who stood near the bottom porch step, and his right-hand man.

Piper narrowed her eyes. "It was my call to make, and I wanted them here. Your little stunt exceeded your authority and cost us valuable information."

"We have one less Whitaker to deal with now, and a sharpshooter at that, right, Silas?" Wyatt grinned.

Silas grunted noncommittally.

Piper continued, "Hannah is still at large and we have no prisoners or infiltrators to glean information from. We're worse off now than we were yesterday. Like I said, you fucked up. You blew an opportunity that we'll never get again."

Silas remained silent, but his head swiveled back to Wyatt, whose grin seemed less convincing now.

"Fuck off, Piper. You're just posturing. Silas, I want to find out why that recon team hasn't returned. Something is going on at that storage complex, and we need to know what."

"Your boy is part of that team, ain't he?" Silas said. A sly tone crept into the raspy voice.

Wyatt replied, "Yeah, Eli is one of the six. They should have been back by now. I get the feeling something is up."

"We don't send out a follow-up team for a full week, Wyatt. That's protocol," Piper said. "You want to make a special exception for your boy? Too bad. That's not how things work around here. I should know about that."

"She's got a point, Wyatt. Piper ain't never got special favors 'cuz of her pedigree." Silas cackled.

Wyatt's eyes narrowed. "Fine. I'll start getting the troops in fighting shape. We need to get ready."

"Exactly. We need to get ready for war with the Whitakers because of you." Piper quickly covered the distance to the lamppost. "This will cost you, Wyatt." She whispered the last words so Silas wouldn't hear.

Wyatt glanced down at the intimidating woman. "Time will tell, Piper. You're not the only intelligent person in this town. Don't forget that."

"You're out of your league," she hissed, before turning back to Silas. "While he's mustering the troops, I'll be working on *strategies*. Wyatt, that word means combining and employing the means of war in planning and directing military movements and operations. In other words, using informed tactics rather than dumb brute force."

Silas snickered, then waved a gnarled hand in approval.

Wyatt watched her walk away, then glanced back at the porch where Silas still perched in a rusted lawn chair. The old man died a little more every day.

Wyatt smiled.

A young woman sat on a wooden stool watching the activity on the weed-choked asphalt beyond the window pane. She would be considered breathtaking if not for the profound sadness in her aquamarine eyes. Most Murdock men didn't notice the sorrow, nor would they care about it if they did. All that mattered was a pretty face, a skilled mouth and tongue, and a strong pelvic floor.

She'd been performing kegels since she was thirteen. Word in Idlewild was that she could smoke a cigarette with her vagina, so strong were her muscles *down there*. It was true. She could do it if she'd been inclined, but she wouldn't waste time on an activity so pointless, not even as a private sex show for Silas. Initiating the vagina-smoking rumor and making sure it circulated had been the point, with the ultimate goal of elevating herself within the Murdock hierarchy. And it had worked. The rumor made people notice her, talk about her, request her. Once she got to Silas, and more importantly, the ear of Silas, she was golden. Golden as in neither a breeder, nor a soldier, nor a sex slave, now that Silas had turned impotent. For a female to achieve such status in the hellhole of Idlewild was just short of miraculous.

Except for Piper, of course. She made her own rules.

Through the filmy glass, Tandy's gaze followed Wyatt as he strolled down one of the two streets bisecting the town. A few seconds later, Levi, Wyatt's right-hand man, materialized out of a clump of dead shrubs directly across from her house. She'd known Levi was there. He usually lurked near the red-light district when he wasn't off doing Wyatt's bidding.

Levi was well known to all the women in Idlewild, especially the young ones. Any female with two brain cells steered clear of him if she could. This informed avoidance was the result of another rumor Tandy had planted. As with the smoking-vagina rumor, it was also true. Levi had raped, or was currently scheming to rape, every prepubescent girl in town.

Tandy could tolerate just about anything. She had survived horrors most women outside the town's perimeters couldn't begin to fathom. But she drew the line at pedophilia. It was the only line she had, and it was wide and long and bright crimson. Nobody was going to cross that line as long as she had breath in her body.

The tricky part of any undertaking, either transparent or covert, was staying under the radar of anyone of importance in Idlewild. As the recently promoted supervisor of the sex workers at the young age of eighteen, she herself had become someone of importance. As Silas's new favorite plaything, her status increased further.

But what kept her safe was convincing everyone she had the brain of a gnat. She'd been working on that cover story her entire life, and it had served her well. Neither Piper nor Wyatt would ever perceive a threat coming from her direction. Sometimes she caught Silas looking at her askance, perhaps wondering if there weren't a few neurons firing behind the pretty face. So she would giggle, reach for his cock, and vanquish any notions he might have of mining for mental acuity.

Because of her status and subtle manipulations, she was able to influence people and situations in ways that benefited everyone, not just the strongest, the most ruthless, and the most politically powerful. That's why the females in the red-light district were enjoying slightly stale Little Debbies for breakfast instead of watered-down chicken broth.

On the street beyond her window, Wyatt had stopped to engage in an animated discussion with Levi. Someone less cautious would have lifted the window an inch or so to listen in. If that person had been caught eavesdropping on Wyatt, she would have been sent to the shed. People didn't always survive the shed, especially in the summer or winter. And the recent cold snap would make for a miserable stay.

Because Tandy analyzed her every move prior to making it, she did not lift the window. She didn't need to. Instead, she read the men's lips, a skill she'd honed over the years and from which she'd gleaned much valuable information. Nobody on earth knew she could do it.

Levi was saying, "Fuck her. We don't need a strategy. We have numbers."

Wyatt replied, "Don't be an idiot. Of course we need a strategy, but it won't be whatever she comes up with. I'll make sure of that."

Wyatt turned his head and seemed to peer directly at Tandy through the glass. She knew for a fact that he couldn't see her. She had carved faint notches into the wood flooring behind which her stool was now positioned. As long as she sat no closer, no one looking in from the street could see her.

Besides, if somebody did catch her there watching the two men, she could always claim to be daydreaming, not spying. *That window is shut! I can't hear what them boys is sayin' anyways.* Rarely a minute went by when she wasn't anticipating a problem and constructing an immediate solution. In her head she could hear the ignorant grammar and ditzy voice she would use to explain her presence there.

"You think it was a mistake to kill Trevor?" Levi said.

"No. It's going to bring things to a head, which is good for us."

Levi's lips were inches away from Wyatt's ear. Fortunately he was facing the window, so the words were easy to read. "Why don't we just kill 'em both?"

Tandy scanned the street in both directions. Nobody was nearby, but saying the words – even thinking those words – was incredibly dangerous. She knew exactly who Levi meant: Silas and Piper, the two people who stood in the way of Levi and Wyatt running things in Idlewild.

Wyatt surveyed the street too, his gaze slowing as he panned her window. She felt a sudden chill on the back of her neck. As bad as Levi was, Wyatt was worse.

"Not yet," Wyatt said. "Come on, let's see what Tandy's got on the menu for today." The perfect teeth in Wyatt's smile reminded her of *Shark Week*, a show she'd seen on television before the end of the world.

There wasn't time to process the most worrisome two words from the conversation. "Killing Trevor" meant she'd be getting a visit soon, and as much as she loved Brock, the timing was terrible. After she dealt with Wyatt and Levi, she would formulate a plan to address the information gathered from their conversation.

She stood, slid the stool back into its corner, placed a delicate crocheted doily on the warmth recently vacated, then moved toward the front door.

A rush of cold air greeted her along with the men. She plastered a dumb grin on her face and giggled a greeting.

Chapter 15

Willadean

"I'm sorry, Cricket. It must suck having a traitor for a daddy," Willa said to the miserable boy sitting beside her.

The plastic milk crate that doubled as a chair in her best friend's house wouldn't bear much more weight than that of the two children. Ezra must have sat on the sofa in the corner when he wanted to take a load off. Decades-old stains covered the disgusting thing, so Willa was quite happy to share the crate with Cricket.

Harlan hovered near the front door, visibly uncomfortable. Willa could relate. What do you say to a person whose father is about to be banished or executed? There wasn't a good way to address the situation, and Willa wasn't good at tip-toeing. Best just to get it all out there and deal with the fallout.

"I can't believe it. I knew he weren't no superhero like your mama, but I didn't know he was a damn traitor."

Willa wrapped her arm around the thin shoulders. In her kindest voice she said, "*Wasn't a* superhero."

"Really? You gonna correct my grammar at a time like this?" Cricket brushed away her arm.

"Sorry. Look at the bright side. You get to come live with us for a while."

"Like I want to live with a mean girl."

Willa felt the sting of the insult, but promptly dismissed it. Cricket was justified in being upset. She should cut him some slack. "You get to live with your dream woman, too. You'll be able to ogle Mama twenty-four-seven."

"I don't care about that. I'm over her."

She stifled a snort. "When did that happen?"

"Probably about the time she had my daddy dragged away with his wrists in zip-ties."

The little hillbilly had a point.

"Did she say when the vote is scheduled?"

Cricket's chin trembled. "At lunch today."

"She'd already been over to talk to Brock?"

Cricket nodded, swallowing hard. "At least his daddy died an honorable death."

This was one of those times when her friend surprised her. Not only did he use proper grammar, he effectively articulated his shame in one concise sentence.

Willa felt an intense stab of empathy for both boys. What would she do if she were in their shoes?

She gently placed her hand on Cricket's face and turned his head, forcing him to look her square in the eyes. "You have nothing to be ashamed of. This isn't about you. Everyone knows what a good kid you are. If it weren't for you and Harlan figuring out where the witch lived, I'd probably be dead right now. You boys helped track down the cabin where me and Mister Fergus were prisoners. I will never forget that, Cricket. You can hold your head high."

The green eyes became misty. "Thanks, Willa. I appreciate you saying that. But just so you know, I ain't coming to live with you. I know how this is gonna go today, and you do, too. I know your mama has every right to put my daddy in the ground. But while he ain't been a good daddy, he's the only one I got. I can't live in the same house as the person who plants him six feet under."

"Maybe the vote won't go that way. Maybe he'll just get banished." Even she could hear the lack of conviction in her voice.

Cricket shook his head.

Harlan moved closer and signed. *Let's go talk to Mama, Willa. Let's see if we can make a case for banishment.*

Willa thought about it for a half-second. "You know that won't work. But maybe there's another way. Come on. Let's go talk to Brock. If there's one person in the village who can sway public opinion right now, it'll be the boy whose father died a hero. If we get enough people in on it, Mama can't bully a majority into voting the way she wants them to, like she usually does."

Several minutes later, the three children stood next to the closed front door of a house on the outskirts of the village. Willa didn't often get nervous, but right now, a swarm of butterflies flitted in her belly.

The door opened to reveal a boy whose handsome face was not tear-streaked and whose eyes were not red from crying.

"Yes?" Brock said. He didn't seem annoyed to see a bunch of twelve-year-olds standing on his front porch.

Willa found that encouraging. She took a deep breath. "We came to tell you we're sorry about your dad, Brock."

"Thank you, Willadean."

She couldn't get a feel for the mood of the young Scout. He seemed oddly tranquil, despite having just learned that the Murdocks had killed his father in cold blood.

"Is there anything we can do for you?"

"No, thank you."

"Can we come in for a minute? I know it's probably not a good time, but there's something really important we need to talk to you about."

"Sure," he said, moving aside to let them enter.

Willa had never been in the house before. Trevor and Brock were nice enough folks but not overly friendly. They kept to themselves in their small house on the edge of town.

"Sit wherever you like," Brock said, taking a position next to the wood-stove.

The interior felt cozy, inviting, and oddly feminine. White lace curtains hung on the windows, and a fancy tea set held a place of honor on a wooden china cabinet.

Willa scoured her memory for insight about Brock and his father. All she could remember was that Brock's mother had died years ago, long before the pandemic. Both Brock and his father were quiet and reserved, but well respected in the holler for their firearms skills. Though they attended the occasional social function, the two of them always left before things got rowdy. Willa knew that because it always seemed to be the same time Mama would send her and Harlan home as well. Sometimes they would share the path with them on the way.

"Are you doing okay?" she said, buying herself a few minutes before diving into the real reason for their visit.

The gaze of the tranquil brown eyes glided from the window and attached to her. She felt a weird sensation, almost like the time she'd poked a bobby pin into an electrical outlet as a toddler.

Brock gave her a sad smile. "Yeah, I suppose I'm doing okay."

"I can't imagine getting the news you got today. If something happened to my mom, I think I would die. Especially if it was unexpected and I didn't have time to prepare for it."

Brock tilted his head; his wavy brown hair brushed a shoulder. Lots of people let their hair grow out these days, and it usually looks scraggly. But this sixteen-year-old could grace the cover of *Teen Vogue* with that hair. Willa wasn't much into boys in a romantic sense, but she knew that day would come.

The way her heart was thumping, she figured the day might already have arrived.

"I had some time to get ready for it," Brock replied. His gaze returned to the window and the forest beyond. She wondered if he was seeing the trees and the sky or something else entirely.

Harlan began signing. *Ask him what that means.*

Willa nodded. "What do you mean? How could you have known something was going to happen to him?"

"Nobody gets out of this alive," Brock said. "Plus, sometimes I get these ... feelings."

"Oh, like Pops. He gets feelings too. Like sometimes he just knows something that he shouldn't have a way of knowing. Is that right?"

"I guess. I've known this day would come for a long time, though."

"How long? Days or weeks?"

Brock shook his head. "Much longer."

"Years?"

Suddenly, Brock seemed to become aware of the fact that three kids were sitting in his house. Kids who might not be trustworthy. Willa noticed the instant he shut down.

He crossed his arms. "So, why are you all here? I think there's another reason than checking up on someone you're really not friends with." The tone wasn't cold exactly, but it wasn't cordial.

Cricket sat at a small metal table. "We need your help," he said in his squeaky child's voice. "They're gonna vote on banishment or death for my daddy for being a spy for the Murdocks. We want you to talk folks into voting for banishment. My daddy ain't a good man like yours, but he don't deserve to die. Willa thinks you'll have some ... what's the word?"

"Sway," she said.

"Right. You'll have *sway* with people 'cuz of your daddy's sacrifice. Will you do it?"

Brock shrugged dismissively. "Why would I? It's your father's fault that mine is dead."

"We don't know that for sure," Cricket said. He rose and puffed out his chest like one of those exotic birds Willa had seen on *National Geographic.*

Brock did the head tilt thing again. "I do know it. That guy Ray, and Hannah, your grandmother," he added in Willa's direction, "Confirmed it. That's what Serena Jo said. But I also know it because I saw it coming."

Willa took a cautious step toward the teenager. "Are you psychic? Is that what you're saying?" The situation had taken a weird and unexpected turn. She felt somehow *untethered*.

"I'm not going to get into that with any of you." Brock waved a dismissive hand. "And I won't help this kid's dad. Sorry."

Harlan had been standing just inside the front door. The situation took an even weirder turn when he chose that moment to vocalize.

"Brock, we understand how you feel. And I probably understand that other business more than these two."

Willa was so shocked she found herself momentarily speechless, a circumstance that didn't happen often.

Brock turned to face him. "Aren't you the kid that doesn't talk? Not because he can't, but because he just doesn't?"

Harlan nodded. "Maybe you could look at this as a kindness to Cricket, not his father. If the situation were reversed, I know he'd do the same for you. Cricket is a good kid. He doesn't want his daddy buried in the cemetery. He'd rather think about him going off on some big adventure, isn't that right, Cricket?"

Cricket nodded, tears threatening to overflow their flimsy eyelash dam. "That's twice I've heard you talk now, Harlan. I wish you'd just decide to do it all the time so I don't have to read your fingers. And yes, it makes me happy to think about daddy goin' off on an adventure, like that Marco Polo guy in one of Willa's stories."

Brock's expression turned contemplative as his gaze flicked from Harlan to Cricket and back.

Brock sighed. "If I agree to this, I want something in return."

Willa felt (something--a wave of concern?) She would be the one to agree to the terms of any deal involving her gang. "What do you want?"

she asked.

"I want to go after Levi. He's Wyatt's man. It was his bullet that killed my dad."

"We don't know which of those Murdocks pulled the trigger."

Brock's brown eyes dilated suddenly as they focused on Willa; a delicate sepia band encircled bottomless black holes. Beneath her sweatshirt and fleece jacket, Willa felt a sudden stirring of the fine blond hairs on her arms.

"I know it was him," Brock said. "And I know we're going to war with the Murdocks. I don't care about that. I only care about killing one person. Do we have a deal or not?"

"What do you have in mind? We need specifics before we agree to anything."

"We set a trap for him in the forest. Lure him there with the exact type of bait guaranteed to do the job."

"What bait?"

Brock stared at her, unblinking. The dilated pupils seemed to have developed a gravity field. Finally he said, "You."

The Ezra vote was close: fifty-three for execution, fifty-six for banishment. If not for Brock's quiet but compelling influence, it would have gone the other way. Cricket was a hot mess. He watched his daddy saunter down the dirt road and out of the village, worldly goods bundled on his back and a middle finger extended to the silent crowd that watched from behind. He didn't even bother waving goodbye to his son.

The three children watched from Willa's front porch. Cricket's tear-streaked face broke her heart.

She twin-signed to her brother: *What a jerk. How can a person be so awful to their kid?*

Harlan replied: *Not everyone is meant to be a daddy. Or a mama.*

"I'll be okay. It's better than seeing him buried," Cricket said with a loud, wet sniff and a shaky smile. His father had traveled beyond the curve in the road and out of sight.

Willa believed her friend. She had always figured Cricket would be better off without his loser father, and it sounded like Cricket had come to the same conclusion.

"Now we gotta honor our deal with Brock," Cricket whispered. "Anybody that likes little girls … in *that* way … is sick in the head. I don't like this plan one bit."

Willa shrugged. "The part I'm worried about the most is sneaking out of the village. Good thing Mama is distracted right now."

"How do you reckon Brock knows stuff, like when his daddy was gonna die?"

"I have no idea, but I believe him," she said. "There's something going on with that boy, and I aim to find out what it is."

Harlan shook his head. *You don't always need to know everything about everyone.*

Willa glared at him but didn't respond.

"I hope your mama don't find out you swiped that photograph from her keepsake box. She'd be mighty mad."

The photography session, carried out just before the end of the world, had been one of the last entries on Serena Jo's 'to do' list before fleeing Knoxville. Pictures of Willadean and Harlan would never be taken again in their lifetime. The lady photographer looked sickly when she posed them in all sorts of positions at a nearby park; probably had been coming down with the plague even while snapping their picture. But Mama had been pleased with the results. She'd printed out the digital images after the session. Hours later, they were on the road.

"I don't even look like that anymore, but Brock said it doesn't matter. Levi wants girls that haven't gotten their period. What a perv."

Harlan nodded, his owlish eyes solemn.

"What's a period?" Cricket said. "Don't that have something to do with writing?"

Willa snorted. "Never mind about that. I'll explain the birds and bees when you're a bit older."

Despite her bravado, she had to admit feeling squeamish about serving as bait to catch a pedophile. But seeing her friend's relief – and knowing he wouldn't have to mourn the death of his father – was worth whatever she had to face in the woods.

"I don't understand how he's gonna get that picture to Levi," Cricket continued.

The crowd was dispersing now, so they had to keep their voices low.

"Brock said he met a woman at the last moonshine barter who'll help him."

"I know, but why would a Murdock lady take your photo to Levi?"

Poor naïve child. When Brock had said the word *madam,* Cricket probably thought it was just a fancy way of saying *lady.*

"Because the woman isn't a lady. She's in charge of the prostitutes. Kind of like a male pimp. Do you know what pimps and prostitutes are?"

"Yes, Willa, I ain't that dumb. I watched movies when the TV still worked."

No doubt Ezra had been too busy being a drunken loser to properly supervise Cricket's television viewing. Willa, on the other hand, had learned about pimps and prostitutes and madams and brothels in a book Mama never knew she'd read.

Willa continued, "So the woman Brock met will get the photo to Levi. Once he approves of me, she'll set up a meeting in the forest. I'm sure Levi will reward her for finding fresh little girl meat for him." She gave an involuntary shudder.

"Okay, I get that part. But why would the ... *madam* ... believe Brock wants to give a little girl to Levi? Ain't she gonna be suspicious that a Whitaker wants to help a Murdock? Especially after one just killed his daddy?" Cricket seemed to finally grasp the situation.

"Yes, exactly. But Brock says the woman hates Levi and wants him dead, so she'll be happy to help."

"How can he know all this, Willa? That's what I'm tryin' to figure out."

Willa shrugged.

Harlan signed: *This is a very bad idea.*

"I know, but we didn't have a choice. You wanted Brock's help too, so I had to agree to it."

An honorable person did not renege on a promise ... ever. She'd never done it before, and she wasn't going to start now.

Chapter 16

Ray

"I have an armory back at the warehouse. You're welcome to all of it."

Ray caught up with Serena Jo on her way home after the brief announcement at the kitchen house. Everyone now knew the Whitakers were going to war with the Murdocks. It wouldn't happen today or tomorrow, but it would happen soon and inevitably.

Why was it always the nature of humans to seek to eradicate each other?

When he didn't get a response, he continued. "I wish it hadn't come to this. There are so few people left in the world ..."

Serena Jo shot him a look of disgust. "Do you think this is what I want?"

"No, of course not. But I'm not convinced we've considered every option."

She stopped and turned to face him. A muscle twitched along her smooth jawline. "We aren't dealing with reasonable people, Ray. That's the problem."

"Hannah told me about the Murdocks," he said.

"What did she tell you?" Gone was the unflappable Serena Jo. In her place was a doppelganger who Ray realized was quite capable of slicing open a throat without hesitating, just like her mother. She stood inches away, so he was able to whisper his response.

"She explained how debauched and heinous they are. She also told me she's one of them. Her father and twin sister run the place."

After a blur of movement, Ray felt a sharp poke at the base of his neck, not forceful enough to break the skin, but close.

The woman whose affections he hoped to win held a blade against his carotid artery. The threat was more overt and immediate than that of Hannah's in the woods, yet somehow it didn't carry as much weight. No doubt Serena Jo was capable of violence, but he knew she wasn't going to murder him in cold blood. At least, not at that moment.

"This goes no further. Do you understand? If people find out I'm the granddaughter of Silas Murdock, I'll lose all credibility."

"I understand. Did she also tell you about the sister?"

"Yes," she hissed. "But not until after the two of you came back."

"Fergus knows, too——at least about Silas. I told him."

Serena Jo made an exasperated noise, then removed the knife from his throat and slid it back into her pocket. "For someone who wants to get into my pants, you're not doing a great job of winning me over."

Ray barked an uncomfortable laugh. "Well, I'm glad we have that out in the open." He reached for her hand suddenly, happy when she didn't resist. "If I can safely keep your secret, I will. But if someone's life depends on this knowledge, all bets are off."

"Let's hope for your sake you can manage it," she said. "We're going to raid your warehouse. I did a cursory tour with Fergus, but I need to get a better feel for what you have. We need an advantage to offset the disparity of numbers between us and them."

Ray tapped his temple. "I have it all stored up here."

"Good. Come with me."

Inside her house, empty of children at the moment and toasty from the woodstove, Ray stood awkwardly by the door.

"Sit," she said, gesturing to the small kitchen table. "Coffee?"

"That would be lovely. You know I have a pallet of it at the warehouse."

He noticed the sudden gleam in her eyes. He was aware of Serena Jo's coffee obsession and was not above using it as another avenue to her heart.

"Where are the kids?" he asked, as she handed him a steaming mug.

"Who knows? They won't go beyond the perimeter, though. Not under these circumstances. They wouldn't dare."

"Willadean is a firecracker, but I'm sure you're right."

Serena Jo sighed. "Yes, she certainly is. Harlan is easier, but he presents his own set of challenges."

"I find him fascinating. I've never known a person, let alone a child, who has simply decided not to speak." He took a sip of coffee, thinking about such an unusual life choice.

"He's not like any other person in the world. Neither of my children are."

"You believe they're extraordinary?"

"Of course. It's not maternal pride, either. Their school in Knoxville couldn't wait to get them into special classes. The administration didn't want to tell me how off the charts their test scores were. They were worried I'd put them in some elite gifted school. But I made them tell me. I wouldn't have moved them anyway."

Ray grinned. "Of course you made them tell you. But why wouldn't you have moved them?"

"I didn't want them to feel more like outliers than they already did. Being extraordinary comes with a hefty emotional price tag. I imagine it feels like a burden to them sometimes."

"You imagine? You're extraordinary, too. Don't you feel the same way?"

She smiled, turning his knees to jelly. "I'm smart, I'm tough, I'm disciplined, and I'm resourceful. But I'm not on the same level as my children."

"I'm not sure I agree."

"You don't have to. It's a fact. They didn't get it from their father, either. His only gifts were six-pack abs and a nice derriere. I was lustful back then. And careless."

"Ah, so the kids weren't planned."

"No, but it worked out for the best. I made sure their sperm donor had no desire to be involved in their lives before I gave him the boot. They've never met him. There was never a need."

"I see."

She laughed. "I doubt that. I don't think you have any idea what you're getting yourself into, Ray."

"You mean in terms of the kids, the war with the Murdocks, or getting into your pants?"

"All of the above." She paused and dropped her eyes. "I thought you were dead, you know."

"That's what you said. Yet here I am."

She frowned, shaking her head. "I know, and I can't explain it. It drives me crazy if I think about it too long. So I'm just going to be grateful."

She leaned over and kissed him. At first it was a playful, light touching of lips. Seconds later, it turned into much more. They stood now, chairs pushed away, bodies pressed against each other, hands exploring, mouths locked in the most passionate moment Ray had ever experienced. He'd known the chemistry was there, had felt it the moment he first saw her framed against a backdrop of sunshine and freedom when he'd been chained up in a cabin in the woods.

Every decision he'd ever made in his life had been guiding him to this very spot … this very woman. He knew it as surely as he knew the sun would rise in the morning. Serena Jo was his destiny.

He hoped she felt the same.

As if reading his thoughts, she pulled away, breathless and somehow vulnerable. He would never get tired of seeing that sudden softness in her face.

"Not now," she said, her voice husky. "The kids could walk in that door any minute."

"I'll wait as long as I have to. I'm not going anywhere."

She gave a girlish, nervous laugh. That nervousness was exactly what he wanted to hear. There was hope.

Then she turned back to business. "I need you to write down everything about the warehouse contents that might be useful to us. Then you should get some sleep. I need to start strategizing."

***

Ray never would have imagined he could sleep so deeply and for so long, especially under the circumstances. Soon there would be bloodshed and mass casualties, perhaps even at his own hands, and the woman of his dreams had kissed him. More than kissed him, actually – groped him as lasciviously as he'd groped her. You only get one chance at a first kiss, and that one would go down in the history books. The thought made him smile in the dark.

He'd been given an abandoned house to use during his stay in the village. Its former occupant had left it reasonably clean, but the small stack of firewood near the stove wouldn't last long. Would he have to go chop down a tree to get more? Where would he wash his clothes? Would chores be assigned to him? And even more pressing, would breakfast be served soon? His growling stomach had awoken him moments ago.

He sat up, noting the lumps in the mattress and the thin blanket barely covering his socks. After fumbling through his backpack, he located a flashlight and switched it on. Hundreds of these devices occupied a pallet at the warehouse, along with the batteries that powered them. He imagined how dramatically the contents of his home could change the way the villagers lived. But Serena Jo had made her position clear on that subject: they were doing just fine without modern conveniences. She only wanted the weapons and other supplemental items to use in the fight against the Murdocks.

Maybe there was wiggle room in that regard, but something told him it wouldn't be much.

The flashlight beam revealed a kerosene lamp and a box of matches on an old wire spool that served as a bedside table. He struck a match and held it to the wick, illuminating the house's small interior.

The lantern light fell upon a shadowy figure standing just inside the front door. Ray leapt out of bed, his heart pounding. He distinctly remembered locking the door before he went to bed.

A deep voice came from the shadows. "I just want to know how those perfect breasts felt. Then I'll be on my way."

Ray closed his eyes in relief at hearing the familiar voice.

Fergus stepped into the lantern's glow. "It's ball-freezing cold in here, Ray. Rule One of living in the boonies: don't let the damn fire go out during the night." Fergus gave a disgusted sigh as he opened the stove grate and prodded the inside with a blackened stick.

Ray glanced at his watch. He'd managed to sleep more than thirteen hours.

"You must have been exhausted after the run-in with the Murdocks followed by your tête-à-tête with the illustrious Serena Jo. I'll get the fire going while you provide all the delicious details of that second part. I've already heard all about the first."

The small man busied himself loading the few remaining logs into the iron belly while pointedly, it seemed, not making eye contact.

"Fergus, I have no intention of kissing and telling," Ray said with a yawn and a stretch.

"Fine, but while you cling to your so-called chivalry, just know you're dealing a substantial blow to our blossoming friendship. I don't know if we can get past it."

Ray smiled at the odd man as he scurried about creating heat. A blazing fire soon chased the chill from the room.

"How did you even know? I haven't mentioned it to anyone, and I'm sure she hasn't either. Were you spying on us?"

"I'll have you know I'm no voyeur. I'm a buyer, not a window shopper. Just understand that you're never as alone as you think you might be around here. You've been isolated in your warehouse for too long. You've forgotten how people, and children, operate in the real world."

"Ah, it was the twins, wasn't it? Damn. I'd have preferred to handle that differently."

Fergus didn't respond, confirming the children must know about the kissing.

"What did I miss while I was passed out?" Ray said. He struck another match and lit the stump of a nearby candle. The warehouse's solar panels and batteries could illuminate the entire village for years to come, but the ambience provided by candles and kerosene lanterns was certainly appealing.

"The Whitakers are going to war with the Murdocks."

"I know that."

"What you may not know is that they will be massacred." Fergus plopped into one of the rusty lawn chairs that served as the cabin's furniture. He rubbed his grizzled red beard, and his blue eyes looked decidedly grim.

"I'm going to give them an advantage. You saw the supplies I have back at the warehouse. With what I'm bringing to the table, there's no way a bunch of hillbillies with sawed-off shotguns can prevail against us."

Fergus snorted. "Like I said, you've been isolated too long. I don't think you have a clue what these people are like——what anybody is like these days. Not only that, you don't understand warfare. You don't understand ruthlessness. You don't understand true debauchery. You lived a sheltered life before the pandemic, and even more so after."

"Gosh, Fergus, tell me what you really think," Ray said, tossing his friend an energy bar from his backpack. Fergus caught it without breaking eye contact.

"I like you. A lot, actually. I don't want you to die in the coming violence. I don't want any of these people to die." Fergus gestured vaguely with his hand. "Not even the Murdocks. Or at least, not all of them."

"I agree, but it seems inevitable. Do you have any ideas about how to stop it?"

"I can't stop it, but I can mitigate the body count."

"Then why do you seem so miserable?"

"Because I'm about to do something I've sworn an oath not to do."

Ray frowned. "Okay. I promise whatever you're about to tell me will remain between the two of us. Like I said, I don't kiss and tell."

"Secrecy is not my primary concern. What I'm worried about is how crazy you'll think I am after I'm done telling my story."

At that moment, a quiet knock came from the front door, and Hannah stepped into the room.

Fergus continued, "I've brought someone to back me up. She doesn't know it yet, but she's here to give credence to what I'm about to say."

Hannah arched an eyebrow. "I better get some coffee for my trouble, then. I know you have some in your pack, Ray. Probably planning to buy your way into my daughter's good graces." She stepped farther into the house and began opening weathered cabinet doors next to the chipped porcelain sink. "Let's see if there's anything to drink it from. Fergus, put the kettle on the stove. I hope our boy here put some water in it before sleeping half the day away."

"I did," Ray said. "I'll have you both know I'm not a complete fuck-up."

Hannah gifted him with a few notes of musical laughter. "No, you're far from that, but you are a naïve city boy wading in some deep waters here."

Once they were settled and the warm air scented with the fragrance of coffee, Fergus took a deep breath.

"One of the reasons I'm telling you the story I'm about to tell you is because I need your help. We need to convince Serena Jo to accept all the assistance she can get in the coming conflict, no matter where it comes from. Or from *whom*."

"You have an army hidden somewhere you've failed to mention?" Ray said.

"Not an army, but they might as well be."

Hannah leaned forward, interest evident on her face. "Who are these paladins?"

"Before we get to that, we need to go back in time." Fergus's eyes narrowed as he stared at Hannah like a mongoose contemplating a cobra. "But first, I want a confession. I want you to admit what you are."

One corner of Hannah's mouth twitched. "I am many things. You'll have to be more specific."

"Are you a current or past resident of my home? Don't deny that you've spent some time there."

Ray was completely confused, but the energy in the space between the two practically crackled. As carefully as Hannah controlled her reactions, micro expressions were nearly impossible to contain. If Ray read them correctly, Hannah seemed to be weighing whether to come clean.

After a long, uncomfortable silence, she said, "I spent a few weeks there. Just enough time to know it was not the place for me."

"Ah *HA*!" Fergus exclaimed, leaping from the lawn chair and sloshing his coffee. "I knew it!"

"Calm down, little man," Hannah said, with a resigned sigh.

"When were you there? Why did I never meet you?"

"I assume you were out doing something similar to what you're doing now."

"Will somebody please tell me what this is all about?" Ray demanded.

Fergus chuckled, delighted to have solved the mystery of Hannah, whatever that might entail. "Just a minute, Ray. All will be revealed." He turned back to Hannah, "When? Give me dates."

"It was the autumn just after the worst had passed ... when everyone who was going to die of the plague had done so." Profound emotion transformed the normally cheerful face into a mask of grief. Ray had never seen Hannah so exposed.

"You lost loved ones ..." Fergus reached out for her hand. She allowed it.

"Of course. Didn't we all? I was recruited by someone who'd witnessed displays of my talents. It was an Asian man who convinced me to 'give it a chance.' After two weeks down there, I was done."

"Ah, that was probably Tung. And yes, you're correct about my absence. I was in Texas, meeting the very people who are relevant to the conversation we're about to have."

"Indeed? I'm eager to hear about them."

"So you didn't like what you experienced down there?"

"Not at all. The lifespans are an abomination ... an affront to my sense of the natural world. Especially in regard to the Ancient Ones."

"I can understand how you'd feel that way. Sometimes I have those same thoughts."

She leaned forward. "How old are you, Fergus? Something tells me you weren't brought into the fold recently."

"Older than I'm willing to say at the moment." Fergus jerked a thumb toward Ray. "You used *langthal* on this one?"

She nodded. "He was worth the effort. Wasn't sure I could pull it off, since he was a goner. But I managed."

"You know that's exceedingly rare."

"I do."

"Your grandson has it too."

"I suspected as much."

"Enough!" Ray yelled finally. "I've been patient. Tell me what the hell is going on." After the bizarre conversation, he wondered if he was mentally prepared for whatever world-shifting revelation was coming next.

White teeth appeared suddenly within the red beard. Fergus squeezed his shoulder. "This is going to take some reality suspension on your part, my friend."

***

Ray's mind reeled. No sane person would believe a word of it: An incomprehensibly advanced race of human beings in an underground sanctuary from which they conducted genetic engineering experiments in an effort to produce new and improved versions of the human race every ten or twenty thousand years. No one aged in this supposed sanctuary. Their minions (the word Hannah supplied to describe people like Fergus) regularly ventured up to the surface of the earth to recruit the successfully engineered humans and harvest their superior DNA, from which new strains of even more advanced humans would be produced. But these ancient beings weren't always successful in this undertaking. Their experiments sometimes resulted in monstrous failures, like the Murdock clan. Sometimes they failed so badly they had to perform an "earth cleansing" and start from scratch. And the most ridiculous part of the story was when all this began.

Millions of years ago.

According to Fergus, the *Cthor* lived when the supercontinent of Pangaea was still intact. Human civilizations had risen and advanced and fallen countless times, all orchestrated by that first tribe of superior beings. And of course, they were so brilliant they didn't forget to remove all the evidence from the geological and fossil records. Ray kept that thought to himself. He had read bargain-basement science fiction books more plausible than the story he'd just heard.

Now the question was how to act like he didn't think Fergus and Hannah were lunatics.

Hannah confirmed the story, but her experience in the alleged underground sanctuary had lasted only a couple of weeks. She'd turned down their offer of virtual immortality, and they allowed her to waltz back up to the surface. No harm no foul.

And now, the two were about to perform an act that would supposedly convince him of the truth of their story. Hannah planned to heal Fergus of a grievous wound – soon to be inflicted – using the same method she had used on Ray himself.

All he could do was sit in one of the lawn chairs, arms folded, facial expression neutral, and let them act out their little play. Afterward, when Fergus required stitches, Ray would be ready with a first-aid kit from his pack. He hoped his friend wouldn't require a blood transfusion. The knife Hannah intended to use was the same one that had slit Myra's throat in the woods. Wearing an unsettling smile, she wielded it now.

"You trust me?" she asked Fergus. Candlelight glinted off the blade.

"Yes. It's the only way to convince Ray of the truth. He must believe what we've told him. His influence with Serena Jo is crucial to convincing her to accept the help from outsiders. And *their* help is crucial to triumphing over the Murdocks. I figure the three of us coming at Serena Jo from multiple directions is necessary."

"It's going to hurt."

"Yes, yes. I've been stabbed more times than the number of years you've lived on this earth."

"Interesting. When this is all over, I want you to tell me how old you really are. That's all I ask."

"Fine. Get on with it, woman!" Fergus said, lifting his shirt and exposing a white belly covered in a smattering of curly crimson hair.

I would have thought he'd be hairier, Ray thought, then shook his head, focusing on the knife.

"This looks like a good spot," Hannah said, pointing the blade in the appendix region. Then she whipped it away and waved it in Ray's face.

"Do you want to inspect the knife first? Make sure it's not one of those movie props?"

"Unnecessary," he replied. His jaws were clenched so tightly that his lips struggled to form the word. She seemed to be enjoying this freak show way too much.

"All-righty, then. Here we go."

In a fluid motion, she sliced a deep, six-inch gash into Fergus's white flesh. Ray watched in horror as the yawning laceration hesitated a heartbeat before filling with bright red blood.

"Gaaahhh, that fecking hurts!" Fergus said, a sudden Irish accent coloring his words.

Hannah laughed. "I warned you. Good thing the blade was nice and sharp. Okay, Ray, do you agree this is a legitimate wound? I didn't fake anything, correct?"

Ray nodded, reaching for a wad of sterile gauze.

"Go ahead and press that against the wound, so you can feel it yourself. Then I'll take over and do my thing."

Ray obliged, alarmed by how quickly the blood saturated the cloth.

"Now sit back down and watch," she said. Her normally low-pitched voice had taken on a subharmonic quality, almost as if two people were speaking at once in the same key. Ray felt chills along his spine.

Fergus's eyes were screwed shut. Hannah pressed both hands against the gash, closing her eyes, too.

Ray scrutinized her hands, then her face, then her hands again. The crackling, invisible energy had returned. He could imagine miniature lightning bolts discharging from her fingertips and striking the wound. The experience was unlike anything he'd ever witnessed.

Minutes passed, perhaps three or maybe twenty. The passing of time might have sped up or slowed down. He had no idea.

Finally, Hannah and Fergus opened their eyes simultaneously, the pupils in both pairs heavily dilated now. They grinned at each other.

Ray had the sudden desire to flee from these strange people. Instead, he waited silently for something else to happen.

Hannah stepped back, taking the saturated gauze with her. Blood smears remained, but Fergus's white skin was smooth and intact.

Ray tried to swallow, but his mouth felt like a desert wasteland. He blinked, rubbed his eyes, and then leaned toward the absent wound.

Fergus startled him by soundly slapping his own belly. "Fit as a fiddle. You can see that for yourself, yes? Anybody want more coffee? Then I'll tell you about the soldiers who will turn the tide in the Whitaker-Murdock battle. You're going to like them. Well, you'll definitely like one of them."

Fergus smiled gleefully. Was it Ray's imagination, or did those white teeth seem vaguely feral now?

Chapter 17

Fergus

"Look, I have the authorization of Serena Jo. You don't want me to tell her you're the one who may cost us the war, hmmm?"

Fergus spoke to one of the newest Scouts, just promoted that morning after barely passing the required tests. The bar for membership had been lowered in light of the upcoming war. The kid was perhaps seventeen, but he'd already donned the stoic façade all the Scouts projected.

It wasn't entirely convincing, and Fergus picked up on all kinds of doubts and insecurities, which he intended to exploit now.

"No, sir," the boy said. "But I have my orders. Nobody gets past me. I'm supposed to shoot on sight."

"Jackson, right?"

He nodded.

"You've been placed in this area because it was a direction the Murdocks won't be arriving from. This is not what they call a high-alert post."

"Doesn't matter, sir. I have my orders."

Fergus blew out an exasperated sigh, then moved in closer. He grabbed the young man's shoulder in a steely grip and sent out waves of virtual endorphins. That always helped to get people to do his bidding. Almost always. A handful he'd encountered in his travels seemed immune to his charm, but they were rare. And this kid wasn't one of them.

After a few moments, Fergus saw his grip beginning to take effect; a minuscule dilating of the Scout's eyes in the late afternoon sunshine confirmed it.

"The two people who will be appearing on the horizon just down those lovely rolling hills," he pointed with his other hand, "Will blow your socks off. Not only are they proficient with firearms and all manner of pointy weaponry, they're strong ... especially the woman, she's a damn freak of nature ... and they move like ghosts. Their targets will never see them, never hear them. They won't suspect anything is amiss until they feel a vein opening in their throat. Wouldn't you love to learn from people like that, Jackson?"

The kid nodded slowly. "Are you sure I won't be in trouble with Serena Jo?"

"Not even a little. Once she gets the full measure of these two, you'll probably get a damn medal. Or whatever passes for one around here."

He'd struck the correct nerve.

"It's called the Bravery and Competence Graph. We get points and demerits based on our accomplishments. I like that it's not all about being the first guy to charge into a dangerous situation. Sometimes just doing a good job, never forgetting your gear, keeping your weapons serviced, stuff like that, is as important as the guys who think they're Captain America or Thor."

Fergus smiled. If there was one way into a young man's heart, it was through superhero movies. And Fergus had seen them all before the world went dark.

After an hour of entertaining movie talk with the surprisingly articulate Jackson, two of Fergus's favorite people on Planet Earth appeared. Not where he expected them, of course. Someone suddenly pressed a sharp object against the back of his neck. He knew it was Dani because Sam stood in front of him now with his perfectly tousled reddish-gold hair and his magazine-cover smile. If Sam weren't the kindest man he'd ever known, Fergus would probably resent that perfect face.

"I thought you died, you sonofabitch," a female voice growled.

The next moment, Dani had twirled him around to face her, then hugged him so hard he thought his ribcage might collapse.

She finally released him, then stepped back wearing a ferocious grin. Fergus would have gasped in shock if not for Herculean self-control. A roadmap of spider-web scars criss crossed her beautiful face. He'd be lying if he said they didn't diminish her former beauty. Mahogany hair pulled back in a smooth ponytail did nothing to cover the ravages. The perfect bone structure remained, however, and the sapphire eyes that could skewer a weaker man with a glance had become more prominent in the scarred visage. The smirk was exactly the same as he remembered.

"I'm Dani 2.0 now. You probably didn't get the memo," she said.

He couldn't help it. A traitorous tear slid down his cheek.

"It's okay, Fergus," she said with sudden tenderness. "I've come to terms with it. Besides, this face makes me even more intimidating than I already was. My foes get a glimpse of this horror show and tuck their tails and run. It works to my advantage."

"We were happy to hear you weren't dead," Sam said. "It makes sense, too, because you know what they say: Only the good die as youngsters, and you were always kinda shady."

"Oh, Sam. How I've missed you," Fergus replied. "And this one too," he jerked a thumb at Dani, who punched him affectionately in the bicep.

"Gah, I forgot how painful it is to be around you, honey badger," he said with a grimace. "Now, tell me all about the trip. We'll talk while we walk. The jet fuel worked?"

"Yep," Dani replied. "Steven's going to be pissed when he finds out Sam and I filched it from the co-op warehouse, but that stuff won't last forever anyway. Turns out refined kerosene gets pretty good mileage in a Ford F-150 diesel engine, also stolen. I have to say, I enjoy imagining the look on Steven's face when he discovers what we've done. Almost wish I could be there to see it in person." She smiled happily, then said, "Wait a sec, there's someone we need to fetch. Come on out, kid."

Chapter 18

Liberty, Kansas

A day earlier

"Let me get this straight: Maddie spoke telepathically to Fergus, who happens to *not be dead*. Who is, in fact, living in Tennessee with a bunch of *Deliverance* yokels and is requesting our help with some kind of hillbilly feud? Does anything about that make sense to you, Sam?"

Sam kissed Dani lightly on the lips and smiled. "Not really, but I believe Maddie. Are we in?"

"Of course we're in. I need a break from Steven-ville and the control freak who runs the place."

"That control freak is your uncle."

"I don't care. I barely care that Julia is my mother." The feigned indifference was evident even to her own ears. "What are you thinking? We sure as hell can't walk all the way to Bucktooth Junction."

Sam laughed. That laughter still had the power to make her heart skip a beat. "You know, just because people aren't as smart as you doesn't mean they're dumb."

She hated it when Sam gave her one of his gentle chastisements, probably because they were always justified and usually necessary.

"Sorry."

He kissed her again, a bit more thoroughly this time, then said, "I think we'll have to steal some of the fuel and a truck from the co-op."

"I can't believe I just heard those words coming from Honest Abe. You're prepared to steal? This must be serious business."

"According to Maddie, it's a like-or-death situation."

Dani frowned, barely registering Sam's usual maxim-mangling. "She gave you the location?"

"Fergus gave her the longitude and latitude since he's not in any town that's shown on a map."

"That'll help. So, we sneak into the co-op tonight, fill up some gas cans with the jet fuel Steven has been hoarding like a fat kid's Halloween candy, hotwire one of the F-150s, and blow this Popsicle stand."

"Yeah, I think that will be necessary since Steven keeps all the keys at his place."

"Hotwiring is one of the many services I offer. I just wish I had a better idea of what we're getting into."

She found it interesting that she had, apparently, bought into the notion of telepathic conversations taking place with supposed dead people. For her, that wasn't even the sticking point of undertaking this adventure. The issue was the absence of any details regarding the feud. Sam had given her a word-for-word recap of his conversation with Maddie, but it wasn't enough.

"Come on. We need to pay Maddie a visit."

"It's dark. She and Pablo are probably getting their little one tucked in."

She ignored Sam's wistful tone. "It'll be all right. I'll take Pablo some M&Ms from my stash. He's an M&M whore."

Everyone walks or rides bikes these days. Motorized vehicles and the precious diesel fuel that powered them were kept under lock and key. And, of course, Steven the dictator held the keys. Dani chafed at the rules and restraints imposed upon Liberty residents. Steven came up with a new regulation almost daily now. Yes, having limited electricity, clean water, and a working sewage system improved everyone's quality of life. But at what price? The rush to return to a pre-pandemic sense of normalcy came at the expense of personal liberty. At least, that was Dani's thinking.

After a brisk twenty-minute walk through deserted residential streets, they stood on the front porch of a small ranch-style house. She pounded on the door.

Pablo opened it a few seconds later wearing an irritated frown. "We just put Willow to bed, and we're about to head there ourselves." Keen dark eyes glared at her. She'd probably pay for the intrusion by ending up as an unsympathetic character in one of his cautionary tales; the townspeople adored his weekly storytelling sessions. She had to admit, Pablo possessed some serious writing chops. But his cut-to-the-chase conversational style endeared him the most. Like her, he wasn't concerned about being polite if it got in the way of clarity or efficiency.

"This will only take a minute. We need to talk to Maddie," she replied. She held up the small bag of M&Ms and laughed at the sudden lust in his eyes.

"Clearly, you know your audience," Pablo said, swiping the bag. "Come in. I'll get Maddie, then I'll let you have some privacy. I know why you're here, and I'm not really interested in this psychic business. She enjoys it, but I'm definitely not a fan."

"Thanks, dude." Dani stepped past him and into the small living room. Sam followed, taking the spot next to her on the sofa.

"Smells like tuna casserole and rugrats," she whispered.

"I think it smells heavenly," he replied in that same wistful tone.

Maddie's sudden appearance provided the perfect distraction from Sam's subtle yet relentless campaign to knock her up. Ankle biters were probably in their future at some point if the stars aligned perfectly and a madman leading a barbarian horde didn't loom on the horizon. But as of today, celestial symmetry had yet to occur, and it may not for some time with the arrival of this tantalizing new challenge.

Maddie's flawless skin and lustrous hair would evoke envy in most women, but Dani liked her too much to be jealous. It simply wasn't possible to resent someone so genuinely nice. Dani had never put much stock in physical beauty anyway, and even less now. Scratching out a place in this dark, desiccated post-apocalyptic world was exactly where she needed to be. It suited her.

"You want me to recap my conversation with Fergus, I assume?" Maddie said, gracing them with her beautiful smile. "I had a feeling you'd need to get it straight from the gypsy fortune teller's mouth."

Dani replied, "Yeah, every word, please."

Maddie touched Dani's arm lightly, then smiled. "Ah, I see. Your issue isn't that I communicated telepathically with your friend Fergus, it's that I didn't provide enough detail about what you're getting yourself into."

Dani opened her mouth to respond but realized she was too dumbfounded to speak.

Maddie laughed. "I keep a lot of the telepathy stuff to myself for just that reason. It freaks people out when they realize I can sometimes hear their thoughts. As a favor to me, maybe you can keep it between the two of you."

Dani nodded. "Of course. But it's remarkable. I had no idea your ability was so ... accurate."

Maddie smiled. "It seems to improve a little every day. Fergus transmits quite clearly, so he must be better at it than me. When his signal came through, I got the impression he wasn't trying to connect to anyone specifically. He wanted to get word to you and Sam, so he tossed out a kind of virtual message-in-a-bottle. With luck, a receiver on a distant shoreline would find it and deliver it."

"And a receiver just happened to be out beachcombing," Sam said.

Dani turned to give Sam an appraising look. He managed to surprise her at least once every day.

"Exactly!" Maddie said. "First, he introduced himself. Then I reminded him who I was. We had met briefly before he left town to join in that ugly business in Hays."

Dani scowled. "We thought he died during that 'business.' I can't wait to get my hands on that little shit for breaking my heart."

"That's understandable, but you should also be thankful he isn't dead." Maddie smiled. "Apparently he's living with some people called the Whitakers in a primitive village in the Smoky Mountains. They're the good guys in this scenario. A short distance away, their rival clan is preparing to attack. They're called the Murdocks. I sensed a lot of dark energy surrounding the surname during our conversation. A long-simmering, generational hostility between the two clans has begun to boil over."

"Like the Hatfields and McCoys ..."

Maddie tilted her head suddenly, then said, '*Our feud makes the famous one look like a community theater production.*' Not sure who that came from. Sometimes disjointed and ambiguous sentences drop down from the ether and I don't have a clue what to do with them. Anyway, Fergus said you must get there right away. He said to use jet fuel in a diesel engine and not to bring much gear. They have access to a lot of firepower and technology."

"What kind of firepower? What kind of technology? I have to know what my assets are before I can plan a battle."

Maddie shrugged. "I can't help with that. I've told you everything he said, word for word. Fergus asked me to get the coordinates and the message to the two of you right away."

"That's all?" Dani pressed.

Maddie nodded. "I think it's clear you have to go."

"Oh, we're going, all right. I plan to give that little red-haired bastard the worst atomic wedgie of his life."

Maddie laughed. "Pablo and I won't say a word about any of this, right, Pablo?" she added toward the empty hallway.

Pablo's voice floated back. "Fine." Of course he'd been listening. Despite his aversion to telepathy, anything that affected the love of his life came under his purview. Pablo was an attentive moon orbiting Planet Maddie.

***

An hour later, dressed entirely in black clothing, Dani and Sam stood next to a building with a sign that displayed *Dillons* in red cursive letters. Steven and his city council had converted the former grocery store into a community co-op. During the day, Liberty residents could gather items they needed from the well-stocked shelves in exchange for work they provided for the town. Nobody used money any longer, and the system worked pretty well, except for a few free-loaders who took more from the co-op than their meager labor was worth.

"Good thing Steven doesn't expect the co-op to get robbed by world-class thieves. This padlock wouldn't stop a toddler," Dani whispered, sliding two open-end wrenches from the waistband of her pants. After placing the sides of the Schlage's steel U-shank in the openings of the wrenches, she brought their handles together, cracking the lock's body and releasing the shank. Easy peasy.

Inside the building, she flicked on her flashlight. A bright beam illuminated the far right corner of the co-op, currently known as the Hardware Store. All manner of garden implements, hammers, and screwdrivers were stacked neatly on a long shelf alongside thousands of nails. On the opposite shelf lay their electric siblings: cordless drills, impact drivers, jigsaws. Now that electricity hummed through Steven's mini grid, those items were no longer just bulky paperweights. Their fragile power plant supplied lighting for homes, as well as electricity for medical devices and infrastructure support. But output was closely monitored and limited to ten kilowatt hours per day, per household. People couldn't use all the electricity they wanted. Not even Steven.

The items Dani sought formed a colorful pyramid at the end of the aisle: the five-gallon gas cans. They would need ten of them for their journey to Tennessee.

"The blue ones, right?" Sam whispered.

"Yes, those are for kerosene. Red is for gasoline, yellow is for diesel. This will just about wipe out the inventory. Steven is gonna lose his mind when he finds out." The notion of royally pissing off her uncle was one of the highlights of her day. The other highlights involved planning their escape from Liberty and contemplating the logistics of warfare between hillbillies. No matter the situation or the odds of triumphing in the Smoky Mountains, *her* hillbillies – the Whitakers, apparently – would win. She would make sure of that.

They loaded the plastic cans onto a flatbed trolley and wheeled it out the front door. The tricky part would be getting that trolley down Main Street to the more secure building where the town's precious fuel was stored ... without getting caught by the patrol.

She knew the patrol routes by heart, as the head of security should. She and Sam had exactly seven minutes to reach the fuel building before the patrol would round the corner of Main and Elm Street.

They made it in six. Sam motioned her in front of him so she could break the locks on the metal rolling door of the commercial building, formerly janitorial supply. Steven's approach to keeping the fuel "more secure" meant adding a second Schlage to the closure. She rolled her eyes, breaching both locks in ten seconds flat. She and Sam ducked inside the building and had the rolling door closed by the time the patrol would have rounded the corner a block away.

Dani flicked on the flashlight.

"Easy cheesy," Sam said with a smile.

Dani gave him a peck on the cheek and flashed the beam along the back wall. Several dozen twenty-five-gallon cans with the words JET FUEL stenciled on them filled half the space. The beam moved to the left wall, illuminating another, smaller assemblage of red, five-gallon plastic cans: the gasoline.

"It's all gone bad at this point," she said. "But the glorified kerosene should still be viable."

Sam rolled the trolley toward the back. It took them another thirty minutes to transfer fifty gallons of jet fuel from two of the large cans to the ten small cans. They took shallow breaths during the process. Sniffing the drying-oily-paint smell seemed vaguely toxic.

"The F-150 is in the back?" she said.

He nodded, wearing an expression of guilt. She draped her arms around his neck and pressed her mouth against his. While she loved kissing Sam more than just about anything else, she'd also discovered a sudden, passionate kiss worked beautifully to distract him from his negative reaction to whatever nefarious business she'd assigned him.

They quickly loaded the fuel into the back of the truck. When Dani slid into the driver's seat, she noticed a key in the ignition.

"I assumed I'd need to hot-wire. Where'd you get the key?"

She shouldn't have asked. In the faint dashboard light, she could see Sam's face turn red with shame.

"Never mind. Look, Sam, the end justifies the means. You understand that, right?"

"I know you believe that, but until we get to the end, you really can't say for sure."

Dani raised her eyebrows but decided to let the issue slide. Even if she could, she wouldn't change a thing about Sam and his integrity. Sometimes, though, it did get in the way.

It had been too long since she'd driven a beast like the diesel truck, and the sudden animal growl of its engine sent a thrill up her spine. She was not only escaping the societal shackles of Liberty, Kansas, she'd stolen fuel and a vehicle. Being a "thrill looker," as Sam called her, was something she didn't advertise, but she didn't try to hide her adrenaline addiction either. You might as well tell Sam not to be a good guy, or Steven to quit being a controlling jerk.

Or Julia to stop compensating for choosing her own education and career over an inconvenient baby all those years ago. Dani had come to terms with it, but she wasn't quite ready to let Julia off the hook. Not yet. It was just too much fun watching her squirm. Plus, she used the uncomfortable dynamic to get favors out of Steven. Dani figured she had another few months of working that angle before Steven got his fill. In the meantime, she enjoyed the occasional perks of being related to two of Liberty's most important movers and shakers.

She glanced at Sam and saw him frowning. "People will hear us," he said.

"Hell yes, they'll hear us." She laughed. "I'm thinking about honking the horn all the way to I70."

"Please don't."

"Fine. But only because you asked nicely. What snacky-snacks did you pack for our road trip?" Food was another good distraction for Sam when he fretted.

"The beef jerky I made last week, the last of the M&Ms we scored from the run to Lincoln in September, and two jugs of water."

"Perfect. Too bad the radio doesn't work. We'll just have to sing Willie Nelson on our own."

On their way out of town, not one person stuck a nose out to see why the hell someone was using precious kerosene at three o'clock in the morning on an errand that wasn't sanctioned. If they had, Dani would have rolled down the window and yelled, "Hasta la vista, suckers!"

Luckily for Sam, she didn't get the opportunity.

Several hours later, with the eastern sky awash in its pastel pre-sunrise splendor, they spied a roadblock in the distance. Dani slowed to a stop on I70's faded blacktop about a hundred yards from the debris pile.

"Doesn't look recent," she said. "The tires on the cars are flat. Lots of dust and rust."

"We're nearing the outskirts of Kansas City," Sam replied, glancing at a Rand McNally. "This may be similar to what we ran into south of Oklahoma City, on our way up from Texas."

"Maybe it was at one point," she said, reaching for the binoculars. "But I think it's been abandoned now. Look for yourself."

"I don't see any movement," he said. "But that doesn't necessarily mean anything. People these days can be sneaky."

Dani snorted. "That's for damn sure." She realized Sam must be feeling nervous; for him to use any kind of disparaging adjective was unusual. But he was right. Everyone these days seemed sneaky, like riptides lurking beneath an ocean or an unexpected step at the bottom of the stairs.

"What does your spider sense tell you?" Sam asked in a low voice.

She thought for a few moments. "I know I'm in a rush to get to the Smoky Mountains. And I know my natural inclination is to plow through whatever stands between me and my goal. But I'll be damned if I'm going to put your life at risk. I can't handle another bullet in your belly."

Sam grinned his beautiful grin. He'd wanted her to come to that conclusion on her own. Sam's lessons didn't smack you upside the head; they snuck up from behind and tenderly squeezed your butt cheek.

"I'll be the distraction, and you'll be the ninja that approaches from the southern flank," she said.

"Dani, for once, let me be the bullet's eye. You be the flanking ninja."

She opened her mouth to argue, but Sam planted his lips firmly against it. His tongue found hers, and soon heat spread between her legs.

Damn it. Sam was using a distraction trick of his own.

He was out of the truck the next second, walking briskly toward the barricade.

"Sonofa ..." She pounded the steering wheel with a fist and fumed for a full minute.

Ninja mode required concentration. Sam was still the best at it, but she was no slouch. The secret lay in blending into your surroundings and moving like a natural facet of the scenery; any impromptu props or disguises gathered from the immediate area added layers of stealth. Misdirection played a part as well. While Sam drew the attention of anyone who might be hiding in that debris pile, she would skirt it and move in from the backside.

She hated taking her eyes off Sam, but it was necessary. After ten minutes, she approached the barricade from behind, carrying a small dead shrub in one hand and her Beretta 9mm with the double-stack magazine in the other. If it looked even mildly dangerous, whatever slithered out of that junk was a goner.

"All clear!" The cheerfulness in Sam's voice felt like a splash of ice water. She'd been excited by the prospect of finally getting some 9mm action.

Dani could see him now as he crawled over the grimy roof of a red Mustang. A few seconds later, he stood beside her.

"There was a tunnel. Looks like someone had been living there at some point. I found this," he added, handing her a small spiral notebook. The purple cover had been decorated with Hello Kitty stickers.

She dropped the shrub, slid the 9mm into the back of her waistband, and took the notebook. After scanning a few pages of elegant prose interspersed by insane ramblings, she flipped to the back. That's where the author would have signed her name.

Turns out, she had not been so inclined.

If you're reading this, I'm dead. Nobody will care, and that's okay. I don't have many regrets, but I do have one. Most of my life, I did the best I could with what I was given, but I betrayed someone who was kind to me. I didn't have to, and I wish I hadn't. SIDENOTE: You know what? Your kinfolk ... your family ... doesn't have to be related to you by blood. They're the people who care about you the most.

I'm going to use this broken Coke bottle and run it lengthwise along the underside of my forearm. That's the correct way. Not the wrist. The wrist is for attention-seekers and those crying out for help. The arm is for the committed.

I don't much believe in an afterlife, so I guess this is it. If someone finds me, I hope you'll stick me in the ground. I don't think I'll mind being dead, but I don't like the notion of animals eating my flesh.

Thanks in advance.

Farewell, cruel world! (smiley face)

"That's really sad," Sam murmured, peering over her shoulder.

Dani nodded, brushing at her eyes. "We can get the Ford around the barricade. I scouted a route. Let's bury her first, though."

"She wasn't in there. Not even any bones."

"Well, damn." A traitorous corner of her mouth pulled down. She would not cry. Not here, not now. Maybe later she would read the Hello Kitty notebook front-to-back after Sam had gone to sleep. In that way, she could honor its author. She inhaled a shaky breath and blew it out again.

"Do you want to talk about it?"

"I do not. Let's go."

"Sometimes it's healthy to share your feelings."

Why was Sam pushing this? "Yeah, well, I've never been much of a sharer. You should know that by now."

"Tigers can change their spots."

"Not this tiger."

Sam chuckled. "Did you know that Bengal tigers make excellent mothers? They're very protective and will attack anything that threatens their babies. I saw that on NatGeo once."

Dani narrowed her eyes, started to respond, then bit back the words. Of course a mother tiger would protect her young. No newsflash there. Sam was just trying to restart the baby dialogue. Again.

"Did you know that I once killed a man in Tijuana just to watch him die? I was three at the time. I used my Care Bears switchblade."

Sam sighed.

They hiked back to the truck in silence, and Dani began to worry that she'd hurt Sam's feelings. It wouldn't be the first time. Not that he was overly sensitive, but it had recently come to her attention that she could be a thoughtless asshole. On occasion. Actually, on a lot of occasions.

"I just have one question," Sam said once they were back in the vehicle.

Oh no. He's using his serious voice. He's going to finally pin me down. I'll have to say yes, because I wouldn't deny Sam the one thing he wants most in life.

"What?" she asked finally.

"Was it a Cheer Bear or a Funshine Bear switchblade?"

***

A glorious, pumpkin-orange moon glowed from the night sky; stars glittered, like ice chips flung from the hand of a reckless god. But all that celestial lighting failed to illuminate the landscape as it flashed by the passenger window. The world seemed especially dark without electricity. Steven's power grid had spoiled her these past months. Funny how quickly people became dependent on modern conveniences.

Dani's metamorphosis from chubby nerd to skilled warrior had been the most difficult undertaking of her life, and also the most gratifying. The notion that she could squander even some of those gains by living in relative ease made her teeth grind. And if she were honest with herself, she'd come to hate that Liberty offered few opportunities for 'thrill-looking' these days. Yet it provided relative safety for anyone wanting to settle down and start a family.

Sam's dream. But was it hers?

He drove now so she could sleep, but there would be no switching off her brain. Dani found the lack of data surrounding her upcoming mission particularly frustrating. How could a general prepare for battle without intel? Without topographic maps, weapon inventories, and head counts?

Her sullen gaze landed on a road sign, caught in the truck's headlights: *Mount Vernon, IL, next exit.* The small, otherwise unimportant town was situated at a pivotal point on the map. Would they take I64 and continue east, eventually approaching Tremont from the north on I75 from Lexington? Or opt for the highway that skirted Knoxville, traveling from the west?

Both routes would have taken about fifteen hours to make the journey under pre-pandemic circumstances. The effortless road-tripping of yesteryear had vanished, however, along with billions of humans.

"Stop!" she said suddenly, peering at a figure ensnared by the truck's headlights. It stood on the highway shoulder, facing the oncoming vehicle. A gloved hand lifted into the night, extending a thumb.

Sam had seen it too and was already slowing.

"What the hell ...?" she whispered. The Ford crept closer, and details of the figure materialized.

Sam parked the truck fifty yards away.

The hood of a fur-trimmed parka framed a toothy grin within a dark-skinned face. Skinny legs extended below the coat, ending at a pair of rugged boots. The grin widened. The other gloved hand waved.

"It's a kid!" Sam said, reaching for the driver's door handle.

"Wait, Sam. This could be a trap, and that kid could be bait."

Dani reached for the Beretta. During the half-second she took her eyes off him, Sam opened the door and slid outside.

Damn it, she hissed. She leaped out of the truck, leveling the pistol at the kid as she approached. She scanned the gloom on all sides, searching for movement or tell-tale signs of warm breath hitting cold air. Nothing stirred or exhaled beyond the highway.

"Oh man. That's some French vanilla right there," the kid said, staring at her as Sam approached.

"Hands up!" Dani yelled.

The gloves reached for the pre-dawn sky. "Don't tase me, bro. I'm just a kid." He turned back to Sam now. "Dude, I hope your boo doesn't have an itchy trigger finger. She's scary as hell. I think I'm in love."

Dani jogged the remaining distance, joining Sam a few feet from the stranger.

"No need to look for anyone else. It's just me," the kid said in a conversational tone. His face appeared perhaps thirteen or fourteen, but she couldn't tell about his build beneath the bulk of the parka. "I'm Kenny. You probably want to frisk me before you let me get into the truck. Not gonna lie. I think I'll enjoy getting a pat-down from the Mistress of Macabre."

Dani felt a knee-jerk grin tug at her own mouth. The waggling eyebrows almost made her laugh. *You're being charmed*, an inner voice warned.

"Out of the coat, kid," she said in a no-nonsense voice. "My partner will do the frisking while I keep you in my crosshairs. Boots, too. What the hell are you doing on a deserted highway in the middle of the night?"

"It's no longer the middle of the night. Sun's gonna peek out any second now," Kenny replied, tugging off the parka. "Who's the Greek god? Jeez, I can't imagine how many notches your bedpost has carved into it."

Sam's blush was evident in the headlights, but he smiled. Dani could tell he already liked the newcomer. She stifled an eye-roll.

"I'm Sam and this is Dani. She's my girlfriend, so don't get any ideas."

Kenny chuckled. "I'll fight you for her. I'd probably get my ass kicked, but it'd be worth a shot."

The intelligent, chocolate-brown eyes seemed candid and honest. Dani felt her inherent distrust start to melt, which made her grip the Beretta more firmly. Charm offensives should not work on her.

"Answer my question," she said as Sam did the pat-down. Based on the skinny frame and scrawny arms, her initial assessment of about fourteen was probably on the money.

"I'm here because I knew you'd be coming this way," Kenny replied. "We have a mutual friend. A certain short fellow with spiky red hair and excellent teeth."

"You know Fergus?" she asked, stunned. "You'd better talk fast, kid. You're making my hackles rise."

"Can we talk in the truck, please? I'm freezing my nuts off out here."

"He's clean," Sam said, turning to her now. "I'll drive. You interrogate."

"Take I64. It's smooth sailing," Kenny said from the backseat a few moments later. "There's a fifty-car pileup on the southeastern route. It'd take a week to get around it. I'm glad you guys finally showed up. Been waiting for an hour. Like Elvis, my gonads have left the building. Hey, you got any snacks? I could eat the ass-end of a porcupine."

Now that Kenny was no longer wearing the bulky parka, he looked like a plucked, tawny-skinned chicken. Utterly harmless physically, though the nonstop commentary may prove lethal.

Dani tossed him some jerky. "Spill it, kid," she said. "How do you know Fergus? Why are you here?"

She watched a mask slide across his previously candid expression. "I can tell you some things, but I can't tell you all of it." A grown man's measured voice emanated now from the teenager's mouth. The friendly eyes turned wise and ancient, like those of a tribal shaman or a sorcerer from a fantasy movie. "What I *can* tell you is that you can use my help in Tennessee. And I can use a break from the place I've been for the last few months. There's a lot I need to sort out about my future, and there are some ... *folks* ... including Fergus ... who thought this might be an educational undertaking for me."

"Why would anyone think a kid can be helpful to me and Sam?" Of all the incredible revelations surrounding Kenny, the fact that someone thought she might need his help pissed her off. Badly.

The teenager's normal voice returned. "You got some 'tude, sistuh. I like it. But seriously, I'm way smarter than you. Yeah, you're crazy smart too, but I'm probably the smartest person left on the planet. At least that's the word on the street." He took a big bite of jerky and watched her reaction with obvious glee, like he might be about to witness Mount Kīlauea blow its top.

She wouldn't give him the satisfaction. "We'll let that slide for now. How the hell do you know Fergus? How is it that he's alive? How did you know we'd be coming this way?"

"I met the weird little dude in Florida. We clicked, of course. Birds of a feather, and all that." Kenny chewed thoughtfully, probably formulating some horseshit answer to her questions. "They gave me a speech to recite when you picked me up. I just nodded politely and let them ramble. It goes something, something, Maddie and her telepathy, blah, blah, life's mysteries, etc. etc. I won't insult you with all that malarkey. Now there's a word we should bring back into the contemporary lexicon. It has a nice old-school ring, don't you think?"

She responded with a look of annoyance.

"Okay, no more stalling. I'll tell you as much as I can because I like you, honey badger. But I won't tell you everything. I took an oath."

"Why did you call me that?" she demanded. There was only one person who claimed that privilege, and the last time she had seen him, he was bleeding out on the floor of an ice-cream shop in Hays, Kansas.

Kenny grinned. "Gives me credibility, doesn't it? Fergus said that should help. Anyway, I was contacted using the spooky telepathic network the psychic chick in Kansas uses. I'd been fidgeting in my new home and needed to get some fresh air to think about things. When this opportunity came up, I decided to take it. Some of my ... uh, roommates ... probably won't be happy about my sudden departure, especially since I got assistance from some of the other roommates. Anyway, I hitched a ride to the spot where you picked me up just now." He shook his head when she opened her mouth to speak. "Don't bother. I can't tell you all the deets."

"Fine, no details. But you said 'they' gave you a speech. Who else besides the suspiciously *living* Fergus told you to meet Sam and me? You can tell me that much."

"Yeah, that should be cool. There's an awesome little Native American woman living in Florida. I spent some time there recently. She's Fergus's off-again-on-again sandwich maker."

"Sandwich maker?" Sam said with a frown.

"Girlfriend," Kenny replied.

Dani gave him her best disgusted look.

Kenny raised his palms. "Sorry. Sometimes the urban thesaurus surfaces at inopportune moments."

Dani bit her lip to keep from smirking, then realized her brain had red-flagged something in the remark. "Wait a minute. Is she short? Dark hair with some gray streaks, usually wears it in braids?"

"Yep, that's our Amelia. She's really good at the telepathy thing. She told Fergus I should join you guys, and he thought I might be useful. The rest, as they say, is history."

"I know Amelia. Sam and I were traveling with Fergus when we met up with Maddie and Pablo in Oklahoma. Amelia was with them. Fergus must have moved on her fast if they ended up together in Florida."

The adult mask slid back onto the teenager's face. "You know Fergus. He's a horn dog."

"That he is. But I don't understand why Fergus thought I needed your help." The words were out before she could stop them.

Kenny guffawed. "There's the crux of it, right? You don't think you need any help. And maybe that's true, but what harm is a skinny black kid going to do? Look, we're killing two birds with one cannon. We're getting me out of the, uh, *neighborhood* where I was living unhappily ever after, and we're adding substantial brain power to your Battle of the Bumpkins. Win, win."

Dani snorted. She couldn't deny it. She liked the kid. Still, these mysteries were piling up, like curbside garbage during a workers' strike. There was some weird shit going on, and if Kenny wasn't going to give her answers, she would get them from Fergus. She'd beat them out of him if necessary.

Kenny's monolog continued. "You need any help figuring out the target destination? I'm kind of a math whiz. Fergus said he gave you the lat and long and I see you have a good ol' Rand McNally there. It doesn't get more old school than that, amiright?"

"You think I can't do the math, Urkel?"

Kenny almost choked on his jerky. "I don't know, Cruella. Can you? There's a lot of long division."

"I can manage," she said. "But if I need your help, Four Eyes, I'll let you know."

"Four Eyes? Lady, you need to update your insults. This is gonna be fun." Kenny leaned into the seat cushion with a happy sigh. "You okay up there, Fabio?" he said to the back of Sam's head.

"Two birds with one cannon ... I like that," Sam replied with a thoughtful expression.

Chapter 19

Idlewild

A faint tapping came from the glass pane on Tandy's bedroom window. She glanced at the wind-up alarm clock, a generational relic handed down from her great-great-great grandmother, then sighed. She'd been expecting him. Her traitorous heart fluttered, and her knees felt like overcooked spaghetti.

Falling in love with a Whitaker boy was perhaps the stupidest thing a female living in Idlewild could do. The risk Brock took by sneaking into town proved he returned her devotion. It also underscored his skill. Very few people could enter Idlewild under the radar. That devotion transcended mere lust on both parts, although the earth-scorching physical attraction played an undeniable part. Their instant connection at the moonshine barter last year had felt like the final two pieces of an exquisitely complicated puzzle snapping into place.

It was probably a past-life attachment, Tandy decided, impossible to deny or ignore and profoundly dangerous for them both. More so for him, though, sneaking into Idlewild for a stolen hour of passion with Silas's main squeeze. Brock would be executed if caught, while she could always play dumb.

Nobody played dumb better than Tandy.

Still, the heart wants what the heart wants. She'd probably die an early death because of the boy, but maybe their next life together would prove less arduous.

She lifted the window and watched her lover crawl into the darkened bedroom. They didn't need light; their hands and mouths quickly found each other. No words were spoken for the next half hour.

Finally, the time came to address Brock's grief. Tandy doubted anyone was good at conversations like these, including her. "I know about your father. I saw Wyatt and Levi talking about it earlier. I'm sorry, my love. I can't imagine what you're feeling. Did you know it was going to happen? Like the other things you've seen beforehand?"

He nodded against her neck.

"That must have felt like an elephant sitting on your chest. You didn't say anything to him before?"

"I couldn't. I didn't want to jinx him in case I was wrong. I know that sounds weird, but that's how it works sometimes. Sometimes I ... misinterpret."

"You've always had the gift?"

Another nod. "It comes and goes, but I wouldn't call it a gift."

Tandy possessed many talents, but precognition wasn't one of them. She let the silence linger as she imagined knowing about events before they happened.

Limbs still entwined, Brock murmured in her ear, "Do you want to get rid of Levi once and for all?"

"Don't tease me," she whispered. "That man is a sticky booger. There's no getting rid of him."

She felt Brock's muffled laugh against her ear. Was there anything sweeter than shared amusement with one's true love? She smiled in the dark, knowing she'd alleviated his sadness at least for a moment.

"I have a plan," he said, serious again.

"If it involves putting yourself in danger, I won't allow it."

"It does, but it'll be worth it. Think of all the little girls who won't be assaulted before they've put on their first training bra."

Next to being with Brock, there was nothing she wanted more than the death of Idlewild's resident pedophile. But would Levi's death be worth risking Brock's life? The once and future little girls would surely think so.

"I'm listening." The words felt like two quick dagger thrusts to her heart.

Brock reached down to the foot of the bed. She felt him fumbling with something, then a sudden match flame assaulted her night vision. He held the flickering light against the photograph of a child.

"She looks like an angel with that flaxen hair and those golden eyes. That one will break hearts in a few years. Who is she?" Tandy would never have used the word 'flaxen' to another living soul. Brock was the only person who knew she wasn't a moron, although a few others might suspect. Recently, a Murdock boy had whispered in her ear that he 'could see through her' as she was taking his virginity. She'd made a point to act extra stupid around him thereafter.

"It's not important who she is. It's only important *what* she is. This picture was taken a couple of years ago, but she still doesn't have any curves, if you know what I mean."

Tandy nodded. She'd already figured out where this was going. Besides playing dumb, she was also proficient at anticipating situations. Generally, people's actions weren't that difficult to predict. Her livelihood required the inherent skill——her life depended on it.

"You want to use her as bait."

"Yes."

"You want to lure Levi into the woods with a beautiful child then kill him."

"I'll be executing him for the crime of killing my father and the crime of child rape."

How could she argue?

"I guess this will delay our escape." Their whispered plans of running off together had always felt like a pipe dream. When Brock's gaze slid away from her face, she knew her fantasy would never happen.

He'd seen something else in store for them.

"What do you need me to do?" she asked. Perhaps she could at least mitigate the danger to Brock. Once he explained his plan, she knew there would be no happily ever after for either of them.

But all the little girls in Levi's orbit may get the chance for theirs.

"Give me two days," she murmured against his hair. In the darkness, she ran a finger along his smiling lips. For the next hour, she didn't think about anything except his young, strong body and its insatiable need. Time spent in bed with Brock was such an exquisite contrast to being with Silas. She never could decide the worst part of lying with the dried-up old husk: his wickedness or his stench.

Chapter 20

Willadean

"Did you see Brock come back this morning? Been gone a while. Wonder what he did with that picture of you?" Cricket stage-whispered to Willa and Harlan at breakfast. A warm front had wrestled autumn back from the jaws of Old Man Winter, so they ate their bacon and cornbread outside. Good thing too. Cricket's so-called whispers could be heard a mile away.

The nice weather would not go to waste. Willa planned to solve a new mystery——one wearing tight black pants and biker boots——that had just sauntered into the village the evening before.

"I don't know, but I'm sure he'll tell us soon," she replied, distracted.

Harlan signed, *Mama sure has been making a lot of exceptions to her rules lately.*

"I know. I think her boyfriend had something to do with letting the new folks in so easily. Guess she figures we need all the help we can get with the Murdocks."

"That new kid seems nice, even though he's colored," Cricket said.

Willa smacked the back of his head. "Nobody uses that word anymore, you little racist."

"What?" Cricket said, rubbing his greasy dark locks. "They don't like being called colored?"

She glared at him in disgust.

"I didn't go to some fancy school in Knoxville like you did, Miss Fancy Pants. We don't have no colored people in the holler, so how do I know what to call 'em?"

Cricket had a point, although it's not like he hadn't had access to television.

"Okay, I'll cut you some slack. The correct term is Black or African-American. I think you're safe using either when you refer to him."

Harlan signed, *Why not just call him the new kid?*

"Good idea, Harlan. Let's go find the *new kid* and pump him for information about the disfigured lady with the kiss-my-ass smirk."

Harlan sighed and shook his head. *You don't want to know about her boyfriend? He seems nice.*

"*Nice* is the last thing I'm interested in. Let's go."

The newcomers had been given the use of a house in the center of the village. Willadean knew the location was no accident; they could be watched more easily there.

The threesome stood in the center of the road, forcing passersby to walk around them. They got a few dirty looks while Willadean surveyed the guest house for signs of life. There were none. Maybe the newcomers were sleeping in.

Cricket said, "We're kinda causing a roadblock here, Willa. Just go up and knock on the door. You don't seem to have a problem with that most of the time."

"Fine," she replied, then charged up the wooden steps.

Just as she raised a fist to knock, the door flew open. The new kid stood on the threshold wearing an amused grin.

"Well hello there, diminutive yokels," the kid said. "I'm Kenny. What's your name, little girl?"

He spoke the last five words slowly, as if he were talking to an idiot.

She crossed her arms. "I'm Willadean. This is my brother Harlan and our friend Cricket. It was a mistake to assume we're yokels. I plan to make you pay for that at some point. We'd planned to invite you into our club, but if you're a pedantic douchebag, the offer is rescinded."

Kenny guffawed for at least thirty seconds. She stifled her own smile as she waited for him to compose himself.

Finally, he said, "Sorry about that, Willadean. I'm new to these here parts. You're a little cherry bomb, aren't you? I bet you cause your mom a lot of trouble. I met her last night, by the way. Ooh-la-la." The waggling eyebrows broke through her reserve. She grinned.

"You got that cherry bomb thing right. How'd you know she was my mama?"

"Because you're her tiny Twinkie. Pretty eyes, nice hair, acerbic demeanor."

"I know what that word means," she replied.

"I figured you did. That's why I used it."

Without bothering to disguise what she was doing, Willadean gave the kid a head-to-toe evaluation. He wasn't much taller than her, he wore good-quality clothing, and based on their cleanliness, his boots hadn't seen much action. Kenny hadn't been roughing it, that was for sure. Yes, he was skinny, but not in a malnourished way.

"We'll let you in our club on a probationary basis. We've already had breakfast, but I'll take you to the kitchen house if you're hungry. First, though, I want to meet your companions."

"Later." Kenny stepped onto the porch and closed the door behind him. "Those two are like peanut butter and jelly. And they look like they want to make a sack lunch at the moment." He glanced at Cricket, then back at her. He was euphemizing sex for Cricket's sake. Interesting that he seemed to instinctively know her friend was naïve in that regard.

She gave him a subtle wink. "Follow us. Hope you like honey and cornbread. I'm sure the bacon's already gone."

"Pity about the bacon. I could eat the ass-end out of a grizzly bear at the moment, but the rest sounds delish. Lead on, my fair maiden. I am in your thrall. Hey, do you all play the banjo?"

***

After an hour-long monolog delivered by their new friend, Willadean realized she knew little more about him than she had before. Yes, he was clearly a genius, and yes, he may well be the smartest person left in the world, as he'd been quick to inform her, but he was also wily. A few pointed questions remained cleverly unanswered. That he could successfully evade her cross-examination spoke to that wiliness. Kenny triggered her internal siren, but the weird part was, she still liked him.

"What's on the agenda for today?" Kenny asked, following her outside. "We gonna rustle up some polecats for tonight's stew?"

"Do you even know what a polecat is?" Willa asked. She didn't take offense to disparaging remarks about native Appalachians in general——only when directed at her intellect specifically.

"Isn't it a skunk?"

"Wrong, Alex Trebec. Did I just discover a chink in the armor of the smartest kid on earth?"

"What is it, then?"

"It's a type of carnivorous weasel indigenous to Europe. It does squirt stinky fluid to deter attacks, but there's no white stripe down its back."

"I'm somewhat correct, then," Kenny said with a smile. He didn't seem to mind being wrong, which earned him bonus points. Most people, herself included, hated it. "How do you know this anyway, Jane Goodall? Have you been living in Europe amongst the polecats?"

Willadean stopped and turned to face him. "No. I started reading the *Encyclopedia Britannica* when I was six."

"Nice. The one for kids?"

"No. The 32-volume grown-up set. My mom kept them in her office. She knew I would discover them some day. She probably didn't realize it would happen so soon."

"Wow. You are a smart cookie."

"Damn straight. Don't forget it, Poindexter."

"I shan't. By the way, I don't really need these," Kenny said, sliding off his glasses and shoving them in a pocket. "I only wear them so people will know I'm a smart black kid. Otherwise, they assume I'm a gang member."

"Interesting. Maybe that's because sometimes you do the ghetto talk thing."

"That's merely a self-defense mechanism. In the company of fellow prodigies, I abstain from the aforementioned ghetto talk." Kenny gave her a wink, smiled indulgently at Cricket, and allowed his focus to settle on Harlan. "You're a riddle, wrapped in a mystery, inside an enigma."

Harlan returned the steady gaze, unruffled. Willadean knew her brother better than anyone, but his expression at the moment was inscrutable. She quickly signed, *What do you make of this one?*

I'm still forming an opinion.

He seems nice.

Harlan shrugged. *There's more to him than meets the eye.*

"Hey, what's going on with the finger gymnastics?" Kenny said. "He can't hear?"

Willa replied, "He can hear and talk just fine. He chooses not to vocalize. You'll get used to it. That is, if you plan on sticking around for a while."

"Ooohhh, the mystery deepens. I'd like to add sign language to my repertoire. I assume it's ASL? American Sign Language?"

"No, it's Swahili sign language. Geez, of course it's ASL, seeing as how we're American."

"I actually speak a little Swahili. And I never make assumptions."

Willa stopped in mid-step. "Is that true?"

"It's true. I never make assumptions."

"No, I mean about speaking Swahili."

Kenny grinned. "That's also true."

Willa felt captivated. She spoke some Spanish only because one of her pre-school teachers emigrated from Guatemala. But the Knoxville Independent School District did not offer foreign language at the elementary school level. It was a facet of the gifted program she and Harlan had been signed up for, but the world ended before they could attend even one day.

Speaking a foreign language seemed almost magical. Or maybe *privileged* was a better word, like being given the key to an exclusive library.

"Why would you learn Swahili? Why not French or German or Portuguese?"

"Because I'd already learned those."

Willa poked the skinny chest. "No way."

"Easy there, Muhammed Ali. Yes, way. As well as Spanish, of course, plus Italian and Russian. I learned Swahili because one of those ancestry websites told me my DNA originated in eastern Africa. I was about to move into the Asian languages when the dooky hit the fan."

"Would you teach me Swahili?" she demanded. "And French? I have a couple of books written in French, and I can't read them. I think they're sexy books, so I know I'll want to someday."

Kenny belly laughed. "Oh, Willadean. You're delightful. Yes, I'll teach you Swahili and French, if you'll teach me American Sign Language. Deal?" He stuck out a hand for shaking.

Willa glanced down at it. "If you want to be part of our gang, you'll have to do better than a handshake."

Chapter 21

Ray

The time had come to put aside logic, science, empirical evidence, and long-held reality-based belief systems in order to embrace insanity.

What choice did he have?

Fergus and Hannah did not fake what he'd witnessed with his own eyes. Even if they could have pulled off some kind of Las Vegas illusion act, why would they? He couldn't see any reason for inflicting a potentially fatal wound on Fergus other than to prove the validity of this mysterious *langthal*. And if Hannah actually possessed this gift of healing, their other bizarre claims may also be true.

He himself was living proof of her ability, if he were to believe Serena Jo. She swore he was dead when she left him. For a spread-sheet and numbers guy, it was a bit much to digest. Still, he would try. For now.

The Whitakers would go to war to avenge Trevor's murder, and they must prevail or be wiped from the earth. According to Hannah, the only prisoners the Murdocks were interested in taking were the women and girls. And she'd painted a graphic picture of what they would be used for.

Fortunately, compartmentalization came easy for him. He banished the unanswered questions and focused on his strategy regarding the newest arrivals.

The "paladins," as Hannah dubbed them, had arrived at the village the night before. Ray would have merely called them "travelers" or perhaps "survivors." The teenager might have been a nerdy fourteen-year old dissecting frogs in middle-school science class. The man could have starred in a string of romantic comedies. Dani, the scarred young woman, had probably been beautiful too – at some point. She sauntered into the village like a leopard surveying its new savanna, exuding confidence, guile, and menace at the same time.

According to Fergus, all three offered unique skills which would increase their odds of prevailing against the Murdocks. Ray trusted Fergus, despite their abbreviated friendship, so he decided to give him the benefit of the doubt.

The contents of Ray's warehouse bought him a place at the table for the meet-and-greet, but according to Fergus, his importance at that moment lay in convincing Serena Jo to accept the help of these newcomers. She'd admitted them into the village, which already pushed the limits of her benevolence. Allowing them to play a major role in the coming conflict seemed highly unlikely.

He would do his best to convince her, though.

He changed into a clean long-sleeved shirt and hiking pants for the meeting. It felt weird to have someone else wash his clothes, but there were villagers whose only job was laundry. It seemed demeaning, but the two wash women didn't mind. When he'd picked up his bundle earlier, they smiled and advised him on the finer points of fabric care as it applied to nylon——which as it turned out, most outdoor wear was made from. It dries quickly and it's durable, but it's not a natural fiber. When nylon clothes are gone, they're gone for good.

Ray's warehouse contained dozens of pairs of REI pants, as well as shirts; the federal government bought enough to clothe a small army in the event of a natural disaster. So he could easily replace the ones he now wore, unlike the holler folk who would probably resort to homespun within the next decade. Serena Jo had wisely included mountain flax seeds in the supplies she'd brought from Knoxville.

What kind of person thinks that far ahead? She was remarkable in every way, but he'd be lying to himself if he thought he was only in love with her mind. Her beauty had lured him in, then the impressive IQ drove the stake through his heart.

He bent down to tie his boots. When he stood up, a figure stood by the door. A spurt of adrenaline jolted his heart rate, even though his brain quickly identified the intruder.

"Seriously, Fergus, you've got to stop sneaking into my house and scaring the crap out of me."

"Sadly, that will never happen. Are you ready for the showdown?"

"Why do you think Serena Jo is going to be obstinate? I've found her to be logical and rational in her decision-making approach. Why would she be different now?"

"You really have led a sheltered life. You think putting two highly intelligent alpha females together in a room is going to end well without some finessing? And these are two of the alphiest females I've ever encountered."

"I'm pretty sure that's not a word."

"It should be. Come, we'll talk while we walk."

They stepped out into the chilly, smoke-tinged air. It was heaven to be able to enjoy being outside. Ray's memories of his life with agoraphobia had already become misty around the edges.

"So this Dani person ... she's a genius at military tactics? What's her background, special forces?"

"Not exactly." Fergus replied. "Her background is unimpressive. What is impressive is her tactical ability. She was probably Hannibal or Alexander the Great in a previous life."

"What about Sam? What's his special skill?"

"Besides looking like Adonis? Sam and Dani both possess an innate ability to move undetected. Sam is even better at it than Dani. I suspect it will come in handy in the weeks ahead. They're both highly skilled at martial arts and with firearms, and their blade work is peerless. Not only that, Sam has some *langthal* ... not the type that heals others, just himself. And remember, neither of them know about any of that other business."

Ray resisted the urge to roll his eyes. "Interesting. What about the kid?"

"He has a mind like a computer and is probably the most intelligent human on the planet. I'm not sure how we'll use him, but we'll find a way."

"And you know that because the mysterious underground people told you?"

Fergus sighed. "The sooner you accept that everything I told you is true, the better this will go for you. Just lean into it, like sliding into a warm bath or caressing a perfect pair of breasts. About those breasts ..."

Ray laughed. "Give it a rest, Fergus."

Fergus's expression turned serious as they stood outside the kitchen house. "Your primary contribution will come later, when you're alone with your paramour. But for now, do what you can. You're a smart guy. I trust you."

A fire burned cheerfully in the dining room's stove, providing an ambience at odds with the serious subject matter. Fergus spotted Skeeter and made a beeline toward him, motioning for Ray to follow.

About twenty people had been invited to this war strategies meeting. Not all the Scouts were in attendance, being busy with their duties to keep the villagers safe, but those present had spread themselves out. More men than women, but Ray was surprised to see the ratio wasn't terribly skewed. The Scouts took up positions against the walls near the doors and windows.

Fergus sat next to Skeeter on a bench, so Ray took the opening on the older man's other side. Serena Jo stood near the woodstove in the center of the room. She scanned a legal pad filled with handwritten notes, her eyebrows crinkled in concentration. A sigh escaped him.

Skeeter snorted. "You got it bad.

"I'd be lying if I said you were wrong," Ray whispered. He glanced at Skeeter's injured hand. "How's it feeling?"

"It's a lot harder picking my nose these days. I been managing, though. Where's them new folks?"

"They'll be here," Fergus whispered.

"You better be right about them," Skeeter said.

"I am."

A few yards away, Serena Jo raised her voice above the muted hum of conversation. "Let's get started."

Of course she wasn't waiting on the newcomers because she hadn't invited them. Serena Jo would never allow strangers at a high-level meeting such as this, no matter what Ray or anyone else said.

"Our success depends on the element of surprise," she said, performing a slow pirouette to catch all the Scouts in the casted net of her focus. "Yes, they'll be anticipating some kind of attack because of Trevor, but they won't be expecting the blitzkrieg that I have in mind. The Murdocks have been allowed to multiply for generations. It's time to exterminate the nest."

The sentiment echoed that of Hannah, and Ray found it almost as off-putting coming from her daughter. *They're cockroaches in human form.*

"Even though there are fewer of us, we'll be far better prepared. We'll have more guns, more bullets, more tactical gear, and more medical supplies, thanks to Ray." She gestured to him on the bench. The small smile when their eyes met was for him alone.

"He must be Santy Claus," said one of the Scouts from a far corner.

Ray turned to study the man, noting the faded flannel shirt and stained ball cap, the corn cob pipe wedged between clenched teeth, and the black eye patch. He looked like a hillbilly pirate. The pipe wasn't burning; surely the tobacco had run out long ago. The man studied him right back.

"He's no Santa Claus, but he is a friend," Serena Jo replied.

"No offense, ma'am, but just 'cuz he's your boyfriend doesn't mean we should trust him."

Ray felt his cheeks get hot. He started to speak, but a sudden, hard pinch to the side of his belly kept the words from spilling out. Even without all his fingers, Skeeter still managed a mean pinch.

"Our relationship has nothing to do with his trustworthiness as it applies to our mission. And my personal relationship is none of your business. What is relevant is that he's giving us the tools to be successful in the upcoming conflict."

"Beg to differ, ma'am. You're the leader here, so it is my business. Pillow talk ain't just an urban myth. It's led to countries losing wars before."

Serena Jo stared at the man for a few uncomfortable seconds, then glanced at her notepad. "Five hundred Remington 870 Express 12-gauge shotguns, three hundred Springfield Armory M1A Scout Squad Rifles, a hundred M9 Beretta 9mm semi-auto handguns, plus thousands of rounds of ammunition for all of them. And that's just the firearms, which I've seen with my own eyes." She glanced back up, clearly enjoying the look of surprise on the face of the hillbilly pirate.

"Should I continue with the inventory, Tobias?"

Tobias chuckled. "No, ma'am."

Ray decided he liked the man.

"As I was saying, success depends on the element of surprise. We surround the town covertly in the dead of night, then attack at first light the following morning. We'll shoot everything that moves."

Ray felt a stirring under the wooden dining table. He glanced down just in time to see a scarred face before it vanished and reappeared beside the table with the rest of its body.

"So you want to lose the war? That plan sucks. Unless losing is your goal, in which case it's an excellent plan."

The scathing tone in the young woman's voice was missed by no one in the room. Ray glanced over at Fergus, who looked like he was passing a kidney stone.

"What are you doing here?" Serena Jo demanded. "Tobias, please escort this woman out the door and then out of the village."

"Pull your panties out of that wad, Barbie, then give me five minutes. After that, if you don't like what you hear, we'll leave without an escort. Eye Patch Dude can't make me leave until I'm ready, trust me."

Fergus squirmed on the bench.

"Seriously, if you'll put your ego aside and listen, you'll be saving a lot of lives. The lives of your people," Dani performed a slow pivot as Serena Jo had done moments before, gesturing to include everyone in the room. Ray couldn't deny the woman's grace; her pirouette looked like something from a gothic midnight ballet. "You want the Murdocks exterminated with minimal bloodshed on your side? Then I'm your guy."

Serena Joe scowled. "Why would I trust a complete stranger with the safety and protection of our village?"

"Because that's what's required to properly get the job done. Now, here's how it will go down."

For the next five minutes, Dani outlined a strategy that utilized several of the eight classic maneuvers of warfare. Ray had read a bit of WWII history, so he found it fascinating that this twenty-something woman had applied some of those tactics to a plan that sounded like it just might work.

Ray scanned the room, observing more than a few heads nodding in agreement. Not that it mattered. There was only one head that must agree to accept Dani's help, and based on Serena Jo's expression, she wasn't leaning that direction.

"The part about kidnapping Silas. How would you gain access to Idlewild? They have guards positioned everywhere."

At that moment, a handsome young man appeared——seemingly out of thin air——to stand beside Serena Jo. Whitaker holler's unflappable leader jumped a foot backward.

"That's how," Dani said.

"Where did you come from?" Serena Jo demanded. Sam merely gave her a warm smile.

"That's for us to know and you to find out," Dani said. "And that's just one of the trinkets in our very big toy box."

Ray watched the face of his beloved as she wrestled with the decision.

Finally, Serena Jo said, "I want to take a vote on this. If folks aren't comfortable putting their lives in the hands of strangers, they need to say so now. All in favor of letting the newcomers help, raise your hands."

It was a testament to Dani's warfare logistics, and perhaps the staged demonstration of her and Sam's impressive stealth, that every hand in the room shot up. Even Ray's.

In the following maelstrom of animated conversation, Ray glanced at Fergus, who dabbed a trickle of sweat with a handkerchief. Skeeter wandered off to chat with Tobias.

"Feel better?" Ray said, scooting over to his friend.

"That's one hurdle of about a dozen, but yes."

"I guess I don't need to utilize my sexy beast skills on Serena Jo after all."

Fergus chuckled. "It would seem not."

"So you spilled your guts about that other business for no reason."

"Nothing I do is ever without purpose, especially something as significant as sharing that *other business*. Don't forget how many more times I've been around the block than you, friend." Fergus looked around. "Speaking of, where is Hannah? I expected her to be here."

Ray shrugged. "I have no idea."

"Hmmph," Fergus said. He stood and left the building.

Ray was wondering if he'd angered his friend when he felt a presence beside him.

"You're friends with the little guy?" Dani asked. Up close, her scars looked even more ghastly than they had from a distance. It was a shame, too. Ray could see what a beauty she must have been.

"Yes. Don't ask me why, but we connected instantly. These days I just don't question things too much. I've found that's best for my peace of mind."

The young woman gave him an indelicate snort. "Who the hell has peace of mind in a post-apocalyptic world? Oh, wait. Probably someone who's been hiding out in a cushy warehouse with central heating and air and all the food he can eat. At least you didn't get fat."

For some reason, Ray wasn't offended by the remark. Dani clearly had no filter, and as someone who struggled in social situations, he found that refreshing. To a point.

"Thanks?" Ray replied with a friendly smile.

"No offense, dude. So you're okay throwing wide the gates and letting people pilfer your dragon hoard?"

"Yes. That's what it's there for. It's not my hoard, by the way. It belongs to the citizens of the United States. Their tax dollars paid for it."

"During my pandemic information-gathering phase, I read about those Strategic National Stockpiles, but the internet went down before I could uncover their locations. And you happened to be working at one when the shit hit the fan. Lucky."

"Yes, lucky for me."

Dani studied him intently for a few uncomfortable seconds, then said, "What finally made you emerge from your little cocoon? Fergus said you were a shut-in for more than two years."

"I saw children with my drone camera. I was worried about them, so I started dropping off care packages at the location where I'd spotted them. Fergus found out and came looking for me to make sure I wasn't some perv."

She rolled her eyes. "Of course, Fergus was involved. It's interesting how he seems to inject himself into all kinds of drama. One of these days, I'll solve the Mystery of Fergus. I thought he was dead, you know. I was there when he was mortally wounded. With my own eyes, I saw the bullet strike him. I watched his life's blood seep out of him. I thought he was a goner, for sure. Cried my heart out because of that little fucker. Anyway, I'm glad he didn't die, but when all this is done," she gestured to Serena Jo, who was engaged in a tense conversation with several of the Scouts, "I'm going to get him drunk and make him spill his guts. He owes me."

So Dani had not been privy to the narrative Ray had heard, a narrative that seemed less wild now with the information about Fergus's near death. Had the little man also been mystically brought back to life?

I have the same plan," Ray said. "I'll provide the whiskey as long as I get a front-row seat."

Chapter 22

Fergus

"Why didn't you attend the meeting?" Fergus asked Hannah once he located her. She'd been hiding out in Skeeter's cabin and had made herself quite cozy. Some of her clothing was neatly folded on the small bed, which she'd likely been sharing with its owner. Her jacket hung on a peg by the door, and her backpack and other belongings were stowed in Skeeter's lovely wardrobe.

It was time for Fergus to find other accommodations. Maybe Ray wouldn't mind having a roommate.

Hannah sat in a chair, legs crossed, sipping on fennel tea.

"There was no need for me to attend."

"You weren't invited?"

"I wasn't *not* invited."

"Even if you'd been barred, you would have showed up anyway if you'd wanted to. You stayed away on purpose," Fergus said, pouring himself a mug of hot water from the tea kettle, then adding some of the fennel from the proffered mason jar.

"I'm trying to keep a low profile," she said.

"For what reason?"

"Because that is my nature, and because opportunities for observation increase dramatically when people don't know they're being watched."

"Interesting. We haven't had a chance to chat since the demonstration with Ray. I have many questions. I'd very much appreciate some answers."

Hannah sighed. "There's really not much more to tell you, Fergus. My time in *Cthor-Vangt* wasn't enjoyable. Yes, I learned a few things, especially about myself and my abilities, but I knew right away it was not going to be the life for me."

"Most people wouldn't pass up the opportunity for virtual immortality."

"Most people aren't me."

"That may be the most truthful statement I've heard from you. And I understand. It's not for everyone."

"Not to change the subject, but I'm changing the subject. Did Ray convince my daughter to accept the help of the newcomers?"

"He didn't have to. They convinced her all by themselves."

"Yes, they're clearly exceptional, but not *Cthor-Vangt* exceptional, right?"

"Correct."

"And what was the plan to wage war against the Murdocks? Please tell me we're not going in all willy-nilly with guns blazing."

Fergus chuckled. "That's what your daughter wanted to do, but Dani presented a vastly superior approach. I like our odds."

Hannah studied him for a few moments. "There is not one person here aside from me who fully understands what we're up against. People without morals don't fight fair. There is no low too low for the Murdocks. They will position their children in front of their soldiers. They will tie infants to their backs so we don't shoot at them from behind. They will sacrifice their own people to win, down to the last toddler. All Silas and Piper and Wyatt care about is being the last person standing. It's not about what's best for the collective. It's about what's best for them individually. Sadly, the rest of the clan doesn't realize that. They just do as they're told. They've been brainwashed by an authoritarian cult for so long that they don't grasp how immoral and self-serving the cult leaders are."

Fergus blinked several times, trying to digest the horrors he'd just been told. "There's nothing we can do to combat depravity, but we'll have the firepower and the brainpower to circumvent it, at least."

Hannah nodded. "I guess that's all you can do, then."

"That's all *I* can do? What are you planning?"

"There's a lot more I can do ... covertly ... to help level the playing field," she replied airily.

"Like what?"

"Don't worry your pretty little head about it."

Fergus scowled now. "Perhaps you need to inform Dani so she's in your loop. I don't want you screwing up her plans."

"I don't really play well with others. Plus, I'm guessing I have about three days. My part will be done, one way or another, within twenty-four hours."

"Give me an inkling of what you're planning."

"You're tenacious for a tiny Irish spud."

"You would know all about being tiny."

Hannah laughed her deep musical laugh. It belonged in a medieval cathedral where its richness could bounce off ancient wood and stone and back down to appreciative human ears.

"Think about it, Fergus. Piper is my twin. What better way to infiltrate the enemy than by replacing one of their key leaders with someone who looks just like her and can orchestrate chaos from within."

He crossed his arms. "That sounds incredibly dangerous. Even if you look exactly like her, you can't emulate her in all other ways. They will see through it. In fact, they may even anticipate it. They're aware of your presence here in the holler."

"I'm going to take that chance."

"I won't allow it."

"You think you can stop me?"

"It's a suicide mission, Hannah. You must know that."

She smiled. "Of course I do. I'm a Murdock too, remember? The world will be a better place when the gene pool has been utterly destroyed. Once I've done as much damage as possible, I'm going to take one for the team."

Fergus huffed in disgust. "This is the definition of insanity. There's nothing I can do to stop you?"

Hannah gave him a kiss just above the wiry beard, then another directly on his mouth. His knees weakened. Skeeter was one lucky bastard.

"Not a damn thing," Hannah said. "I'm leaving tonight. Please keep that to yourself until I've gone, then you can tell your friend Dani. She'll need to factor my potential success or failure into her equations."

"I'll do that, but there's something you can do for me first."

"What's that, Sweet Lips?"

"Let's establish a *scythen* connection now. If we do it in person, it's easier to find it again later."

"Kind of like blading an inroad on rural acreage?"

Fergus nodded. He didn't trust himself to speak.

"Fine. But I can shut it down and probably will if I find you too intrusive.

I had to do that with my grandson recently. He's a natural, you know."

"Yes, I discovered that recently."

The impish smile vanished. "Don't you dare take him to *Cthor-Vangt*. I won't allow him to live in such an unnatural place."

"Well, don't get yourself killed. Then you can weigh in on the decision when the time comes. As of now, he's a prime candidate."

Hannah placed her hands on her hips and studied his face for signs of a bluff.

Harlan certainly possessed the inherent gifts to qualify for *Cthor-Vangt*, but there had been no time to conduct the proper tests. Even if the boy passed with flying colors, would he be willing to take a perfectly happy child away from this woodland paradise?

"You're bluffing."

"I don't bluff."

The grin was back. Hannah had broken through his *scythen* block. "Yes, you do. You're still on the fence about it and have been too distracted with other matters to continue your 'harvesting' duties."

"Damn, woman. No wonder they wanted you."

She laughed. "Everybody does."

Chapter 23

Idlewild

"Hey, darlin'. I was hoping you'd stop by today," Tandy said in her high-pitched dumb tone. The only time she spoke normally was with Brock. "I got something to show you." She motioned Levi through the front door.

He followed her down the hallway and into her bedroom. His eyes grew wide at the sight of the beautiful little girl in the photo. "Who is this?" he demanded. Weak sunshine filtered through the window, glinting off fresh saliva pooled at the corner of his mouth.

Tandy swallowed a surge of bile, then replied with a ditzy smile. "Nobody special. She's my gift to you ... for the Little Debbies you brung us last week. I'm hoping maybe you'll get us something even better next time. She's a little older than in the picture, but not much. She ain't got her period yet."

Levi struggled to tear his gaze away from the photo, but he finally managed. There were few things in life Tandy hated more than being the target of those dead, soulless eyes.

"Well, how kind of you. What hoops do I gotta jump through to get her? She's not from around here, I know that. I would have noticed that little beauty if she was a local girl."

"One of my girls owes me a favor and said she'd arrange for ... a meeting ... tonight."

"That sounds easy enough," Levi replied. His hand slid down to the growing bulge in his pants as his focus returned to the photograph. "Here at the house?"

"No. That's the only hoop you gotta jump through. The child is her niece and lives with her mama in a little cabin out in the woods. We gotta meet her in a clearing close by. It ain't far, though. She'll be ready for you."

"Why can't she come here?" Levi demanded.

"Cuz mama ain't a fan of the Murdocks."

Levi narrowed his eyes. "How is it we've never come across this cabin containing two defenseless females in all of our recon missions?"

Tandy had been anticipating this question. "Because Piper didn't want Wyatt to know about them."

The easiest way to distract Levi was with a reference to his archenemy.

"You're saying Piper somehow made sure no missions were conducted where they live?"

Tandy giggled. "Yep. I guess she was just being mean. Don't ask me how she done it neither, cuz I can't keep all the particulars straight about how you men run things. Don't seem right that a woman should have so much say about important stuff, if you ask me."

It pained her greatly to speak those words, but speak them she must. Framing herself as an ally to Wyatt and Levi was paramount. She would deal with any fallout from Piper later; or maybe she wouldn't have to, if Silas held on a bit longer. She despised the old man, but he kept her safe as long as she kept him happy.

"All right. When is the meeting?"

"Tonight. That's why I was hoping you'd show up today. We gotta leave right after dark."

Levi continued to study the photograph as the seconds ticked by. Finally, he tucked it into a shirt pocket and took her by the shoulders. He squeezed so hard she felt her bones grind.

"I gotta go do a couple things 'fore I can leave. I'll be back by dark. Do not fuck with me, Tandy. I don't care how good you are at sucking the old man's cock. I'll find a way to make you pay."

He turned and left.

Tandy's heart felt like it might beat out of her chest. She took ten deep breaths and chanted her mantra: *You are a survivor. You have endured much and will endure more. You will outlive them all.*

When she uttered the last words, a nagging voice in her head said: *Are you sure about that last part?*

"No, I'm not sure," she whispered to the voice. "But it doesn't matter. If I do one good thing in my life, it will be this. No little girl will ever be despoiled by that demon Levi again. Even if I have to die. I've made my peace with it. Amen."

She rubbed the silver cross pendant tucked under her blouse for good luck. She didn't much believe in Jesus or God or any of that religious stuff, but she found the trappings of Christianity comforting. And at this moment, she needed all the comfort she could find.

Chapter 24

Willadean

The sun had set, and Pops was making Willa and Harlan get ready for bed. For once, Willa didn't argue. Far from it. The next few minutes would be tricky.

"I hope Mama has a good time with Mister Ray," Willa said in a casual voice.

Pops chuckled. "Well, she took that bottle of wine she's been saving for two years. I think they're gonna have a very good time."

"Maybe since she's having the wine, you should get some Old Smokey."

His pale eyes took on a suspicious cast. "Why? You usually tell me you don't like the way it smells."

Willa turned her back on her grandfather, then reached for the moonshine bottle and a mug from the kitchen cupboard. When she turned around again, she'd arranged her face into an expression of empathy.

"Pops, I know how much you're already missing Hannah. She probably won't be coming back, since she pretty much abandoned you for the last few decades already. It's okay to have a snort or two to drown your sorrows."

"Snort? Who taught you that?" Pops replied, but he didn't argue when she began pouring the liquid into Mama's coffee cup.

"I guess I just picked it up somewhere. You know how I am about learning new words."

"That's true enough." He took a large gulp. His eyes watered for a second, then he finished off the rest in a single swallow.

"More?" Willa said.

"No, that was plenty," her grandfather replied. "Next time you want to slip someone a sleeping herb, don't use so much. I could taste it."

"Wha ...?" Willa began.

"Don't waste your breath, child. I already seen you goin' into the woods tonight, and I know you're gonna be okay." He tapped his remaining index finger against a bony temple. "Everything's a bit blurry these days, but that's comin' through clear enough. Just be as safe as you can. That goes for you, too," he called toward the bedroom where Harlan was pretending to get ready for bed.

"You knew I dosed you with valerian?"

"Yep."

"Why did you let me?"

"Cuz I figured I could use a good night's sleep. And like I said, I know you and your brother are gonna be okay. I don't know the particulars ... probably some kid's club initiation thing, I'm guessing. Anyway, it don't matter. Just be home by sunrise before your mama gets back. Wear your heavy jacket, too. A cold front's comin' through tonight."

Willa nodded wordlessly, then dashed into her bedroom before Pops changed his tune.

She was already sweating from the down jacket when she and Harlan closed the front door behind them. Pops' snoring had begun by the time they stepped off the front porch, out of the circle of lantern light, and into the night. As they walked toward Brock's house, their eyes adjusted to the weak starlight. At the bend in the dirt-packed road, an inky shadow peeled away from the giant oak tree whose branches she'd climbed dozens of times when she was younger.

"Who's there?" she hissed.

"Nobody but us ghosts," a now-familiar voice replied. Kenny appeared the next moment, his grin shining in the darkness like a lighthouse beacon.

"What are you doing? You're supposed to be inside. It's after curfew."

"I don't remember signing any contracts when I arrived. Are you under a curfew?"

"There's no contract, just accepted rules. You'll get kicked out of the holler if you're not careful. Go home."

"No can do, cherry bomb. I don't know what you two have planned, but I'm coming. I performed the blood oath and am officially the oldest member of the gang. That gives me some authority."

"That gives you zero authority. Now go away before you get us all caught."

Kenny stopped, reached for her arm and pulled her gently to a stop.

"Willadean, I don't know the particulars of your plan, but I know it's dangerous. I'm coming with you."

"Oh no you're not."

"I have rights. I'm an officially sanctioned gang member."

"Cricket is, too, and you don't see him with us," Willa snapped. "He's in bed, same as you should be. This is a three-man job, and you're not the third man." Willa began walking again. Harlan followed soundlessly.

"Who's the third man? I think I'm jealous."

"None of your beeswax," she said, slowing at the front steps of Brock's cabin.

Kenny glanced up at a figure moving inside, illuminated by flickering candle light.

"That weird dude is your third man? He's a creepy sumbitch."

"Brock isn't weird or creepy. He's ..." Willa pondered descriptive words and realized Kenny had a point. Brock did seem a little freaky when his eyes got all dilated. "He's okay," was all she could manage.

"He doesn't have your interests at heart. He has his own agenda. That's why I'm going."

The 'and that's that' tone in Kenny's voice would normally make her hackles rise. But for some reason, she considered allowing him to join them. Something in his words rang true. Brock did have an agenda. She was merely a tool with which to get the job done. And not just any job. Tonight's business was *wet work*, a term she'd read in a book——a euphemism for violence and bloodshed.

"How do you know about Brock's agenda?" she demanded.

Kenny surprised her by taking her hand in his and holding it for a moment before answering. "I can't say how I know. I just know. I think you understand that on some level, yes?"

Surprisingly, Harlan nodded vigorously.

"See? Your brother agrees, right, Champ?"

Harlan surprised her again by flashing a thumbs-up sign. She had never seen him do it before. Usually he brought his index finger and thumb together in an 'okay' gesture.

"Two against one."

Harlan grinned, then answered Kenny's raised palm with a resounding high-five slap. Willa narrowed her eyes at the annoying display of male bonding. Still, she didn't entirely trust Brock to keep her safe.

"Fine, but you need to stay out of sight. I don't think Brock wanted anyone else to come."

A voice came from the porch. "He can come. It doesn't matter. His presence won't change the outcome."

Brock closed the door behind him and stepped onto the dirt road.

"Let's go," he said simply, then took off at a brisk pace toward the forest.

At sixteen, Brock was practically an adult, even though he might grow another inch or two and his muscles would fill out some more. In a post-apocalyptic world, everyone achieved adulthood faster than they would have in their old lives. Losing one's parents surely made a person grow up even faster. Willa felt a wave of sadness for the young man navigating the spectral woods ahead of her. As much as she might butt heads with Mama, she loved her with all her heart. A world without her was incomprehensible.

Kenny whispered from behind, interrupting her morose thoughts. "He moves like a wolf. And that fabulous hair screams *lycanthrope*."

She suppressed a giggle. This was neither the time nor place for humor. Every ounce of concentration was required to keep from tripping and falling on her face. It was one thing to wrangle with the vines, rocks, and brush in the daytime, but quite another to do so at night with just the stars and a tangerine-wedge of a moon lighting the way.

"What's the plan, cherry bomb? I know you haven't undertaken a dangerous outing like this without working out a strategy."

Willa kept her eyes on Harlan's back. She'd lost sight of Brock, but her brother was a savant at this wilderness business. Between his acute hearing and billy-goat feet, she trusted him more than Brock anyway.

"It's simple," she replied. "Once we arrive at the predetermined location, I'll be tied up to a tree holding a flashlight. I'm supposed to shine it on my face so Levi can see me. Brock will take up a position nearby, maybe in a tree Once Levi is in range, Brock will shoot him."

"What about your brother? What's his job?"

"I'm not sure. Brock didn't say what he wanted him to do, only that he wanted him to be there. Just in case."

"Oh, Willadean. This stinks to high heaven."

She wanted to feel scathingly annoyed, but found herself alarmed instead. Brock's plan wasn't much, but she'd agreed to it because of her promise. Brock had extracted that promise from her, then marched into the village and saved Cricket's daddy from execution. He'd made good on the bargain, and so must she.

She would never renege on a promise. Never, ever.

"I know, Kenny, but I didn't have a choice."

"Maybe not then, but you have a choice now. Let's grab Harlan and run the opposite direction before somebody gets hurt. Or dead."

"I can't." She hated the spineless tone in her whisper. "I *won't*!" There. That was better.

She heard Kenny's dramatic sigh as she hurried to catch up with Harlan.

They trudged through the woods for what seemed like half the night, but was probably only two hours. Finally, they reached a clearing and gathered in a close circle just inside the tree line. The moon had risen higher in the night sky, and its light turned Brock's eyes a weird grayish orange. As had happened before in his presence, her skin suddenly tingled. She shuddered, partly from his odd, unblinking gaze, but also from the chilly air. Pops was right. A cold front was moving through, carried on sudden, violent gusts of dead leaves.

"That tree is where I'll tie you up." Brock pointed toward a lone birch in the center of the clearing. Its pale, papery trunk glowed in the moonlight; whenever the wind kicked up, the tree's doubloon-shaped leaves fell from its limbs like confetti. In the daylight, those leaves were painted with butterscotch and honey, but night had drained their glorious colors, tinting them in ashen shades of gray and darker gray.

Willa nodded, then tried to swallow around the lump in her throat.

"You're not going to tie her with real knots, right?" Kenny said in a reasonable voice.

Brock's eerie gaze glided to him now. Willa felt lighter somehow now that she was no longer the focus of those eyes.

"She'll be tied with real knots. Levi would see through any trickery."

"Look, let's talk about this man to man," Kenny began.

Brock waved a dismissive hand. "Stop talking, newcomer. This has nothing to do with you. It's not your fight. If you don't shut up, I'll just kill you."

A knife blade suddenly glistened in the moonlight. Kenny glanced down at it, then up at Brock. His chocolate-brown eyes narrowed, but thankfully he didn't offer a retort.

"Very good," Brock said, then turned to Willa, "Let's go. Levi will be here in a half hour. If you need to pee, do it now."

She did have to pee, but hell would sprout icicles before she urinated in front of three boys.

"I'm good. Let's get this over with." She marched out of the forest and into the clearing, feeling like she carried a bullseye pinned to her back.

Brock had her stand against the rough birch bark, then looped the nylon rope around her a half-dozen times. As with other acts of physical prowess, he was quite good at tying knots. She couldn't wiggle anything but her flashlight hand.

"You still have some movement," he said. She held the small flashlight, switched on now, in a tight grip. If she dropped it, Brock would be furious. He whispered that to her as he tied the knots. She was sure he didn't want the other boys to hear him threatening her.

"The only thing I can move is the hand with the flashlight," she said, angry now. "You didn't tell me the rope would be so tight or that I'd have to stand the entire time. I feel like a cartoon character tied to a train track."

Brock shrugged. "That's what we want. You need to look helpless and weak. Try not to scowl. Levi likes compliant girls."

"I should never have agreed to this," she mumbled.

"No, you shouldn't have. But you did. Good luck, Willadean. You're doing a heroic thing." He turned and walked into the woods.

She could no longer see any of the boys among the trees now, which made her even more scared. Kenny and Harlan's presence had been comforting on the journey here. She had only just met Kenny, but it didn't matter. They had connected on a level she didn't question. Brock was supposed to be one of the good guys, yet he'd threatened Kenny's life.

The peril of the situation finally sunk it. Kenny was right: it stank to high heaven. If something awful happened to him or Harlan, it would be on her.

Her ears straining to pick up any sounds of human activity, Willa swiveled her head from side to side as far as possible, scanning the clearing and the tree line that fell within her limited range of vision. An owl hooted from somewhere close by. Between the sudden wind gusts, no other animal sounds could be heard. In late fall, the frogs had probably gone into hibernation, and the crickets would be dissolving in the stomach acid of the frogs.

The sound of dead leaves crunching beneath footfalls came from the left. Willa strained her neck for a glimpse of the person approaching, but it was impossible to see anything with the flashlight shining in her eyes. Surely Brock would be distracted at the moment, not staring at her to make sure she kept the flashlight in place. She counted ten heartbeats before she pointed the flashlight toward the sound, just in time to see a man emerge into the clearing.

He wasn't in a hurry. It was almost as if he were taking his time, savoring the vision of Willa tied to the tree. When a wide grin appeared in the gloom, she knew she was right. Levi was enjoying every brushstroke of the living portrait before him: a young girl in distress, tied to a tree in the middle of an eerie forest at night.

And she had no confidence in Brock, her would-be knight in shining armor.

Pops had 'seen' that she and Harlan would be okay, but what about Kenny? Or what if Pops and his second sight——or sixth sense or whatever it was——was wrong?

"Hello, little girl," Levi said when he was ten feet away. His face looked clean-shaven, unlike most men's these days; starlight reflected off a white scalp visible beneath his crewcut. He stopped and stared, enjoying what he saw. She felt his gaze slither down her body like it had scratchy cockroach legs.

Brock's whispered directive penetrated her fog of terror: *Act helpless. Pretend to be weak. Look scared.*

She didn't have to fake that last part; her bladder let go.

"I ... I ... don't want you to come any closer."

"We don't always get what we want." Levi gave her a horrific wink and started walking again.

He was a yard away when a sudden commotion in the woods drew his attention. Three quick, sharp retorts echoed through the night.

Much to Willa's dismay, Levi's attention settled back on her the next moment. He grinned. "That would be Wyatt killing your friend Brock, and anyone else who came with you."

Willa's mouth fell open, and an undignified squeak slipped out. In her lifetime, she had read a few books she wasn't supposed to read. It didn't require much imagination to visualize what would happen when Levi got the rope off her. Even now, his hands had begun the task, trembling slightly in anticipation, like a kid unwrapping a Christmas present.

She closed her eyes, swallowed hard, and summoned courage from a hidden reservoir. "You're not a real man. A real man wouldn't do this to a child. You're a monster. A weak, spineless, *flaccid* monster." It was a word she had learned recently, and she saw its instant effect on Levi.

"I'll show you flaccid, you little bitch." He jerked hard on the rope, drawing it firmly against her throat. "You and Brock thought you were so smart. Too bad you underestimated me. Tandy already paid the price for that mistake. I wrung her neck, with Silas's blessing. Now it's your turn. What kind of dumbass falls for a trap like this?"

Willa tried to swallow but couldn't summon enough moisture. "I'm guessing the kind of dumbass who wants to rape a child," she choked.

Levi contemplated her for a moment, then suddenly punched her in the belly, driving all the oxygen from her lungs. She gasped, frantic for replacement air.

"Maybe that'll shut you up," he mumbled, then continued untying the rope.

Finally, her lungs decided to cooperate, and she drew a painful breath. When Levi unwound the last loop of the rope, she fell to her knees on the cold, rocky ground. Her palm landed hard on an angular object the size of a plum. Her fingers skittered over the dead grass, feeling for something more in the pear or apple range. Seconds later, her fingers located a grapefruit. It would have to do.

Levi stood next to her, hands on his hips. "Stand up, bitch. You're older than in your picture, but you'll do."

Her fingers curled around the rock. It was large enough for him to see, so she'd have to be lightning fast. Her knees began to unfold, pushing her body up off the ground; the rock arm remained behind her as she turned. The position would be good for a kind of softball fast-pitch once she stood fully erect.

She forced her body to move slowly, allowing her brain time to do the calculations. The rock needed to slam against Levi's skull with enough force to do serious damage. Anything less, and this would not end well for her.

One ... two ... three ...

Her knees locked into position, and she began executing the arcing movement with the arm holding her best chance of survival.

She saw the moment Levi noticed the rock. How a human could move so fast, she would never know. His hand caught her arm just before she could release the coiled-up energy.

"You're a fighter!" he said, followed by a dumb-sounding guffaw. "Normally, I don't like that, but you might be an exception."

The leering grin was inches from her face now. He was tugging on the zipper of her jeans when another gunshot rang out from the tree line.

The next moment, half of Levi's head exploded in a burst of night-black liquid.

Gore splattered across her face. Levi's soulless eyes stared up at the stars. His mouth hung open in comical disbelief.

"I guess you didn't plan on ending up like this." A manic giggle escaped her as her knees buckled. All the adrenaline-triggered energy drained out of her. She imagined it pooling alongside Levi's blood, then swirling around the fragments of skull and chunks of brain matter.

She turned to the side and threw up.

"Willa, you okay?" Cricket's voice called out of the darkness.

That snapped her out of her reverie. What the hell was Cricket doing here? What had happened to Harlan and Kenny?

She stood on trembling legs and stumbled toward Cricket's voice. The crescent moon had fully risen, and she could see the tall figure walking alongside her friend. Ezra held his rifle in the two-handed ready-carry. Hunters used that method when they might need to kill something quickly but didn't want to accidentally shoot a 'friendly.' She'd learned all about it during target practice.

Who would have thought the worthless Ezra would be worried about safety measures?

"What's your daddy doing here? He got banished."

"Ain't you glad he didn't go far?" Cricket said with a face-splitting grin.

"Where's Harlan and Kenny?" Her brain and her legs were working better now. She darted toward the tree line where she'd last seen the boys.

"I don't know. We come in from the other way. We was followin' y'all," Cricket hollered after her.

As she entered the gloom of the forest, she realized the lit flashlight was still in her hand. Its erratic, quivering beam illuminated brush and pine trunks and fallen branches before finally landing on the boys. One lay face-up on the forest floor. The other knelt beside him, expressive fingers splayed out on the skinny chest below.

"Kenny got shot?" Willa whispered, kneeling next to her brother.

Harlan nodded.

"In his chest?" she almost choked on the words. She reached out to adjust her new friend's glasses, even though he said he didn't need them and even though his eyes were closed.

Harlan nodded again.

"What are you doing?"

"The same thing I did to Cricket when the witch shot him. Now be quiet, Willa. I need to concentrate."

Willa didn't know which was more shocking: the words themselves or the fact that Harlan was vocalizing again. Three times in the last week was surely a new record for him.

A thought intruded. "Was it Wyatt? Where is he?" she whispered as she scanned their surroundings.

Harlan made an irritated noise. "Yes, it was Wyatt, but he's gone. Brock is dead, so I can't help him. I'm not that good yet. But I can help Kenny. Now go away, Willa. Find out what Cricket and his daddy are doing. Come back in ten minutes."

"Fine, but I will have questions."

When she reached Cricket and Ezra in the clearing, she shined the flashlight beam in their faces.

"You've got some explaining to do, Cricket."

"Before that, maybe you ought to say thanks to my daddy for saving you."

Willa's gaze traveled down to Ezra's rifle, then up to the man's face. "Wyatt's gone?" she demanded. She believed her brother, but she wanted to have it confirmed by an adult, even if that adult was Cricket's daddy.

"Yep."

"How do you know? Did you see him leave? He might still be out there with his gun pointed right at us."

"He ain't. If you want to do a search of the woods, help yourself."

Cricket tapped her shoulder. "I know you been through a lot, but ..."

"Fine. Thank you for saving my life, Mister Ezra. Now why are you here?

You're supposed to be banished."

"I don't owe you nothing more than what I just did, and that includes explanations." The rifle shifted from ready-carry to cradle-carry. That meant Ezra didn't perceive an immediate threat. While he was no Scout, he was still a Whitaker and an Appalachian. He knew about firearms and hunting in the forest, even if he was a drunk.

"He don't drink no more, Willa," Cricket said, reading her mind. He took a deep breath. "And I'm leaving the holler to be with him."

"What? No, Cricket, you can't!"

"I can and I am." Cricket thrust his chin out and crossed his arms. "There ain't no place for me in the village, Willa. And there ain't a place for my daddy in Idlewild after what he just done for you."

The full picture came into focus. Ezra had been covertly helping the Murdocks, who might have provided him a sanctuary after he'd been outed as a spy in Whitaker holler. Now that he'd killed Levi, there would be no sanctuary for him. In fact, because of his decision to help her, he was likely a dead man walking.

"I can see you get it," Cricket said. "I knew where my daddy was staying, and I went to him when you agreed to Brock's crazy plan. I knew it weren't going to end well if someone didn't step up." Willa couldn't help but smile at his use of one of her pet phrases. "My daddy stepped up. Never forget that. And promise me you'll never let the Whitakers forget that."

Willa nodded, and Cricket continued. "So I'm going with him. We're leaving Tennessee. Gonna get a fresh start somewhere where there ain't any Murdocks or Whitakers. Don't try to talk me out of it, Willa. You know it's best for everyone."

Cricket was right. And for once in her life, she chose not to belabor a point.

"You're leaving now?" she said, frowning. *I will not cry. Not in front of Cricket and his daddy.* Human emotion overcame her stubbornness, and the tears flowed anyway.

"Yep," Cricket said, his own unshed tears turning the green eyes into glassy emerald marbles. "Maybe I'll come back and visit someday when we're both older."

"You better, you little bumpkin," she said, then wrapped Cricket in a hug.

Cricket's chin quivered so badly, Willa knew he wouldn't trust himself to speak.

"It's best for you two to be out of the area when the sun comes up," Willa said. "Thanks again, Mister Ezra." He gave her a nod.

The two shadow figures, one small and one tall, quickly traversed the moonlit clearing and melted into the forest beyond.

Willa didn't have the psychic gift of seeing into the future like Pops and Brock, but something inside told her she would never see her best friend again. The thought of Brock prompted her to spin around and run back into the forest, where Harlan was doing whatever he was doing to Kenny.

The mysterious procedure had worked. Kenny sat up now, holding his glasses in one hand and rubbing his eyes with the other.

"Willadean, can you please not shine that light into my eyeballs? It feels like a blast furnace."

She shifted the flashlight beam to her brother, still squatting beside Kenny and grinning like an idiot.

Harlan, who definitely was *not* an idiot, chose that moment to speak again. "I think I did a better job on him than Cricket. His injury wasn't as bad, though, so that might have helped."

Willa shoved the flashlight into Harlan's hand, then grabbed for Kenny's shirt and tugged it up to his neck.

"Whoa, there, little filly," Kenny said. "I'm not old enough for that kind of stuff, and you certainly aren't."

She was too focused on her task to be amused. Kenny's chest was smeared in bright red blood, but there was no gaping hole.

"Where did the bullet go?" she said to her brother.

Harlan pointed at a spot on the unblemished skin covering Kenny's rib cage.

"There's nothing there, Harlan. You're mistaken."

"No, I'm not mistaken. I fixed him. I fixed the bullet wound, and I fixed what was damaged on the inside too."

It was at that moment when all the horrific events Willa had experienced that night crashed into the weird, inexplicable occurrences that had been happening in the holler recently. It all suddenly became too much.

"Where the hell is the hole, Harlan?" she screamed.

Kenny's mouth formed a silent "o" of surprise. Harlan winced at the sudden, ear-piercing outburst. Then he stood and drew his sister into a hug, holding her for a long time. When he released her, she felt sane again … grounded and calm.

"Is it another gift, like the ability to travel in your sleep?" she asked in her normal, non-screaming voice.

Harlan smiled. "Yes. I'm not sure what it's called though. I'm able to send calm feelings into others. It's kind of nice, isn't it? Mister Fergus can do it too. I think I'll get better with practice. Maybe I should call myself The Willa Whisperer. Whatever this thing is seems to work especially well on you."

She shook her head, feeling as if the world was shifting under her feet. Not in a rumbling, violent, earthquake-shifting way. More like the ground transforming into an ocean swell and she clung to a rubber raft.

Rather than plying her brother with questions, she squeezed his hand; it felt feverishly warm in the chilly air. She lifted the back of her palm to his forehead; his temperature felt fine.

"Maybe you *should* call yourself that," she said, staring into the golden eyes so similar to her own. "Let's go home, boys. Harlan, we need to be in bed when Mama gets back from her visit with Mister Ray. I just might sleep for a week."

Chapter 25

Ray

Ray hoped no one would order him to stop smiling today. He didn't think it would be possible.

Serena Jo had left an hour ago after a night of passion and intimacy he thought he'd never experience. Even back when there were still plenty of women in the world, he hadn't felt the profound connection with any of them that he felt with her. His butt would be dragging today, but he would have no regrets.

As he walked past her house on his way to breakfast, Skeeter emerged. Ray grinned at him, helpless to do otherwise. His expression evoked an interesting sound from the older man——something between an amused cackle and a disgusted snort.

"Reckon you worked up an appetite," Skeeter said as he fell into step with Ray.

"I love your daughter," Ray blurted.

"Son, I don't think there's a living soul in this village that don't already know that. There's probably tribesmen in the Amazon jungle that know it."

"Do I have a chance?"

Skeeter gave him a sideways glance. "You mean to marry her? I doubt it. Probably the best you can do is about what you got right now. Serena Jo's got matters more pressing than a new husband. If you're smart, you'll bide your time until all this Murdock business gets resolved. *If* you're still around then."

"I guess I have extra incentive to stay alive."

Skeeter wasn't amused. "Best keep behind a Scout, then."

The remark stung a bit but did little to deflate Ray's euphoria. "Listen, I've been practicing. I'm better than the last time you saw me shoot. Are you going to the warehouse with us today?"

Skeeter shook his head. "No. I'm staying here to watch the kids. That's my job, these days, while the younger folks go charging into danger." He made an annoyed sound, then hawked a loogy and spat it on the ground.

Ray pointedly averted his eyes. "That sounds like a pretty important job to me."

"Don't patronize me, young man."

As usual, Ray was surprised to hear a rather high-brow word from Skeeter's mouth.

"And don't look surprised to hear me use a word like that."

"Sorry," Ray said. "I'm still trying to overcome an inherent bias."

"I know you are," Skeeter replied in a kinder tone. "Try harder. Anyway, I don't have a good feeling about this mission today, but it's gotta be done. Keep my daughter in your sights at all times."

"Of course."

Fergus caught up with them from behind.

"Good morning, gentlemen. I hope you slept better than me. Never mind. I can see by the cow-eyes this one is making he got less shut-eye than I did."

Did everyone in the damn village know what had transpired between him and Serena Jo last night?

"Hannah isn't coming back, Skeeter," Fergus added in a low voice.

"Don't you think I know that?" Skeeter barked. The pale eyes watered suddenly as he looked away. Finally he said, "You're still welcome to bunk with me, especially since this one," a thumb jerk in Ray's direction, "is courtin' my daughter."

"Thank you. I guess we head out after breakfast?" Fergus directed the question at Ray.

"Yes. There will be about twenty of us," Ray replied. Serena Jo had outlined the details of today's mission between their first and second rounds of lovemaking. When he pictured her golden hair splayed out on the pillow, his stomach felt like he'd stepped off a stair tread and into thin air.

Skeeter interrupted his daydream. "And a lot of toe sacks."

Ray nodded. "That's what Serena Jo said. I've always called them gunny sacks." Just saying her name out loud prompted a goofy grin; he'd lost all control of his facial expressions. He hoped he wouldn't have to play poker anytime soon.

"Good grief," Fergus said with amused disgust. "Try to dial down your enthusiasm, please. I'd like to enjoy my breakfast. Do we know what's on the menu?"

Skeeter said, "You boys are lucky this morning. Thelma always make somethin' special on mission days."

Skeeter was right. When they entered the cook house, a heavenly aroma filled the space.

"Mmmm ...smoked ham, fried potatoes, and corn fritters," Fergus said. "If we have to die today, at least our last meal will be memorable."

They elbowed their way onto one of the benches, placing their loaded cafeteria trays on the table. There wasn't much background chatter this morning; everyone was enjoying the meal too much to talk.

Ray glanced about the room, noting the people wearing threadbare clothing. He felt a surge of affection for them. At that moment, he fully understood Serena Jo's insistence on maintaining their primitive lifestyle.

"We're just going to the warehouse," Ray said, fully registering Fergus's words along with Skeeter's concern. "That shouldn't be especially dangerous. You're not coming with us?"

"No. I've been delegated the task of training semen demons to shoot firearms. Don't forget, Ray. We left dead Murdocks in that warehouse," Fergus said between bites.

"But the living Murdocks don't know that," Ray replied.

Skeeter gave him an appraising look, as if deciding whether to share what was on his mind. Finally, he spoke. "We don't know what the Murdocks know. That goon posse they sent out to your warehouse was probably due back by now. Don't you think they're gonna start lookin' for 'em? Don't you think before them boys left they were told where to go? One of them dead Murdocks in your warehouse fridge is Silas's nephew. And Hannah shot Eli, Wyatt's son. That means his body is out in the woods somewhere and will be easy to find 'cuz of the smell. Wyatt's a human turd, but he's still a daddy. He ain't gonna be happy findin' his son dead. You pickin' up on a theme yet?"

Ray swallowed and nodded. "I still have a lot to learn, don't I?"

Skeeter raised a wiry gray eyebrow. "You have no idea. But I appreciate that you're tryin'."

They ate the rest of their meal in silence.

***

Later that day, after tripping over briars, brush, and fallen logs for eight hours, Ray arrived at the outskirts of the warehouse compound. Serena Jo and a troop of Whitaker Scouts navigated the forest with stealth and grace. In contrast, Ray's movements probably sounded like a stampeding elephant. He was fairly certain he'd heard someone hiss *city boy* at least twice.

But the journey had been otherwise uneventful. Fifteen armed people strategically positioned around the industrial complex did little to dispel its vague feeling of menace. When he gazed at the warehouse, he contemplated how quickly and completely his new provincial home had supplanted this sterile version.

The two newcomers lurked nearby as well, but nobody knew exactly where. As stealthy as the Whitaker Scouts were, Dani and Sam out-stealthed everyone.

Ray stood next to Serena Jo, who peered at the warehouse through field glasses. As far as he could tell, it hadn't changed since he'd last been here. But from their forest vantage, they couldn't see the HVAC unit.

"Team Black Bear goes in first through the ductwork," Serena Jo said to the three Scouts who flanked her. "Once they've confirmed the interior is safe, we'll follow. Gray Wolf will remain outside until then."

The three stoic Scouts——two older men and a young woman——nodded in unison. Ray knew they belonged to Team Night Owl, but he had no idea the significance of the names. He did know that in order to make it onto any of the Scout teams, one must prove proficiency in all facets of outdoorsmanship. Not only with the flashy stuff, like firearms and blade work, but also mundane endeavors like clean water procurement and safe food storage techniques.

He hoped their impressive skill sets would be enough against the Murdocks. It gave him added comfort knowing the contents of his warehouse would provide them a huge advantage in the dangerous days to come.

Just as the mental spreadsheets began scrolling through his mind, a thunderous explosion pummeled his eardrums, sending a shockwave through his bones and sparking a wave of anxiety he hadn't felt since

Hannah had resuscitated him.

"Oh, no," Serena Jo whispered.

"What's happening?" Ray said, scrambling to get beside her as she continued peering through the binoculars.

"The doors on the warehouse just blew, the rolling one in the front and the one on the roof, too. Smoke is billowing out on the HVAC side of the building."

"Shit," said one of the Scouts, a grizzled man who could have served as a stunt double for Sam Elliot.

Serena Jo lowered the binoculars, then glared at Ray. "Was there anything chemically unstable in there?"

"No! I mean, yes, but not in close proximity. The people who designed the layout knew what they were doing. They didn't store the Class Ones near the Class Twos."

"What does that mean?"

"We don't keep the mercury fulminate next to the bullets."

"What the hell do you need mercury fulminate for?" she demanded, lifting the binoculars back to eyes that glistened now. Members of Team Black Bear may well be dead.

"In a natural disaster, sometimes we have to blow up stuff that might stand in the way of helping people."

"We need to get down there, ma'am," Sam Elliot growled.

"Not yet, Luke. If this is the Murdock's doing, it could be an ambush. The Black Bears can take care of themselves. We'll hold our position for a few minutes."

Luke grunted a vague response. Ray noticed the man's fingers twitching near the trigger of his rifle. He looked like he should be guzzling whiskey in a Wild West saloon.

"There's someone coming out onto the roof now. Wait, three some-ones. Those are not our people," she said. "Is there a way for them to get down?"

Ray nodded. "There's a fire escape ladder on this side. Pan down ... you should see it."

"Damn it. They're getting away."

"Is there a clear shot?" Luke demanded, raising his rifle.

"No, those trees are blocking. Wait, something's happening."

Ray watched Serena Jo as the binoculars tracked movement at the complex. The *pop-pop-pop* of rapid handgun fire reverberated. Another round evoked a squeal of delight from Serena Jo.

"Two of them are down!"

"What's happening? Who got who?" the young female Scout demanded. In a perfect world, she would be marching in her high school band or practicing for a youth soccer game. Instead, she held a Remington bolt action mounted by a Vortex scope that probably cost more allowance money than the rifle. She pointed the barrel in the opposite direction of the warehouse and swiveled it slowly back and forth. She was in charge of 'watching their six' in case enemies attacked from behind.

"The newcomers just shot two of the three Murdocks. Looks like the third got away. Flames are coming out of the building. Let's move."

On the way to the warehouse, a second explosion blew out a section of the roof. Chunks of galvanized steel and gravel-imbedded tar rained down on the asphalt where Ray had parked his Toyota a lifetime ago.

"Oh no," he whispered as he ran, imagining flames engulfing the priceless contents of his former home. They rounded the final corner of the back of the building.

Team Gray Wolf stood spread out in a half circle fifty yards from the HVAC unit. Hannah's magical tarp lay on the ground like the discarded wrapper of a giant's Twinkie. So much for cutting-edge cloaking technology.

Serena Jo jogged over to a woman wearing full woodland camo——Patsy, Ray remembered. She looked like she could bench press most of the men on her team.

"Report!" Serena Jo commanded.

"Sonsofbitches must have seen Black Bear coming. We were holding back, covering from the parking lot, when the first explosion happened. The Bears were either on their way inside through the ductwork or already in. I don't see how they could've survived this." She waved a hand toward the building just as another explosion erupted from the opposite back wall.

Ray groaned. It was the location of the firearms and ammunition.

"This is a rescue mission now, ma'am," Patsy said, motioning for her team to follow. She took off at a trot toward the building.

"Stop!" Serena Jo yelled.

"We can't let them burn," Patsy roared in reply, then started running again.

"You'll all die, too. Then the Murdocks will kill the rest of us, including the children."

That's what did it. Ray watched Patsy's shoulders droop, and she stopped running.

Serena Jo trotted over to her. She didn't hug the other woman, didn't attempt to comfort her. She simply pressed her forehead against Patsy's, letting the contact convey her own despair. They remained that way for a few heartbeats while Team Gray Wolf gathered around.

Ray held back, watching from twenty yards away. He hadn't yet earned a place in the circle.

Suddenly, he felt a presence beside him. When he turned, he wasn't surprised to see Dani's scarred face. She wore a grim expression; streaks of ash and blood on her cheeks amplified the menacing vibe she always projected. Was that her own blood? Probably not.

Sam spoke from his other side. Ray hadn't even known he was there.

"One got away," he said, watching the Scouts, who seemed to be holding some kind of prayer session now.

"I need to have a convo with the Big Kahuna," Dani said quietly. "You think it's cool to barge in on the Jesus circle?"

"Give them a minute," Ray replied, watching Serena Jo drape an arm around Emma's shoulders. The youthful face was wet with tears.

"Okay, but this is rather pressing," Dani said with a scowl. "I'll give her two minutes. Best I can do."

Ray gave Dani his full attention. "What happened?"

"Sam and I had been tracking three hostiles. Followed them here ... your warehouse, I presume?" Ray nodded. "Waited while they gained access to the interior and were just about to follow them inside when the first explosion occurred. We saw them on the roof right after, then Sam and I were on them like stink on shit when they came down the ladder. We could tell they weren't *our* hillbillies."

Ray winced.

"Got one of them, but just winged the second and had to finish him off with my knife. The third dude got away. He's a fast fucker. I'm guessing he's the one that orchestrated the explosions." Her gaze left Ray's face and darted to the warehouse. Orange flames and coal-black smoke belched through every breach in the structure. It must surely be fully engulfed on the inside. "I'm guessing you had either mercury fulminate or ammonium nitrite in your adorable Strategic National Stockpile."

He nodded. Despite knowing there were people dead or dying inside, he couldn't stop his brain from scanning those mental spreadsheets. The contents of his former home had been valued at more than three hundred million dollars prior to Chixculub. In today's post-apocalyptic world, its worth couldn't be quantified. How many sick people could his medicines have cured? How many starving people could his food have nourished? How many Murdocks might his firearms have eliminated? The answer was unknowable, of course. And now it didn't matter.

Because in his gut, Ray knew the Whitaker clan——Skeeter and the kids, the ladies who did the laundry, the folks who cooked breakfast and dinner, the laborers who toiled in the fields, the Scouts who hunted for meat and kept everyone safe ...

... and Serena Jo. All were now utterly and irrevocably screwed.

***

"We're not totally screwed," Dani said a short time later. They'd lost nine Scouts in the fire. Those remaining gathered close to Serena Jo and the newcomer. Ray noticed Dani's partner, Sam, standing a few yards away from the group. He seemed to only half-listen to the discussion while he kept an eye on their surroundings. They'd withdrawn back into the forest, which was a relief. Ray couldn't bear watching his building collapsing upon itself, rendering its priceless contents worthless.

Serena Jo's eyes were filled with cold fury, but her voice was calm. "As long as there's a Scout left breathing, we're not defeated."

Did she truly feel that way, or was it just cheerleading? Perhaps a bit of both, Ray decided.

"Let's skip the hyperbole and get down to business," Dani said.

Ray found himself wincing a lot when Dani spoke. He winced again now.

Serena Jo's eyes narrowed. "You're the military expert. What do you propose?"

Dani openly scrutinized Serena Jo. People with no filter tended not to conceal their thoughts well. Ray could see Dani was conducting an evaluation ... trying to gauge strength or resolve. He could have saved her the effort. Serena Jo was as tough as they come.

"I propose we continue as planned. Sam and I will head to Idlewild and swipe the old fucker in charge. Then we'll meet up with you at the originally designated time and location. As for what happens after that, it will depend on the information we extract from said old fucker, but I'm certain we'll need to switch to guerrilla tactics. That's what you do in a situation with a disparity in numbers."

Serena Jo nodded.

"In the meantime," Dani continued, "train every non-Scout villager, including any rugrat out of diapers, to shoot a gun. Capeesh?"

"We're doing that already. Not the children under ten, though. That wouldn't be appropriate."

Dani placed her hands on her hips and arched a dark eyebrow. "I've heard stories about the Murdocks. It's appropriate now, sister."

Chapter 26

Fergus

"'Course I got a ghillie suit. Ain't one of them fancy ones, like you buy at Cabela's. I made it myself," Skeeter said, shuffling toward his armoire. "Get us some light over here."

Fergus noticed Skeeter shuffling more lately. He wasn't sure of the older man's age, but he was certainly well into his seventies. Yes, his health seemed otherwise excellent, and he'd healed quickly from Lizzy's torture. But while they'd been imprisoned in her basement, Skeeter had mentioned memory issues. Memory issues and feet-shuffling: the calling cards of Alzheimer's.

The damn *Cthor*. Why couldn't they have genetically engineered that horrific disease out of humanity's DNA?

He struck a match and lit the kerosene lantern Skeeter had left precariously close to the table's edge. Fergus shook his head, dismissing thoughts of Skeeter in the throes of full-blown dementia. His cognitive decline might be a moot point anyway if they didn't survive the war with the Murdocks.

Skeeter opened one of the doors and withdrew a tangled pile of netting that looked like something a beachcomber might find washed up on the shoreline.

"It's supposed to look like that," he said. "I used autumn colors, so it won't work so great for snow."

"It won't have to. I need it for tonight."

Hannah had been gone for a day. It was time for him to follow her.

"You gonna go after her?" Skeeter said. "She won't like that."

"We've agreed to stay in touch, so to speak."

"*This* is one thing," Skeeter replied, tapping his forehead. "But *this* is something else." He handed the camouflage net to Fergus.

"I'm trying to save her."

"I don't think that's what she wants." The sadness in Skeeter's voice was heart-breaking.

"I know that's not what she wants, but she's not the boss of me. I'm going to try not to interfere or intrude, but I want to be close. Just in case."

"Okay, then. I wish I could go with you, but I gotta stay here and keep an eye on the kids. You're supposed to be helping me with firearms training, by the way. That business at Ray's warehouse is gonna … *escalate* everything. I had a bad feeling about it. That feeling ain't getting any better."

"You'll have to cover for me, Skeeter."

"I won't lie to my daughter. Not this time. It's hard enough keeping my thoughts straight, but weaving deception into the dialogue makes things damn-near impossible to keep up with."

"You don't have to lie. Just wait until morning to tell her I've gone."

The bald head dipped. "I can do that. You need anything from under the floorboard 'fore you go?"

Of course Skeeter would know about the items Fergus had hidden there.

"Now that you mention it, I'll take that vial of Midazolam and the syringe. I don't know if I'll need it, but it's useful to have a strong sedative hidden somewhere on one's person at all times."

Skeeter snorted. "Don't let any of the ladies hear you say that. Wouldn't want you gettin' kicked out for being a pervert."

"Long before that happens, I'll probably die in a blaze of glory: the pivotal character in the triumphant battle of Whitaker holler."

The bald head dipped to one side. "You ain't gonna die. 'Least not in this war. But plenty of others will." A teardrop navigated the crevasses lining the older man's cheeks.

"I don't want the details," Fergus muttered.

"Wasn't going to share 'em."

***

It hadn't been that long since Fergus had been positioned in the branches of a large oak tree on a chilly night. Previously, he'd been waiting for a serial killer. This time, from a similar lofty and leafy vantage, he could keep an eye on the outskirts of Idlewild.

He'd packed enough supplies for at least two days: water, a few squares of cornbread, and smoked bear sausages. That last item had been a gift from Skeeter, freshly pilfered by one of the ladies at the kitchen house. Skeeter said she was sweet on him, and Fergus didn't doubt it. Skeeter possessed a profound decency that most people sensed on a subconscious level, even those without *scythen*.

Fergus had never tasted bear meat, which was surprising considering his unnaturally long life. He'd sampled many exotic varieties of flesh – camel, guinea pig, iguana – but somehow had never had the opportunity to sample black bear. After biting off a piece, he allowed the flavor a few seconds to permeate his taste buds. Whether it was the meat itself, the added spices, or the smoking process, Fergus decided black bear was delicious. According to Skeeter, bears that survived on a diet of berries, acorns, and honey tasted the best. A diet of salmon and carrion rendered bear meat nearly inedible. The sausage he enjoyed now was definitely of the honey bear variety.

He hoped the meat wouldn't give him the runs. He could easily empty his bladder from up here, but pooping would present logistical problems.

He sipped from a canteen recently filled with spring water and settled in for the night. The spot he'd chosen in the tree provided adequate limbs to break a nasty fall if he fell asleep on the job. He'd gotten lucky in terms of the weather. A chilly breeze puffed through the branches, but it lacked teeth, and no snow-bearing clouds obscured the midnight canvas overhead. The stars began to twinkle now, and the moon would be rising soon.

He let out a deep sigh, thinking about his love of being outdoors, whether at the beach with Amelia or alone on a tree limb in Tennessee. The thought of going back to the claustrophobic, hyperbaric chamber that was his home felt distinctly unappealing at the moment. Despite the dire situation, he was quite enjoying himself. This excellent location also provided a *scythen* boost; the treetop served as a combination sensory deprivation tank and cell tower site.

Just as he closed his eyes and prepared to send out a ping to Hannah, a rustling noise below jerked him into high alert.

"Well, well. Look what we have here, Sam. A kitten got stuck in a tree.

Wait a minute ... that's no sweet little pussycat. That's a spikey-haired leprechaun with an overactive libido! Pa, grab the camera!"

Fergus rolled his eyes, but couldn't deny the pleasure he felt at hearing Dani's voice. "Quiet, Honey Badger. I'm on a stakeout."

"Okay, we'll come up."

Several minutes later, two of his favorite people perched on nearby branches. He couldn't stop a grin of pleasure from spreading across his face.

"What are you smiling about, Lucky Charms?" Dani said in an affectionate tone.

"Just happy to see you both," Fergus replied, reaching over to squeeze Sam's shoulder.

"We're happy to see you too," Sam said. "Although Dani is still kind of mad that you're not actually dead. I'm not mad. I'm just glad our story together hasn't ended."

"Sam, are you waxing poetic these days?"

"He's been hanging around Pablo too much lately," Dani said.

"I'm not hanging around Pablo," Sam replied. "I'm hanging around the baby."

"Indeed?" Fergus said. "You have a hankering for a fidget monkey, Sam?"

"I do. But it takes two to tap dance, if you get my drift."

Dani scowled and remained silent.

"Very well, then. Let's change the subject," Fergus said with a chuckle. "You're going into Idlewild to capture their leader?"

Dani nodded. "We've been conducting reconnaissance."

"Before you go, you need to know that Hannah is also on a covert mission within the town." He outlined Hannah's plan to replace her twin sister Piper as one of the Murdock leaders. During the explanation, he realized just how ill-advised the strategy was. Surely people would know she wasn't the same person. No matter how identical twins can be, there must be infinite tiny differences in speech patterns, clothing preferences, facial expressions. Anyone who had been part of Piper's life would surely see through the subterfuge.

The expression on Dani's face mirrored his thoughts.

"That's insane," she said. "I'm glad you told us. We'll be on the lookout for her corpse. I doubt it will affect what Sam and I plan on doing, though. We've figured out which house belongs to Silas. We'll sneak into town, render the old fucker unconscious, and sneak back out with a human-shaped tarp draped over Sam's shoulder. The only sticking point is keeping him quiet. I could do my version of the Vulcan nerve pinch on him, but apparently in addition to being an old fucker, he also has a terminal illness. We need him alive. A few times when I've performed the pinch, my subjects didn't wake up, so I'm hesitant to go that route. We'll figure it out, though. Never fear."

Dani's bravado was legendary, yet there was nothing false about it. Still, Fergus needed to be certain she and Sam didn't fail. For the Whitakers to prevail, nothing about their plan could go wrong.

He reached into an interior coat pocket. With a dramatic flourish, he produced the Midazolam and the syringe.

Dani's eyes widened. "Holy shit! Is that what I think it is?"

Fergus nodded.

"You're a damn wizard!" She snatched the items and then kissed his cheek. "Let's go, Sam. See you on the flip side, Lucky Charms. Stay alive this time."

Then they were gone, and Fergus was left alone with his thoughts. Sam wanted a baby, and Dani clearly did not. Interesting. What kind of gifted child would two such exceptional people produce? He speculated on the baby Pablo and Maddie had created. All four of these adults were special, but none of them possessed the criteria necessary to be recruited by the *Cthor*.

What if two *Cthor* candidates existed even now who conceived a child together? The *Cthor* manipulated human DNA all the time to achieve their desired results, taking a pinch of this trait and a sprinkling of that trait. The union of two incomparable intellects and two diverse ethnicities may result in human perfection. Or as close as humanly possible.

The notion became more thrilling by the second, but Fergus knew the stars would have to be aligned perfectly in order to create such conditions. At that moment, he felt a shadow of what the *Cthor* must have experienced for millennia: the exhilaration of playing God. His mission clarified itself further: Kenny and Willadean must survive the war with the Murdocks, get through puberty, and then fall in love.

The thought of a world repopulated ... eventually ... with the offspring of those two made his heart sing.

Chapter 27

Idlewild

Everyone of importance in Idlewild had been summoned to the emergency meeting at Silas's home. The place stunk to high heaven, as usual. Apparently, when a human body rotted from the inside out, it produced a pungent odor. The stench had not only permeated the rugs and curtains, it had soaked into the wood paneling of the wall Piper currently leaned against.

Or maybe it wasn't the cancer that created the stench. Maybe it was the perfume of evil.

"Jesus, it reeks in here," she whispered under her breath. "I don't like this any more than you, Wyatt," she added to the man standing nearby. Nobody enjoyed getting one of these middle-of-the-night summons. They never boded well. Piper figured Silas chose the timing just to fuck with people.

"You'd be liking it a lot less if I hadn't destroyed that building and all the shit the Whitakers would have had access to."

He was right. The Whitakers didn't stand a chance against them now. After generations, the feud would finally come to a head, and the odds of prevailing lay solidly with the Murdocks.

Piper formulated her next words carefully. "I'm sorry about your son, by the way. I despise you, but I wouldn't wish the loss of a child on anyone."

Wyatt flinched but continued staring straight ahead. He didn't bother to respond. They both knew Silas wasn't long for this world. The air in Idlewild felt viscous and murky somehow, like a chum-filled ocean.

The two largest killer whales in the sea were both going after the same floundering great white.

Silas's raspy voice came from his throne positioned near a wall in the center of his living room; it was the only place in the entire space where someone could sit. The chair was actually an ancient hand-carved rocker, but the old man had been holding court from it for decades. He fancied himself a king surrounded by ambitious, ruthless courtiers, all willing to strangle their own grandmothers for power.

Silas rapped a dented tin cup on the handle of the rocker, his version of a spoon-tap against a crystal wine glass. The low-pitched conversation in the room came to an abrupt halt.

"Wyatt, give us a report," Silas commanded.

The younger man began to speak in his elegant, high-pitched voice. Wyatt would have been perfectly at home behind a pulpit asking for money from an enthralled television audience.

"Levi was approached by Tandy with a scheme meant to lure him into the woods. He realized instantly that was her goal and notified me. We extracted her true intention, as well as the location of the bait. Levi was then given the honor of executing the traitor." Wyatt had been moving through the gathering of more than a dozen people as he spoke, working the crowd with an occasional shoulder squeeze or friendly wink. At the word traitor, his gaze darted back to Silas.

Tandy had been Silas's beloved whore. Though he'd sanctioned the execution, it didn't mean the old monster was happy about it.

Silas's skull-like face wore a dispassionate expression. The death of his favorite plaything aroused no visible emotion, maybe because the days of physical arousal had departed long ago for him. The loss of a toy that could no longer be enjoyed didn't leave much of a void.

"Levi and I took a team into the woods. We dispatched the boy, Brock, who had planned to exact vengeance on Levi for killing his father. The Whitakers are now down two valuable Scouts." Wyatt smiled, his Hollywood teeth gleaming in the candlelight. "Then, recklessly, Levi exposed himself before the area had been cleared, and a sniper took him out. I don't know who did it or how many there were. It was a Whitaker, of that I'm sure. Since our mission was complete, we bugged out before we could lose any more men."

"Stupid of Levi. That's what *exposing* yourself to a little girl will get you," Piper said in a bored voice. A low-pitched titter rumbled through the gathering. Silas snorted.

Wyatt shot her a murderous look before continuing. "After that, we went to the last known location of the recon mission whose members hadn't returned."

"Why was that?" a young man interrupted. "They weren't technically overdue." Colton was distantly related to Silas and had been elevated within the ranks before he'd actually earned his way. For some reason, Silas had taken a liking to the swaggering youth. Maybe he saw glimpses of himself at a similar age.

Piper couldn't stand the kid, but she always enjoyed watching Wyatt get called out.

Wyatt pivoted to face the boy, his back to Silas and the megawatt smile gone. "Go fuck yourself," Wyatt said, his face inches from the kid's. Colton lifted a reflexive hand and pushed Wyatt back a step.

Any other man in the room would have come back swinging. Not Wyatt. Self-control dictated his every move. Beating the shit out of Colton served no purpose at the moment. "Get out," he said. "This meeting is above your pay grade." Then he pivoted back to Silas once the kid had slunk out the door.

"We found the remains of the recon mission, one member outside in the woods and the rest inside the building. They'd been assassinated and put in cold storage." Wyatt's voice remained steady and strong, despite describing the death of his only son.

Piper pounced. "So you decided to destroy *literally tons* of valuable items in order to exact revenge on the Whitakers. How carelessly self-indulgent."

Wyatt didn't usually make dumb mistakes, but revealing the contents of that building to one of his confidantes had been an enormous fuck-up——especially since the confidante happened to be one of Piper's assets.

Silas chuckled. "She's got a point, Wyatt. Don't ya think we coulda used all that treasure?"

Wyatt shot Piper another venomous look. "There's a military term called *scorched earth*. Ever heard of it, Piper? It means to destroy everything that might be useful to the enemy. I knew we couldn't get our people there to gather it all up before the Whitakers. Yes, it's a loss, but for them, not us. We don't need it. We've been doing fine without it. And now they won't have it."

"How'd you lose your other two men?" Piper asked, pushing people out of the way and positioning herself next to her father's chair. She placed a hand on his bony shoulder, a message not lost on anyone in the room.

Wyatt crossed his arms. "Two people ambushed us when we came out of the building. I got away. The other two didn't."

"You're telling us two strangers happened to be nearby and attacked while you fled from a burning building filled with priceless items. These strangers killed your men, but your heels sprouted wings. And here's the kicker: you weren't able to grab any of that treasure and bring it back for the rest of us. See where I'm going with this, Wyatt? I know what scorched earth means. I also know what a steaming pile of horseshit smells like. I'm smelling it now."

Barely restrained laughter circled the room.

A spark of rage sputtered across Wyatt's face, then quickly faded. One corner of his mouth twitched as he gazed at Piper. He didn't respond.

"Gotta say, I ain't happy about that, Wyatt," Silas said. "You got anything else? You're the one that wanted this meeting. Make it worth my time."

Wyatt paused for a few heartbeats, then addressed the room in his honeyed voice. "Folks, we're going to war with the Whitakers. It's a conflict that's been brewing for generations. We *will* prevail. I'll make damn sure of that." He emphasized ownership of the boast by placing a hand on his chest. The meaning of that hand was clear: Wyatt personally would assure a win for the Murdocks. Not Piper. Not Silas.

Piper glanced down at her father with raised brows. Silas was already looking up at her. Neither said a word.

***

She could have left decades ago, like her sister had, but Piper had chosen to stay for reasons that weren't entirely clear even to herself. She'd put up with a lot of bullshit during her life, but there had been payoffs. One of those dividends loomed before her in the dark. Her house was the most opulent in all of Idlewild. Actually, it was the only house that could be considered opulent at all. It sat on ten wooded acres on the outskirts of town. She'd personally overseen its construction, from the foundation to the shingles. Silas didn't care for the trappings of wealth and power, but she did.

She liked nice things.

The wrought-iron gate swung open silently on its well-oiled hinges. A flagstone path leading to a graceful Georgian structure beckoned her to the only place in Idlewild that felt safe. The tiny hair she'd placed on the doorknob hadn't fallen off in her absence. Good. It wasn't much of a security system, but it was the best she had now that the electronic version no longer worked. The additional locks, bolts, and booby traps inside gave her comfort. A few minutes later, she'd checked them all and assured herself nothing was amiss.

She lit a candle and sank onto the living room sofa with a tired grunt. After leaning her head against the creamy leather cushion, she closed her eyes.

"You haven't aged well," a voice said from the shadows.

Piper didn't bother opening her eyes. "I knew you'd show up eventually."

Hannah chuckled. "You have some balls, sister. Normally when I make these kinds of entrances, my targets react with more alarm. Are you truly so blasé, or are you faking it?"

Piper sighed, then opened her eyes. "Maybe both. Come sit where I can see you." She gestured to a wingback chair near the marble fireplace.

Hannah complied, careful to keep the silencer of her MK 23 pointed at her sister's forehead.

"So you're a hit man? Or I guess that would be hit woman," Piper said in a conversational tone.

"I do what needs to be done. That's why I'm here in this dump." Hannah grinned, waving her hand at the elegant setting.

An identical grin appeared on her twin's face. "Pretty fancy, huh? It's one of the perks of wallowing in our father's shit all these years."

"You didn't have to wallow in it. You could have left."

"You could have taken me with you."

Hannah sighed. "I should have. But at the time, I didn't think it would be possible for both of us to leave without repercussions. I knew Silas would send out a posse if both daughters ran away. We'd be carted back to Idlewild secured in duct tape. When we were seventeen, I had an epiphany. It occurred to me that he might let one of us go without too much fallout."

Piper's eyes narrowed. "Turns out you were right. After you ran, he focused all his attention on me. Can you imagine the crushing weight of that soulless bastard's attention? The inexorable burden of his scrutiny?"

"Yes, I can. And I'm sorry."

"*Sorry* doesn't do a whole lot coming from someone pointing a gun at my head."

Hannah didn't respond, but the business end of her MK 23 dipped a few millimeters before righting itself. "We're both killers," she said. "The difference is I kill people who have it coming, and you take innocent lives, directly or indirectly."

Piper gestured toward the cigarettes on a side table, waiting for her sister's approval before reaching for the pack. She struck a match, inhaling deeply of stale tobacco smoke. She blew a plume in her twin's direction.

"There's not one innocent soul in this godforsaken place," she said.

"The children are innocent. Some of the whores aren't evil. Hell, a few of the men might even have turned out honorable if they'd gotten out of this shithole. And, of course, there are all the people outside the city limits who once crossed you or Silas. Some of them were surely innocent."

"Perhaps. But we can't escape our destiny, sister," Piper replied. "We're cursed. This town and every one of its citizens, down to the fetuses in their mothers' wombs. We Murdocks are a fucking pestilence. It's written in our D ... N ... A." She drew out the letters, as if one might explode in close proximity to its neighbors.

"On that we agree. I concluded that myself recently. The ideology led me to an even more monumental decision."

"Indeed? Do tell."

"In time. First, I want to look at your face and hear your voice. Did you know I'd been checking up on you? For decades, I've been monitoring your activity ... your rise in the hierarchy."

Piper gave a disgusted snort. "Hierarchy. That's an elegant term for what we do here. What we used to do back when there was still meth and oxycontin and heroin."

"You earned your place in the syndicate. Silas gave you no free passes just because you were his daughter."

"That's true. I had to take down a few troublemakers along the way." Piper's expression turned dreamy.

"Too bad you couldn't get rid of Wyatt."

"No shit. Trust me, I've tried. He's the cockroach that survives a nuclear holocaust."

"That's an interesting metaphor. I've applied it to the Murdocks myself recently."

Piper took a deep draw on her cigarette and gazed at her sister from beneath lazy eyelids. "You plan to wipe us all out, sister? In one fell swoop? I don't think I'd try to stop you."

"That's good to know."

"How will you do it? Assuming you assassinate me first, how do you bleach the collective shit stain known as the Murdock clan?"

Hannah gazed for a long while at the face so similar to her own before reaching into the pack she'd left on the floor. She unzipped a pocket and removed a large glass bottle, factory sealed, with a pharmaceutical label on the side. The label didn't exhibit a little skull and crossbones symbol, but it might as well have.

"Clever," Piper said as she read the label. "I can't imagine how you could have gotten hold of that much botulinum. Did you blow a pharmaceutical tech?"

"No. I killed him. The end justifies the means, right?"

"So you do kill innocents."

"Only as a last resort. He wasn't interested in a blow job."

"Hypocrite," Piper said affectionately. "So your plan is to sneak in here and poison everyone? How? Slip it into the moonshine? I don't think you'll get away with it. However you're going to do it, you can't just waltz around town."

"I can if people think I'm you."

Piper snickered. "That's ridiculous. Even if we switched clothes, nobody would believe you were me. Look at us. I could be your mother, thanks to these." Another long drag on the cigarette.

Hannah sighed. "That wasn't really my plan ... it was more of a cover story. Mostly, I just wanted to see you. After our visit, I'll head over to the water tower."

"Ah, the water tower. That makes a lot more sense than poisoning the moonshine. You'll get everyone that way."

"Yes. The Murdocks will be obliterated once and for all."

Piper nodded, stubbed out the cigarette and lit another. "The problem with your logic is, as long as you're still alive, you haven't fully eradicated the nest."

"That won't be a problem. I'll see to it."

Piper raised her eyebrows. "Is this some kind of murder-suicide thing?"

Hannah's laughter resonated off the walls.

Piper smiled. "I've missed that. I used to have the same laugh——until I took up this nasty habit." She flicked the cigarette ash into a crystal bowl. "Am I right?"

Hannah stood, the MK pointing to the polished mahogany floor now, and moved toward her sister on the sofa. She opened her mouth to speak, but a clicking sound from the fireplace drew her attention, terminating the words on her lips. She'd heard that sound before.

Well, shit.

She reached for her sister's hand a heartbeat before the house exploded.

***

Wyatt watched burning debris from Piper's house fall out of the sky like fragments of a meteorite. He thought he'd estimated a safe distance from which to execute the explosion, but he was off by about fifty feet. Still, the branches of a giant hemlock kept him safe.

A piece of a finger, the nail bed still intact, landed next to his boot. He recognized the polish color and smiled.

"You weren't able to grab any of that treasure and bring it back for the rest of us?" Piper's voice said in his head.

"I actually did bring back some treasure ... just for you," he whispered. "I hope you enjoyed it." He turned to the man standing behind him. "Send the teams to the holler. Remember, three teams of three each."

Colton nodded. He gazed at the finger now, perhaps processing that the various body parts spread among the chunks of smoking drywall and roof shingles belonged to a distant relative. Not that it mattered. Just about everyone was related to everyone else in these parts, and the Murdocks never let a bit of shared DNA get in the way of ambition.

Wyatt studied the youthful face, wondering what was going on in that head. He trusted Colton as much as he trusted anyone ... which wasn't much. But a man couldn't be in two places at the same time, and some tasks must be delegated. "Good acting job during the meeting. And nice work with the explosives."

"Told you I knew what I was doing," Colton replied in that overly confident tone of youth.

"Stick with me, kid, and you'll go places." Wyatt clapped him on the back.

"I'm a sticky booger." Colton replied, deadpan.

Wyatt chuckled. "Guess you'll have to find a new whore to moon over now that Tandy's gone."

"I reckon so." Colton walked off into the night.

Wyatt watched him vanish into the gloom, pondered their conversation, and headed toward Silas's house. With a curt nod, he acknowledged the two guards who materialized out of the shadows. A third, stationed beside the door, allowed him inside. None of them asked about the explosion. Silas had trained them to keep their eyes and ears open and their mouths shut.

In the living room, Wyatt noticed a flickering lantern. Strange that Silas hadn't extinguished it before going to bed. He contemplated what he was about to do now that Piper's assassination had set in motion the coup d'état. There would be no going back now.

He withdrew a garrote from his jacket. Most killers preferred a knife or a gun, but Wyatt enjoyed the sensation of slowly strangling a person to death. He imagined he could feel their life force——their souls——draining from them as he deprived them of air. He loved witnessing the terror in their eyes just before the whites turned red from asphyxiation. At that point, they were beyond intellectual terror, and their lizard brains took over. That's when he lost interest.

He hoped to stretch out Silas's death. He'd been putting up with the old man's shit for far too long.

As he walked down the hall, his footfalls were soundless on the braided rug. The bedroom door stood ajar, which gave him pause. He knew Silas always slept with that door closed and locked; Wyatt had brought tools for the purpose of getting past the locking mechanism.

Something was amiss. A rush of adrenaline compelled him to reach for the Glock nestled in a shoulder harness. The gun's nozzle entered the bedroom first. Enough lantern light penetrated the interior to see that it was empty. Rumpled sheets lay in a pile on the floor. The flame from his

Zippo revealed nothing under the bed nor in the closet.

A wintry breeze fluttered the stained curtains, transforming them into spectral sentinels to the open window beyond. A quick search of the rest of the small house revealed no evidence of the Murdock clan's leader, nor any apparent sign of a struggle.

"Fuck," he whispered to himself, standing in the living room again. He opened the front door and beckoned to the nearby guard.

"Where did he go?" Wyatt demanded in a hushed voice.

"What do you mean?" the idiot replied. "He's in bed. I saw him myself twenty minutes ago."

Wyatt smacked the greasy head. "No, he's not, you fucking moron. Find him, but do it quietly. We don't want to alarm anyone." He was already formulating a cover story for why he'd come back to the house, one that had nothing to do with assassinating the current leader of the Murdock clan. He would say he'd witnessed a group of people running from Piper's house just before it exploded. And one of those people might have been Colton. Why not throw the kid under the bus? Something about the boy's behavior tonight made his hackles rise.

Until Silas was well and truly dead, preferably by Wyatt's own hand, he posed a risk. It seemed Wyatt would have to play the loyal lieutenant a while longer.

Chapter 28

Willadean

"Harlan, what are you doing?" Willa whispered in their darkened bedroom. She couldn't make out her brother's face, but she could see that his eyes were open. He sat stiffly upright in his bed.

He didn't respond.

"Harlan," she hissed, louder. Pops would be sleeping nearby, perhaps in a kitchen chair or maybe stretched out on the floor. There wasn't a lot of space to sleep in their tiny cabin except for the beds, and mama's was empty. She'd gone off with most of the Scouts to deal with the Murdocks. Mister Fergus had also vanished, but to where she had no idea. Pops had stayed behind with a handful of folks, most of whom weren't particularly skilled with firearms, to keep an eye on the kids and the village. Now that so few Scouts remained, almost all of them would be needed in the Whitakers' offensive near Idlewild.

She kicked off the covers and tiptoed over to her brother. Starlight revealed tears on his face. She sat beside him and draped an arm around his shoulders.

"Was it a nightmare?" she whispered. "Or did one of your astral adventures turn scary?"

Instead of signing, he whispered back. "Hannah is dead."

"What? How do you know?"

"I felt it. Or saw it with my mind's eye. It's hard to explain, but I know she's dead. Her ping is gone. Not just far away, but truly gone."

"Well, damn. I was starting to like her."

"I loved her. She was our grandmother."

Willa didn't care for the accusatory tone in her brother's voice. "I know. But how can you love someone you just met, even if she is related to you?"

Harlan wriggled out from under her arm. "How can you not? She was

... *extraordinary*."

"That's a big word for a little boy."

"Shut up, Willa. You're being a brat."

Her attempt to make Harlan feel better was failing miserably. "I'm sorry. I guess sometimes it just takes me a while to like people."

"You liked Mister Fergus and Kenny pretty fast."

He had a point, but since she couldn't explain that even to herself, she didn't bother answering.

Finally, he gave a shaky sigh, his way of saying he forgave her.

"How did she die?" Willa asked. "Do you know?"

He shook his head. "Only that it was very sudden. Her light was snuffed out. There one second and gone the next."

"Well, that could be anything. A bullet to the head, brain aneurysm, heart attack ..."

"It was none of those things. There was thunder around her."

"You think she was struck by lightning? That's possible, I suppose. And it's a quick way to go."

"You're the worst." Harlan rubbed his wet face with the edge of a blanket. "Not that kind of thunder."

"Hmmm, maybe a bomb then. That would make for a very abrupt death."

Harlan nodded slowly. "Yes, that feels right."

"Damn," she whispered thinking of her grandfather. "Pops isn't going to handle this well. Guess we need to tell him."

She tiptoed through the bedroom doorway. No snores emanated from the cabin and no grandfather-shaped figure slept in a chair or on the rug.

Willa struck a match and placed it against the kitchen lantern's wick.

Pops was nowhere to be seen.

"Get dressed," Willa told her brother. "Put on your cold-weather adventure clothes."

"I'm doing that now," he said from the bedroom.

Adventure clothes were worn on days when they planned activities in the woods. The garments were stretchy for climbing trees and dodging evil fairies, neutral-colored for the purpose of camouflage, and warm for staying outside for extended periods during the chilly fall and winter months. Mama didn't know there were distinctions in their wardrobe, and Willa intended to keep it that way. Mama didn't need to know everything about everything.

By the time they were dressed and standing on the porch, the sky had begun its transformation from gray-black to pink. If not for the situation they were in, she would have taken time to enjoy the sunrise, her favorite time of day. Early mornings always held the promise of *what might be*, and the possibilities seemed especially endless today if you were a girl who craved excitement.

Pops was gone. Mama would be furious with him for abandoning his charges. There must be a good reason for his absence, and Willa aimed to find out.

Their first stop was the kitchen house. Pops could be there sweet-talking Thelma for a breakfast appetizer. If he wasn't, Thelma probably would know where he was. She'd been sweet on Pops for ages.

As usual, the heavenly aroma of cornbread greeted them when they opened the door. The fact that nobody was sitting around making small talk while they waited on their breakfast revealed two things: many of the villagers were elsewhere, and it was damn early.

Willa sidled up to Thelma, who was pulling an enormous cast-iron skillet off the woodstove.

"Goodness, child, you scared the bejesus out of me!" Thelma was nowhere near Pops' age, but that didn't keep her from crushing on him. It was a weird notion that someone could have romantic feelings for her grandfather, with his bald head and missing fingers, but Thelma didn't seem to mind the physical shortcomings. Recently, Willa had caught her staring at Pops with puppy-dog eyes and wearing a dreamy smile. It was both adorable and disgusting. Mostly disgusting.

"Thelma, do you know where my grandfather is? He was supposed to be staying with me and Harlan, but he wasn't there when we woke up. And he's not in his cabin either."

Willa watched the play of emotions on Thelma's homely face. Before the woman opened her mouth to speak, Willa knew she was going to lie.

"I ... I have no idea," she said.

"Cut the crap, Thelma. I can tell you're lying."

Thelma's hazel eyes narrowed. "Such impertinence!" Her outsized jaw was set firmly now, and her pale lips pressed together in disapproval. Thelma was stonewalling. It was written all over her face.

Willa was about to go ballistic when she felt Harlan nudge her aside.

"Miss Thelma, we're real worried about Pops," he said, reaching for the woman's callused hand. "It would be mighty helpful if you'd tell us where he is."

Harlan, who had just recently decided to vocalize, was also now using hillbilly talk. *Mighty helpful?* Willa turned away, rolling her eyes. Fine, she would let Harlan schmooze the woman, but when this was all over, she was going to have a come-to-Jesus meeting with her brother. All these weird talents and now the sudden decision to speak was just too much to process right now.

Thelma regarded Harlan's earnest face, then sighed heavily. "He went to Idlewild. I don't really understand all of it, but it seems that ... *woman* ... was in danger. The damn fool thought he might be able to save her."

"He went to save Hannah?" Harlan prompted.

"Yes, even though he said he didn't have a good feeling about it. You know about those feelings, right?" She whispered the last part, and her gaze darted about the empty dining hall.

"We do. Some of that runs in the family." Harlan gave her one of his rare smiles, and Thelma just about melted into the wood floor.

Good grief.

"Come on, Harlan," Willa said, tugging her brother away from the transfixed woman and back into the cold morning air.

Kenny stood at the bottom of the steps, arms crossed, wearing that cute, cocky smile.

"Good morning, bumpkin buddies. What's on the agenda for today? I'm assuming some shenanigans may be imminent since all the important white folks in the village are MIA."

"Pops is gone," Willa replied. "We think he went to Idlewild to help Hannah. Mister Fergus is gone too. Do you know where he is? Don't lie. I'll smell it on you, like that polecat stew you seem to be enamored of."

Kenny chuckled but didn't answer. He just stared at her with a goofy grin. She felt her cheeks getting warm, so turned away before he could see her blush.

Her brother seemed amused, but then his elfin face took on a serious cast. "You know those feelings we were talking about?" he whispered, drawing the other two in closer.

Willa nodded. Kenny remained silent.

"I'm having one now. I think the game is afoot."

"Nice reference, Sherlock. What's happening?"

"I think we may be sitting ducks."

Willa did a slow pivot, noting the lack of activity in the village. Just a few chimneys exhaled curls of wood smoke, and the only person they'd seen so far was Thelma. "Firearms practice isn't scheduled for at least another hour. Could be folks decided to skip breakfast and sleep in."

She instantly realized how ludicrous that sounded. Nobody skipped breakfast in the holler.

"This way." She grabbed the boys by their sleeves and darted back toward Pops's cabin. Inside, she said. "Let's assess."

"Don't mind me. Assess away," Kenny said, snooping around in Pops' armoire.

"You can't just paw through people's private belongings, Kenny. Were you raised in a barn?"

"Says the girl with figurative straw in her hair and a penchant for tossing metaphorical manure."

Harlan giggled. His hero worship of the new kid was becoming tiresome. Still, Kenny's presence had proven entertaining——and something else … a bit more abstract. Something difficult to articulate, which Willa would analyze when she had more time.

"It doesn't seem possible that everyone who can protect us would be running off to Idlewild. Mama wouldn't have made such a colossal tactical error."

"Neither would Dani," Kenny replied, removing an item from a shelf and examining it covertly.

"What is that?" Willa demanded. Kenny turned his back to her, silent. "Whatever it is, it belongs to my grandfather. Put it back."

Finally, he turned and handed her a piece of notebook paper, creased and smudged.

Together, Willa and Harlan read the spidery, archaic cursive.

Dear Family, my time has come to an end. I'm sure you noticed that my brain ain't working so good these days. Instead of waiting for it to turn completely to mush, I'm going on a quest. That's one of your words, Willa! Anyway, me and Josie have one last job to do while I still got my wits about me. Since I lost them fingers, she and I have been at odds, but I think we can still manage it. This is one of those times I know it ain't gonna end well, but I gotta do it anyway. I'm sorry to leave you kids alone, but it can't be helped. I know you will be okay, but things may turn out a bit different than you expect. I love you more than I can say. Even Willa's words ain't enough, so I'll just end with this: Serena Jo, Willadean, Harlan, you all are my heart walking around outside my body. I'm a lucky man to have a family like you. All my love, Pops.

Willa's eyes filled with tears. She looked at Harlan. The moisture distorted him into a weird underwater version of her brother, but his hug felt normal. Felt wonderful, just like the other night when he'd cured her hysterics.

"It was his time, Willa," he said softly. "You know Pops can't handle feeling useless, or worse, like a burden. I don't know what he's planning, but this is his path. We have to accept it."

She sniffed, rubbed her nose with a dry sleeve, and nodded. It was strange to feel so profoundly sad but at the same time so content. Harlan was right. Pops would never want to be a burden; episodes of cognitive issues had been starting to stack up. She had no idea how fast Alzheimer's took over a person, but Pops seemed to be on a fast track.

Kenny reached for her hand and gave it a gentle squeeze. "I'm sorry about your grandfather. He seemed like a righteous dude. Who's Josie?"

"Josie is his shotgun. And he's not dead yet," she said.

A pristine white handkerchief appeared in Kenny's hand. He offered it to her.

"Thanks," she muttered. It smelled like freshly mown grass, or maybe the first snowfall of winter, or perhaps starlight. The blissful scent almost made her head spin.

"What did you wash this thing with? Heaven-scent Gain?"

Kenny chuckled. "The woods are lovely, dark and deep. But we have promises to keep. And miles to go before we sleep. Let's get moving, Willadean."

Good grief. A cute, smart boy who spouted Frost poetry.

Willa knew a lot of things. And now she knew one more thing: This boy was even more special than she'd thought.

***

"You're the only adult we can find," Willa said a few minutes later. Despite the sadness of Pops's letter, her stomach growled, triggered by the smell of smoked ham and corn fritters. Thelma had even given them a smidge of honey butter this morning when she loaded up their trays.

"Surely I'm not the only grownup here. Your grandfather and mother wouldn't have done such a thing." Thelma made a 'tsk' sound when she turned away.

The door opened then, and a young man glided in on a chilly draft.

"Jackson!" Willa said, using her most authoritative tone. "Please tell us what's going on. Everyone is gone." She gestured to the empty bench beside her. Kenny and Harlan sat on the opposite side, too busy eating to pay attention to the Scout.

"Give me a minute, Willadean," Jackson replied, then made a beeline for the tray Thelma was loading up.

A giggle escaped the kitchen. Thelma was being schmoozed again, as evidenced by Jackson's heaping tray. Willa studied the nondescript boy as he slid in beside her. She hadn't had a single conversation with him in the two years they'd lived here.

"What's going on? Where is everyone?"

"On their way to Idlewild."

"What if the Murdocks attack the village while there's nobody here but kids and cafeteria ladies?"

A loud tsk came from the kitchen.

"I'm here to protect you," Jackson said, his mouth full of ham.

"No offense, but you're just one boy."

"I'm seventeen, so technically I'm a man."

"Who else?"

Jackson swallowed. "There are three other Scouts nearby in the woods positioned as lookouts. We're taking six-hour shifts. I just got off mine, and I'm as hungry as a bear, so if you don't mind ..."

He went back to eating. Everything about the frustrating boy was unremarkable. Willa thought she wouldn't look at him twice if she passed him on the street.

"Four Scouts to protect our entire village? That's absurd," she grumbled.

"Your Pops is here. And that Fergus guy," Jackson said between bites. A few crumbs stuck in his sparse beard.

"No, they're both gone."

"For real? Well, that sucks."

"That's all you have to say?" she demanded. "What if we're attacked? Four Scouts aren't enough to hold off an invasion."

"I think you underestimate us."

"It comes down to a numbers game. Do you understand that? Four Scouts protecting the kids and the other grownups who can't fight? It's madness!"

Harlan reached across the table and squeezed her hand. She suddenly felt calmer. The Willa Whisperer had struck again.

"Are you finished with your meltdown?" Jackson asked wryly.

"Yes, I think so."

"Okay, so we've set up booby traps in the woods along all the trails the Murdocks would use. For that reason, if not a million others, you'd best stay put and not go venturing out like you kids usually do when your mama isn't looking."

"I don't remember you being put in charge of me."

Jackson shrugged. "Suit yourself. I hope you don't fall into one of the punji traps. Dani, the scary girl, told us how to make them."

"What's a punji trap?"

"Imagine a pit with a bunch of pointy stakes in the bottom——pointy end up——covered by a camouflage of branches. If you step onto the branches and fall into the pit, you'll be pissing out of your belly for the foreseeable future. That is, if you're not killed right away."

"Dang," Willa said.

"Feel safer?" Jackson grinned.

"Somewhat, but I'd feel a lot safer if we all had weapons. This seems like an extraordinary situation."

"I wasn't authorized to let anyone keep their weapons after firearms practice."

"You're still not in charge of me, Jackson."

"No, but I am in charge of the firearms cache. That's because inventory control and weapons maintenance is squarely in my wheelhouse."

Willa had to laugh. That was the first time she'd heard someone from the holler use the trendy term.

"Don't laugh. Being organized and thorough may not be glamorous, but people like me provide critical support for all the showoffs. Where would Batman be without Alfred Pennyworth? Or Superman without

Jimmy Olsen?"

"I'm not into that superhero stuff, so your metaphors aren't helpful," she replied with an eye roll.

Kenny said, "I am. Or was, I should say. And you make a valid point, Jackson. Those flashy guys need a solid support system. You seem capable ... reliable."

Willa watched the nondescript boy transform into a slightly less nondescript boy. Praise and recognition could have a remarkable effect on people who craved it. Being supremely confident in herself, she sometimes needed a reminder that other people could use an occasional ego boost.

And of course, she saw what Kenny was doing. There were times when it was best to keep her mouth shut, so that's what she did as she watched Kenny and Jackson's nerd fest play out.

"Who's your favorite super villain?" Kenny was saying. "I like the smart dudes. Mine used to be Lex Luthor, but now I'm partial to the High Evolutionary because he developed his own brain to its full potential. Virtually unlimited knowledge and intellectual ability is definitely in *my* wheelhouse."

Clever throwing Jackson's own phrase back at him; it was something she would have done herself. Harlan gave her a ghost of a wink from across the table. He knew what was happening, too.

"I like Magneto," Jackson said with enthusiasm. "He's not a villain all the time. Sometimes he helps the X-Men, and of course, he's friends with Professor X. Cool that you're into comics. Most people just like the movies, but I like all of it. Every time my mom took me to Knoxville, I'd add to my collection. When all this is over with the Murdocks, I'll let you read them, if you want."

"I'd like that," Kenny said with genuine warmth. "You know what Alfred Pennyworth would do in a situation like this?"

"A situation like what?" Jackson said, still stuffing his pie-hole.

"Finding ourselves responsible for keeping everyone safe."

"I already mentioned the punji traps and the lookouts."

"But *thoroughness* demands a bit more, don't you think?"

"Maybe. I have to admit, I like backups to my backups. What are you thinking?"

"Everyone has received firearms training, right?"

Jackson nodded. "Pretty much, except the littlest ones."

"Do you feel comfortable with their level of training? Like, can they shoot straight and not accidentally murder their comrades?"

Jackson laughed. "Yeah, everyone in these parts has lived around guns since they were born. The training isn't really a new thing, but it is more structured than just a dad teaching his kids how to hunt. We start with the basics, like proper cleaning and maintenance. Then we work up to target shooting."

"So why not let everyone keep their firearms after the training class this morning?"

"I don't know. I mean, I get your point, but I have my orders."

Harlan stood up, walked around the table, and draped a skinny arm across Jackson's shoulders. "Alfred Pennyworth would do what he thinks is best, despite Batman's orders. And Batman would respect that."

Jackson nodded slowly, then his eyes became owl-like. "Hey, when did you start talking? I thought you only used sign language."

Harlan gave Jackson a shy smile that carried a megaton of mountain-toppling charm. With Harlan's help, the Transcontinental Railroad would have been completed in half the time. "I've evolved, just like that comic book guy. It's time for me to start talking like normal people do."

"Okay. Yeah, I think you're right about the guns. I'll make an inventory list, though ... who is given what and how much ammo. Gotta cross all the Ts and dot all the Is."

Kenny grinned now, too. "Certainly. That's what smart people do."

Willa watched with narrowed eyes. She approved of the manipulation, of course, but she didn't like that Kenny and Harlan were better at it than her.

Chapter 29

Ray

Ray stood a few feet away from the unfolding drama. Something told him to keep his mouth shut. His input was not needed in whatever grim resolution was forthcoming.

"You're absolutely certain Hannah and Piper were killed? You saw it happen?" Serena Jo demanded of Fergus.

"Yes," Fergus replied.

He was lying. Fergus had already told Ray he hadn't seen it first-hand. He'd witnessed it with his *scythen*, the supposed telepathic channel of communication he had established with Hannah. But he certainly couldn't explain all that to Serena Jo without being banished to the holler's version of a loony bin.

Fergus said, "I saw Piper enter her house, and Hannah followed soon after. The structure exploded minutes later. Nobody walked out of there alive, trust me."

"Can you confirm this?" Serena Jo said to a sack of bones sitting on the ground cocooned in a wool blanket that surely hadn't seen the inside of a washing machine during its lifetime.

"Told ya already. I don't know nothin' except these two assholes kidnapped me from my bed," Silas hissed. His teeth had begun to chatter.

Ray watched Serena Jo take notice of the old man's discomfort, then turn away. He'd be lying to himself if he said her obvious lack of compassion didn't bother him a little.

"I believe him," Fergus said. "He's clearly a psychopath, but he doesn't know anything about the explosion. Just trust me on this. I've never let you down before."

Serena Jo seemed to consider his words but remained silent.

Dani stood on the other side of the blanket-wrapped bones, which had assembled themselves cross-legged on the frosty ground. She had gone oddly quiet. Ray hadn't been around her much, but he'd picked up on a few of her behaviors. Remaining silent during a discussion that involved warfare and the interrogation of an enemy combatant seemed out of character for the woman.

Serena Jo, on the other hand, frequently went quiet as her impressive brain wrangled with conundrums. She faced one now as she gazed at the loathsome creature on the ground——who happened to be her grandfather. She'd processed the news about Hannah's death with the stoicism Ray had come to expect. Within the small group gathered in a wintry meadow several miles outside of Idlewild, it seemed he and Fergus were the only ones who acutely felt Hannah's loss. To be fair, though, the two of them had spent more time with Hannah than her own daughter, who had never known her until now. Being related to someone didn't guarantee a bond. Those had to be forged through time, shared joy, and shared adversity.

Finally, Serena Jo spoke. "Yes, he's a psychopath, and he's our enemy. We'll interrogate him and extract every scrap of information he has. Now that we've lost our advantage, we need intel more than ever. Get started, Luke," she said to the Scout at her side.

"Using all means necessary, ma'am?" Luke asked, his tone deadpan and menacing.

Ray would prefer not to witness whatever "means" the Sam Elliott look-alike might engage in.

"Yes." Serena Jo replied.

Dani finally spoke up. "You're wasting your time. This putrid old fleabag will never talk. He's half-dead already, and he knows it. If you start torturing him, he'll just stroke out."

"Would that be such a bad thing?" Serena Jo asked, staring at her grandfather dispassionately. The man's reptilian eyes returned her gaze without a shred of affection or even humanity. Fergus glanced at Ray with a raised eyebrow that said: *No love lost there.*

"My point is, why expend the energy? Let's just kill him now and move on. We have shit to do," Dani said.

While he didn't condone torture, Ray recognized the necessity of it under these circumstances. If Silas died from the duress, so be it. But to murder him in cold blood crossed a line. That sort of thing always would, no matter how justified.

"Maybe he doesn't deserve an easy way out," Serena Jo said, still facing the prisoner.

Ray imagined he could see waves of malevolence emanating from the silent leader of the Murdock clan. At that moment, he knew he was in the presence of pure evil.

Dani glanced at Sam, who gave her a quick frown followed by a head shake. She made an exasperated sound, then became a blur of movement.

The next moment, Silas Murdock, a man responsible for an unquantifiable number of deaths, lay supine on the frigid ground. A widening pool of blood framed his cadaverous skull, forming a grisly crimson halo. The body temperature liquid collided with the chilly air to produce steam. From Ray's vantage, it created an effect that looked like poisonous vapor. He took a step backward, not eager to inhale whatever evil escaped the old man.

"There. Now, can we move on, please?" Dani said.

Ray glanced at Fergus, who merely shrugged. The red beard twitched once, then was still. Ray knew what that meant, and he sighed. He would never understand people. Was he the last person on the planet who didn't condone murder in any form?

Sam suddenly appeared beside him, and they briefly made eye contact. *No, there's at least one other,* Ray thought. Sam gave him a shoulder pat and moved away.

"This old fucker was on his way out in terms of control of the Murdock clan," Dani said. "We know that from Hannah. Now that her sister is dead, we have our clear target."

Serena Jo nodded. "Wyatt." She didn't seem unhappy to have her authority usurped by the younger woman, at least in regard to dispatching Silas. In fact, they seemed to have developed an almost extrasensory connection in their mutual desire to destroy the Murdocks.

Ray understood Serena Jo's motivation. Her family had clashed with the Murdocks for generations, and that animosity had recently escalated to the level of existential threat. Dani, on the other hand, simply seemed to enjoy warfare. Or perhaps she enjoyed a challenge. Either way, Ray hoped the young woman would go far away once the mission was over. She made him profoundly uneasy.

"Something tells me Wyatt may be worse than this one," Dani said with a gesture toward the blanket.

"You're probably right. I've met Wyatt a couple of times during the annual moonshine barter. With Silas, what you saw is what you got: crass vulgarity and animal cunning. In contrast, Wyatt has a slick veneer. He's handsome and eloquent and charming, but he wouldn't bat an eye while sticking a knife in your back. And he'd be wearing a dazzling smile the entire time."

"I know the type," Dani said. "Makes me want to take him down even more. If there's one thing I hate, it's a phony. What would be his first move?"

"The smart thing would be to hunker down and let us bring the war to him. Maybe we should have done that," Serena Jo added.

"No, that's too limiting. Being mobile gives us flexibility. As I mentioned after this dude's warehouse blew up, the disparity in numbers requires a change of plans."

"Wyatt may not yet realize he's in charge. You all seem to think he was behind the explosion that killed Hannah and Piper, and I agree that makes sense. But he doesn't know that Silas is permanently out of the picture. So, the smarter question is, what would Wyatt do if he thought he was still answering to Silas?"

"Good point," Dani replied. She glanced at Sam, who was frowning now. "Wyatt may assume that we're holding Silas hostage as a bargaining chip. If it were me, I would want a few bargaining chips of my own."

"What do you mean?" Serena Jo asked. Her lips barely moved as she spoke. Ray had identified this as one of her tells: she was anxious. More so than she'd already been as they prepared to launch guerrilla attacks on Idlewild.

"According to Hannah, the Murdocks will stoop to unimaginable depravity to win," Dani said.

"Yes, she told me they would use children for shields and strap babies to their backs. I figured that was hyperbole, but maybe it wasn't," Fergus said, grimly.

"That was no exaggeration. The Murdocks are capable of all of that and more," Serena Jo said. "When I returned to the holler and assumed leadership, I was informed of their heinousness."

"The Whitakers are the opposite in that regard," Dani said. "Children are precious ... priceless. Even more so when those children are Whitaker holler children. Catch my drift?"

"My god," Serena Jo whispered. "They're going after the kids."

"That's my guess. They'll send some troops to the village, knowing it's not fully defended, and snatch a few ankle biters for collateral. The punji traps might not stop all of them. Look, Sam and I can get back to the village faster than anyone. You and the Scouts stay here. Keep everyone spread out, and don't do anything until we get back."

"You think I'm just going to stand idly by when my children are in danger?" Serena Jo demanded, hysteria creeping into her voice as she closed the space between Dani and herself.

"You'll just slow us down, girly," Dani drawled. A muscle twitched in her scarred jaw.

Fergus intervened when he saw the possibility of a brawl between the two women. He squeezed Serena Jo's shoulder.

Ray knew the intent behind the gesture. Fergus was sending forth 'serenity vibes' that apparently worked like a fentanyl injection. It was another of the gifts he'd either been born with or learned from the supposed underground dwelling in which he and his genetically enhanced brethren resided. Ray hoped he lived through the next few days if for no other reason than to get Fergus alone and make him spill his guts.

This time, though, the serenity vibes didn't seem to work fully. Serena Jo visibly calmed, but she didn't concede.

"We're leaving," she said firmly. "You and Sam can go ahead, but we'll be right on your asses. Go."

Dani's shrug said *you're making a mistake*. Within seconds, she and Sam had disappeared into the tree line.

A shrill whistle pierced the air. Scouts emerged from their camouflaged positions from within the surrounding forest, answering the call of Serena Jo's lieutenant.

Their numbers didn't inspire confidence.

"We're returning to the village. There's been a change of plans," Serena Jo said. She started off in the direction of Whitaker holler.

The Scouts hesitated, exchanging nervous glances. Serena Jo had gone ten paces before she realized no one was following.

Ray felt guilty. He should have been right behind her.

Her eyes blazed. "What's the problem?"

"Why are we leaving?" one of the younger Scouts asked. His discordant voice revealed a boy recently past puberty.

"It's not your place to question me," Serena Jo snapped, storming back toward the group. "Luke, do you want to handle this insubordination?"

"No, ma'am. It may be insubordination, but the boy's right. That ain't the right call."

"Explain," she said through clenched teeth.

"We're already set up here. We have gear, food, water, and firearms, all positioned in well-camouflaged locations. We're ready to start picking off those bastards like ticks from a hound. That Dani girl is right. If we just pull up stakes and run home, we don't know what we'll come back to. Might be walking into a nest of Murdocks hiding in our foxholes. We stay put, we hold the ground here. We're in good shape going forward. You don't need all of us to secure things back home. We don't even know there's a *problem* back home. You're making this decision because you're afraid for your kids, which I understand, but it ain't the right call."

If Serena Jo clenched her jaw any harder, she might break a few teeth. Ray held his breath.

Fergus broke the tense silence. "He's right. I'll stay with the Scouts. You and Ray go. Follow Dani and Sam. Those two are better than a battalion of Marines. In the meantime, we'll make sure no Murdocks leave or return to Idlewild with their throats intact."

Serena Jo closed her eyes. When she opened them again, a different kind of fire had replaced the previous one.

"You're right, Luke. Of course, you're right."

Luke nodded, then exhaled in relief.

"If they've touched a hair on the head of any Whitaker child, we'll be bringing back their balls in a sack. Come on, Ray," she said, grabbing his bicep and pulling him along. "I'm ready to kill somebody."

Ray glanced back at Fergus, whose beard had begun twitching furiously.

***

"It was the right decision," Ray said as he trudged behind the love of his life, occasionally tripping on vines and dead branches. Her graceful movements ten yards ahead were a bit distracting. Memories of their night together threatened his ability to concentrate. He'd begun to lag behind. Rather than thinking about her taut body or her perfect breasts, he should be constantly scanning the perimeter looking for threats. Fortunately, all the bears would be hibernating by now——but human predators could be anywhere.

"Yes, I know that. Can you walk faster, please?"

Her tone was equal parts tense and annoyed, but he took no offense. She was worrying about her kids.

Ray worried too, but he tried to calm her. "They'll be fine. First, we don't know that there's even a threat. Second, those traps are a huge deterrent if any Murdocks try to approach the village. Third, Dani and Sam could easily dispatch a handful of assailants. Those two seem quite competent."

"I know you're trying to make me feel better, and I appreciate it. But if you stop talking, you can walk faster."

"Did it work? Do you feel a little bit better?"

She stopped abruptly and spun to face him, her eyes blazing.

"You've never had children, Ray. You couldn't possibly understand the gut-wrenching, utterly consuming terror of thinking your children could be in danger. I have no room left for rational thought. Every minute that passes while I'm trying to get home could be the moment where the Murdocks slink into the village. We left the kids like sitting ducks, thinking a few Scouts and some holes dug in the woods would keep them safe. How fucking arrogant was that? Feeling better isn't an option I'm interested in at the moment. Do you understand? I'm going to start jogging now. I'm going to focus on pushing my body to the limits of endurance instead of picturing a Murdock knife held against my children's throats. Please try to keep up. If you can't, catch up when you're able."

His smile vanished. What an idiot he'd been. The only thing that could make her feel better was seeing her children safe and unharmed, and that wouldn't happen until they arrived at the village.

"I'll keep up," he said grimly. "Let's go."

Chapter 30

Fergus

"You sure came up fast in the ranks for an outsider. How is it that you wormed your way into the thick of things already?" Luke asked, his eyelids half-closed. Not half-closed in a sleepy way, more in a way that said: *the smell of your bullshit is burning my corneas.*

Luke's graying mustache and beard looked like he trimmed them with hedge loppers. When the Appalachian drawl emerged through the drooping facial hair, black holes appeared where teeth had formerly resided. His heavily patched clothing might have been generational heirlooms. The rifle he held, an M-1 circa WWII, never left his hand. Never.

Luckily, Fergus knew better than to judge intellect by regional dialects, old clothing, or a few missing incisors.

"I guess Serena Jo is a good judge of character. Perhaps she sees something in me that will prove useful to her." It would have to be enough. As nice as it felt to be liked and accepted and to earn a person's respect, at the moment, he didn't give one fuck about any of that. All he wanted was to get the people he cared for safely through the coming storm.

And if that happened, he just might lift a middle finger in the direction of *Cthor-Vangt* and spend the rest of his days on a golden beach with his beloved Amelia. Every time he thought about it, the dreamy image came more into focus.

"Uh-huh," Luke replied, polishing the gleaming wood stock of his rifle.

"Is that an M-1 Garand?" Fergus asked, only half-interested.

"Yep. You know firearms, I reckon."

"Yes. In a war filled with bolt-actions, the Garand semi-automatic stood out. Patton called them the greatest battle implement ever devised."

Luke nodded but said nothing, which was a relief to Fergus, who knew a lot more about the rifle but wasn't in the mood for small talk.

He'd organized his personal gear in a small wash-out next to a six-ty-foot chestnut oak. Some of the tree's roots had broken through the side of the concave space in the ground. The small, cave-like opening would provide some minor protection from the elements, as well as camouflage in the forest. A small person could wriggle behind those roots and become practically invisible to any passersby. Fergus was just small enough.

Luke's gear rested nearby within a tangle of rhododendrons. Two other Scouts were setting up their personal camps twenty yards in either direction. The strategy of spreading out was a smart one. If Luke hadn't suggested it, Fergus would have. Yes, there was safety in numbers. But there was also safety in scattering human targets across a hundred-yard grid instead of clustered within a fifty-square-foot camp that could be obliterated with a few automatic rifle sweeps.

A gruff voice suddenly came from behind him. "I'm thinking about beginning the raids at midnight. Just a couple targets at the east and west end of town, then fast withdraws. Start softening things up for when the *generals* get back."

Fergus had just situated his sleeping bag and was inventorying his food. So when the deep baritone sprung from three feet behind, he jumped. Like Dani and Sam, Luke must possess the stealth gene. And it would seem Fergus's rifle knowledge had scored a few points with the Scout; he acted downright friendly now.

"Aren't we under orders to stay put?" Fergus asked, careful not to inject any hint of disapproval.

"Yep. But those orders came from a young gal that I don't know and a slightly older gal I do. Serena Jo is an admirable woman, but she's no military expert."

Fergus struggled to keep from smiling. Luke had placed no emphasis on the words gal or woman, and he didn't need to in order to make his point. Sexism wasn't alive and well in Whitaker holler, but with some of these older men, it might still be on life support.

"You're suggesting we disobey a direct order?"

"I'm suggesting some creative interpretation."

Fergus snorted. "Go on."

Luke warmed to the task. "We take two small teams of five Scouts each, armed to the teeth, and hit the guard stations at both ends of the pissant state highway that runs through that shithole. Stagger the attacks ... the east about five minutes after the west." He withdrew a hand-drawn map of the tiny town of Idlewild and pointed a callused finger to the left side, then the right.

"We make a lot of noise only on the western front ... controlled rifle bursts, a few of those black powder bombs, and lots of Comanche war party screaming. Their attention will be focused where the noise is, so our second Scout team can pick off a few distracted Murdock guards on the east. Then we fall back. Leave them alone the rest of the night. They'll be on high alert until dawn and unrested by the time the next attack comes. When the sun rises, they'll find casualties where they didn't expect. That'll be a bit disconcertin', don't you think?"

"So how is this in any way a creative interpretation of the direct order to not engage?"

"'Cuz we're not taking all the Scouts. Just a handful. More Scouts will be unengaged than engaged."

Fergus chuckled. "I'm not hating it. We can create a lot of confusion within the enemy's ranks, which is always a good thing. They'll be thrown off when we fall back and withhold follow-up assaults for unknown hours. However, I would add one more element to your plan."

"What's that?"

"We insert a covert operator here," Fergus pointed to the top of the paper, "whose task will be to quietly infiltrate the town and eliminate any handy targets he encounters while the firestorm is happening to the west and the assassinations are happening to the east."

"I like it. I got the perfect man in mind for the job."

Fergus shook his head. "You're already looking at him. I'm going in under their radar."

A slow smile spread across Luke's face. "You're definitely the right size for that."

***

Fergus hid within a cedar copse on Idlewild's northern city limit. He'd chosen the position for its proximity to the town via a secondary dirt road that ribboned in and out of the surrounding woods. Clouds obscured much of the moonlight, making the road's ankle-breaking potholes more dangerous. Behind the sporadic clumps of dead Johnson grass, a Murdock guard might be positioned. The length of a football field separated Fergus from Idlewild's northernmost building, an antiquated gas station boasting two rusty pumps. A faded dinosaur smiled benevolently from atop a crooked signpost.

Idlewild, barely a speck on his U.S. map, was in fact a shithole. He beheld the shitholeness with the help of night-vision goggles. The town had certainly never been charming, despite its location nestled within thousands of acres of Smoky Mountain forested glory. There were no quaint antique shops, no neatly landscaped town squares, no early 20th century cabins converted into cozy B&Bs.

Instead, a characterless strip mall had attempted to take root on either side of a sixties-era Piggly Wiggly. A few dozen houses existed just beyond the commercial district on Main Street; their weed-choked lawns were covered with abandoned cars, stained mattresses, shredded sofas, and even a toppled metal swing set. The Murdocks wanted to make certain no pleasure-seeking, sightseeing travelers would ever venture to Idlewild.

Bloody overachievers.

Fergus sighed in disgust as he panned the glasses from left to right. Five teams of two Murdocks each patrolled the streets. The night vision feature transformed them into green specters. After half an hour, he had memorized their pattern.

Additional adversaries would be patrolling the nearby forest as well. These were the ones to worry about, but the ghillie suit Skeeter had lent him would provide excellent cover. Anyone who happened to glance in his direction might think they saw a shrub swaying in the breeze.

But this shrub was armed to the teeth and hellbent on bringing down the de facto leader of the Murdock clan. Fergus planned to incapacitate anyone he encountered on the way to his primary target. With any luck, Wyatt would be inside Silas's house. A usurper who wants to assume the throne would predictably set up housekeeping in the castle of the missing king.

He smiled as he pondered the notion of a hellbent shrub, then frowned when he realized he would probably have to kill a few people tonight. When next he reported in to *Cthor-Vangt*, he would have to confess. Maybe if he was lucky, they would banish him forever and save him the trouble of a nasty breakup.

At that moment he realized he'd made the decision. Perhaps he'd made it long ago but didn't want to admit it to himself. Suddenly, the oppressive burden of living for ten thousand years (and counting) fell from his soul.

So this is what it feels like to be free. I'd forgotten. The shrub sighed happily. The next moment, it zigzagged its way toward Idlewild.

✶✶✶

An hour later, the shrub no longer felt happy. Fergus hunkered a mere ten yards from the back door of Silas's house. He'd yet to be challenged, which made no sense. Hannah had described the location of the house and explained that it was always heavily guarded. Wyatt would have kept those sentries in place.

Worse, when Luke's fireworks show exploded on the town's western border, barely a handful of people took to the streets. Those who did were malnourished women. Not even the patrols slowed in their orchestrated pattern. And worse-worse, now that Fergus was closer, he could see the patrols were as small as himself——children or adolescents dressed up as soldiers. No light escaped through the window panes of Silas's house. No one stirred from within when the cacophony occurred to the west.

The jockey-shorts stain of a town was practically empty except for costumed kids and females who didn't look like they could lift a chihuahua, let alone shoot a rifle.

A sickening feeling sprang from the region between sphincter and colon. The Murdocks hadn't sent a small contingent to Whitaker holler with the intent of kidnapping a few kids.

They had sent the bulk of their army——with the intent of annihilation.

Chapter 31

Willadean

It had been a very long day and an even longer night. Yesterday morning, Jackson handed out firearms and ammunition to everyone over the age of eight who could half-ass shoot straight. Then they took up defensive positions around the village. The four Scouts who'd been left behind to protect the village were stationed just beyond it, hidden in trees and ready to shoot anything that moved. Nobody was on rotation now. If you wanted to eat or take a pee, you did it in situ.

Every Whitaker in the village, including kids, cooks, and crones, had gotten an instant promotion to *soldier*. A few of them weren't happy about their sudden elevated status. Thelma had to be enticed by Harlan to stick a revolver in her apron. Even then, he couldn't persuade her to leave the kitchen house. The cornbread would be safe, though the rest of them might not be around to eat it.

Willa expected an attack within the next few hours——she just didn't know when it would come or how intense it would be. Harlan and his freaky psychic third-eye had seen it ... had picked up on the thoughts of a Murdock assailant as he crept toward the village. Then he'd picked up a few more. He called them blips, and he was utterly certain they were approaching.

She didn't doubt him for a second. Her brother was a weirdo extraordinaire, but he wasn't a liar. Nor was he prone to flights of fancy, unless he was pretending to track fairies in the woods. Once he'd told her about the blips, using actual speech with vocal cords and everything, she had Kenny and Harlan work their manipulating magic on Jackson. In the end, it hadn't taken much effort. Jackson quickly agreed that something felt off. Maybe Jackson possessed some level of freaky psychic talent. too.

For the rest of the day, they waited. Then for the rest of the evening, they waited. Then for the rest of the night, they waited. A person couldn't stay on high alert indefinitely, so by the time the eastern sky over the mountains began to brighten, every soul in the village was tapped out——and royally pissed off that they'd missed lunch, dinner, and a good night's sleep.

Harlan's conviction in those blips didn't waver even a tiny bit. So even though everyone was grumpy and hungry, they grudgingly took turns loading up gunny sacks with dried apples and smoked venison, then returned to their concealed positions.

Willa knew they couldn't hold out for long, so it was almost a relief when she saw movement on the outskirts of the village just beyond where Brock and his father had lived.

"Get ready," she hissed to the boys. Willa, Harlan, and Kenny hid in the crawlspace beneath Serena Jo's cabin. Early morning sunlight crept through the criss-cross lattice panels covering the open space between earth and floorboards. Willa and Harlan had spent count-less hours here——sometimes hiding, sometimes pouting, sometimes avoiding chores——but usually they came here when they wanted to spy on folks without being seen.

It was the perfect spot from which to kill any Murdocks who came into view. With a thumb sore from all the firearms practice, Willa cocked the rifle hammer. Jackson had given her the Winchester she'd been using for target practice. She could hit a grasshopper off a dandelion fifty yards away with that gun.

"Lock and load, boys," she whispered grimly. It would have sounded fierce if not for the slight quaver in her voice.

"What the hell ...?" Kenny said the next moment.

Jackson and another young Scout prodded a band of six Murdocks up the main road. All the Murdocks' hands were locked behind their heads in an instantly identifiable posture of surrender.

"Willadean!" Jackson called. "Come on out! We need to have a parley!"

"What a minute, Willa," Kenny said, grabbing her ankle before she could scramble out into the light. "You're the heir apparent in this back-water. Princess Hayseed doesn't just waltz out into the open without knowing what's what. I'll go. If this is some kind of trap, the only prisoner they'll snare is a smartass ghetto boy."

Before she could stop him, he squirmed out from the crawlspace and jogged toward the group.

"Damn it!" she muttered, forcing herself to stay put. But she knew Kenny was right. As much as Willa hungered to be involved in whatever was about to happen, the shrewd move was to play it safe. After the close call with Levi, she would think twice about charging into danger from now on.

Or at least this time.

In a weirdly fatherly gesture, Harlan mussed her hair. Then he returned his attention to the unlikely congregation in the center of the village. It had come close enough now so Willa heard every word.

"Willadean isn't taking new clients just now. I'm her personal assistant. How can I help you?" Kenny said. He used what Willa had come to think of as his Poindexter tone.

Harlan snorted softly.

"These dudes are on the level, Kenny," Jackson said. "They want to escape from the Murdock clan and join forces with us here in the holler."

Kenny lifted an eyebrow. "Color me skeptical, Jackson."

"They hate the leadership, and they especially hate Wyatt. They're tired of eating shit sandwiches for breakfast, lunch, and dinner. Those were his words." Jackson prodded a young Murdock who happened to be the one Willa's focus had gravitated to. Something about the teenager demanded notice. He reminded her of Brock; strange energy waves seemed to emanate from him.

"I see," Kenny said, nodding comically for effect. "And yet, I'm not convinced. Listen here, Jackson Brown, these villains may be blowing fairy dust up your bloomers. How can we be sure they aren't lying their redneck asses off?"

"Because there were nine of them to start. Colton here," Jackson dipped his head toward the enigmatic young Murdock, "Executed the others before my very eyes. He said he did it to prove he had no loyalty to the Murdocks. And also because they weren't part of the contingent who wanted to defect. Just these six were."

"Jackson, my good man. No offense, but this stinks like a serial killer's basement."

Harlan scrambled out from the crawlspace and jogged toward the group.

"Harlan!" Willa whisper-screamed, but it was too late.

Her heart trampolined from her chest to her throat at the sight of her slight, otherworldly, half-pint brother standing an arm's length away from Murdock cutthroats.

He stopped directly in front of the one called Colton. From her vantage, she could only see the back of her brother's head, but she could read his body language like it was a first-grade primer.

When Harlan began to speak using his silvery new voice, her attention shifted to Colton's face.

"Why should we believe you?" Harlan asked, placing his little-boy hand on the chest of the Murdock teenager.

Colton's eyes never left Harlan's face. "All the reasons that you already heard. You're too young to have gone to the moonshine barters, so you don't know what those people are like. Calling them animals is an insult to animals, so I refer to them as monsters. We've been planning our exit strategy for the past year, thinking we'd high-tail it this summer. But then something happened that changed our timeline."

"What was that?" Kenny demanded.

"They executed a girl I loved. Tandy was the sweetest, kindest, most beautiful creature ever to walk this earth. And they fucking strangled her right in front of everyone. That's what they do. Public torture and killings are how they keep control. So when Wyatt put me in charge of a mission to kidnap a few kids from the holler," the boy gestured directly toward Willa in her hiding place, "I knew this was our opportunity."

Harlan's body remained motionless for a full minute. No words were spoken. Kenny merely smiled at Harlan.

Finally, Harlan broke whatever spell had held them frozen.

"Come on out, Willa," Harlan yelled. "It's all clear."

Jackson gave a loud whoop.

Kenny folded his arms and watched with keen interest as Willa joined their ranks.

Harlan grinned.

Colton slid his right hand from its locked position at the back of his sandy-haired head and thrust it toward her.

"You must be Willadean. You look just like your mama. I pledge on my honor that in no way will I seek to bring harm to you or your kin. We all pledge. We won't let you down."

Shockingly, Colton kneeled on one knee; the remaining five Murdocks followed suit.

The silence became deafening except for the pounding in her ears. Everyone stared at her. She felt heat rising in her cheeks. Finding herself the subject of Kenny's fiercely expectant gaze forced her to locate her missing tongue.

In a brusque, authoritative voice, she said, "Jackson, they're yours now. Place them wherever you think best. You're the highest ranking Scout here. I guess we can all take a breather, get some sleep finally." She yelled so everyone hiding could hear too. "It's all over, folks!"

She felt Harlan's presence beside her suddenly. He shook his head.

"It's not over, Willa. About a hundred more blips just popped up in my head."

Willa called for an impromptu meeting inside the largest structure in the village: the kitchen house. Two dozen exhausted people, mostly very young and very old, sat on the wooden benches. Jackson leaned against one wall, holding his rifle in the two-handed 'ready' position. The other Scouts had returned to the woods. The Murdock deserters leaned against the opposite wall. Jackson didn't exude any overt hostility toward the former enemies; he'd witnessed the dispatching of three loyal Murdocks at Colton's hands. A triple execution tended to be convincing.

But the folks sitting on the benches hadn't seen it, and they didn't seem inclined to let go of a generational blood feud. For that reason, Jackson had wisely decided to withhold the Murdocks' firearms so they would appear less threatening. Even so, Thelma looked like she wanted to pop a cap in the forehead of all six of them.

Willa felt the heat rising in her cheeks again, but she powered through. Even though she was just a kid, she knew she was a natural-born leader. And because of her elevated social status within the holler thanks to her mama and her grandpa, folks didn't question her authority. At least not these folks. They sat quietly on the benches and waited for whatever speech was forthcoming.

Willa had been writing it in her head for the last ten minutes. She figured the height gained by standing on one of the dining tables might bolster the impression of authority. She ignored Kenny's grin as he gazed at her from below.

Just as she opened her mouth to speak, the door slammed open. Standing in its frame was the scarred-faced Dani holding a high-caliber handgun, which she pointed at the Murdocks.

Like a ghost, her boyfriend Sam appeared next to Willa. "Are you okay?" he whispered.

"Yes, I'm fine!" Willa snapped. She couldn't deny the relief she felt at seeing the two of them.

"What the hell is going on here?" Dani asked with a furious glance at Kenny.

He shrugged in response. "Ask the little cherry bomb up there."

"You mean the *child* standing on the table? Who the hell is in charge? You're Jackson, right?" Dani snarled over her shoulder. She kept her gun trained on the Murdocks, who hadn't moved a muscle or blinked an eyelash. They recognized a pro when they saw one.

"Yes, ma'am. We have a lot to explain. These guys aren't a threat, so you can holster your weapon," Jackson said.

"And you can go fuck yourself." In a slightly less strident tone, she said to Willa, "Start explaining fast, young lady. I'll give you thirty seconds before I start making chunky gray soup out of Murdock brains."

Kenny snorted.

Suddenly all the tension of the last twenty-four hours drained away, leaving Willa's legs weak and noodly. She took a seat.

"Here's what happened ..."

Chapter 32

Wyatt

"They're late," the idiot said.

"I realize that," Wyatt snapped.

"How much longer should we give 'em?"

Wyatt pivoted to face the moron, the same sentry who had seemingly misplaced Silas. Now that Levi was dead and Colton was off on a mission, Wyatt had to dig deep into the ranks of people he considered trustworthy. Hank had been on duty when Silas went missing——or been kidnapped, or summoned by Satan to the bowels of Hell——and therefore shouldered some responsibility. Wyatt provided him with a way to redeem himself: blind loyalty to Wyatt himself. Hank seemed thrilled to step into the power vacuum left by Levi's death. The elevated position of being Wyatt's new right-hand man brought him instant prominence. Hank better enjoy it while it lasted; Wyatt didn't expect the man to make it through the day.

Wyatt had decided it didn't really matter where Silas was, so they had stopped looking. He was in charge now and everyone knew it. In hindsight, the coup d'état had been easier than he'd expected. With Silas vanishing into thin air and Piper blown into a thousand pieces, the entire Murdock clan swiveled to Wyatt like a field of sunflowers reaching for the sun.

He glanced at his watch. "A few more hours. It might have taken Colton and his team longer than expected to acquire the leverage I asked for."

"Okay, but we don't want to wait too long. The Whitakers could get back here 'fore we expect 'em."

Wyatt gave the man an open-faced slap. It was the most humiliating of all Wyatt's rebukes, especially when directed at a man. Next to a good strangling, he favored the slap for its unique ability to instantly degrade and dominate.

"The Scouts won't be here for another day, you half-wit. Maybe two. They still think we're hunkered down in Idlewild waiting for them to attack. The Whitakers have no clue that we flanked their little guerrilla encampment on the way to the holler. It was a stroke of genius. I'm pleased to have thought of it."

That last part was a test. Hank had actually made the suggestion.

As expected, Hank replied, "Yessir. Fucking genius of you. So a couple more hours? We don't really need any of their kids. We got them out-manned two to one."

This time Wyatt merely smacked the man's head. "How much fight will it take out of them if we have their children held captive? I don't want to lose any more of our people than necessary."

"That's true, sir. We'll just wait for your order, then."

"Yes, you fucking will. Now, go get me one of the girls. I need a distrac-tion."

"Yes, sir."

Wyatt watched Hank scurry away. It wasn't just any child Wyatt need-ed for leverage. The bargaining chip he desired was one of the two children belonging to Serena Jo, Whitaker holler's arrogant, haughty, condescending leader. Either of her kids would do.

Wyatt hadn't been able to stop thinking about the woman since he'd seen her at the moonshine barter two years ago. The way she held her head high while looking down her nose and delicately sniffing, as if she found his mere presence repugnant. What a fucking bitch. It wasn't sex he desired. Well, not *just* sex. His need to dominate Serena Jo Whitaker more completely than any woman he'd ever known was what he thought about constantly. That image was just about the only thing that got him hard these days.

And once he'd pummeled his sworn enemies into the ground, he would take Serena Jo as his personal sex slave. He wondered idly how long she might last under those conditions. A year? Two? The notion was so exciting that he was more than ready for the whore Hank tossed at his feet.

That was why they must wait for Colton to return with the necessary leverage. Even if it took all fucking day.

Chapter 33

Ray

Ray had experienced happiness on more than a few occasions. But the joy he felt watching Serena Jo hug her children so fiercely that Harlan yelped and Willadean's eyes bulged was hands-down the best thing he'd felt in his life.

"I was so worried," she whispered into their hair.

"We're okay, Mama. You can let go now," Harlan said.

Willadean added, "Folks are looking, Mama!"

The villagers had gathered to witness the reunion. Dani and Sam stood to the side; Sam wore a wistful expression, while Dani's was one of impatience.

"Clock's ticking, people!" Dani yelled when she could no longer contain herself.

Serena Jo released the children, then rocked back on her heels and sat down hard on the ground. Her face was the picture of exhaustion. Ray could relate. He had no idea how he'd been able to keep up with her. But he had, and in the process, he felt like he had passed some kind of test. Not one Serena Jo had placed on him, one he'd placed on himself.

And one he planned to never repeat. Every inch of his body screamed. He desperately hoped there would be time for a bath, food, and a few hours of sleep before they had to return to the Scouts' camp.

"No time to waste," Dani said. "Let's go powwow in the mess hall. You can eat while I talk."

***

"At least we have a few more soldiers," Serena Jo said ten minutes later as she nibbled bacon and sipped black coffee. Ray didn't nibble; he gobbled down every morsel Thelma had placed on his tray.

"Yes, but I don't feel good about them, even though your son swears they're aces," Dani replied, her blue eyes narrowing when they located Harlan, who stood nearby.

His delicate eyebrows pinched together as his gaze drifted from Serena Jo to the fierce young woman opposite her. Willadean stood beside him, looking as exhausted as Ray felt. Her silence seemed to underscore her fatigue; Willadean was rarely quiet.

"Harlan is a special boy," Serena Jo replied. "I've only recently begun to realize how special. Both my children attended gifted classes in school and tested off the charts. And while my daughter possesses an IQ higher than any the school system had ever seen, my son's gifts are more esoteric. I don't even understand them myself." She sighed. "If he says he can sense a hundred assailants heading our way, you'd better believe it."

Dani pivoted to face Kenny, who'd been following the discussion wearing a fascinated expression. Ray knew nothing about the teenager, but for some reason, he liked him.

"Is this more of that cryptic horseshit you were feeding me on the drive here?" she demanded. A mask slid over the youth's features. Whatever he was going to say may be the truth, but Ray knew it wouldn't be the whole truth.

"Yes."

"Can you elaborate?"

"Only to say this: Believe the boy. He's one hundred percent on the level."

Dani made a disgusted sound, then stalked away. Everyone watched her pace the length of the kitchen house, chewing on a ragged fingernail.

Ray started to say something, then stopped when he felt a light pressure on his shoulder.

"Leave her be," Sam whispered. "If you interrupt her thought process, she may shoot you." He flashed a weak grin that said he was only half-kidding.

After several minutes of pacing, she stopped and glared at everyone in the room. "It can't be done. We can't win based on the current situation. I can work a few minor miracles, but I can't conjure soldiers and guns from thin air. We can't retrieve the Scouts and get back here before the Murdocks are on our doorstep. And we can't beat more than a hundred armed invaders with less than twenty trained people. I assume the Murdocks wouldn't honor some kind of humane or civilized treaty?"

Serena Jo snorted. "If we can't prevail ... if there's absolutely no possible way to beat them ... then we're better off not being here when Wyatt shows up."

"I thought about that. Maybe it's bug-out time," Dani directed the last sentence to her partner. Sam gave her a quick nod, relief written on his face.

"So that's that, I guess," Serena Jo said to no one in particular.

Harlan moved toward his mother and wrapped an arm around her weary shoulders. "Mama, I don't think that's that," he said in his lilting, newfound voice. "More blips just showed up in my head, but these ones ... they're *our* blips. And they're coming home."

Chapter 34

Fergus

"I hope your Scouts are capable of a forced march beginning immediately," Fergus said between gulps of oxygen. After realizing the pissant burg of Idlewild was essentially empty, he'd backtracked to the Scout camp in record time.

Luke's bushy eyebrows came together. "Are you familiar with Marine recruit training?"

Fergus nodded. For the moment, it was easier than talking.

"That's what we go through before we can call ourselves Scouts. It's customized for the conditions here." Luke's hand gesture encompassed the woods and the mountains and the dangers and hardships they embodied.

Fergus smiled. "I thought I caught a 'former military' whiff when I first met you."

Luke ignored the comment and brought an index finger and thumb toward his lips. Fergus had just enough time to press his hands over both ears. He'd come to recognize many of the varied whistles within the Scout repertoire. Luke let fly the one that said, "Get your asses to me." The Scouts complied. Within three minutes, several dozen Scouts encircled their captain, their gear neatly packed and on their backs.

"We're double-timing it back to the holler. The Murdocks left a skeleton crew at Idlewild while the bulk of them are heading to our village. I don't have to tell you how important it is for us to get there first."

Every Scout responded with a silent nod that conveyed their utter loathing. Fergus liked that there was none of that *sir-yes-sir* business. Neither Serena Jo nor Luke demanded displays of allegiance or subservience. And while the chain of command was clearly respected within their ranks, each Scout was practically a self-contained one-person army.

Fergus doubted the Murdocks could make the same claim. Yes, they had superior numbers and superior firepower, but from what Hannah described, their triumphs depended on overwhelming their adversaries with relentless barbarity rather than competence. The approach had worked against state police and competing crime syndicates for generations.

Fergus desperately hoped that strategy would fail them now.

"Send up some prayers, folks," Luke growled. "We're gonna need 'em. Let's roll."

"You go ahead," Fergus said quietly to Luke. "I have some business to attend to first. I'll catch up."

"Best make it fast. And stay out of the poison oak. The last thing we need is a soldier with an itchy ass rash."

Fergus just chuckled. He would let the Scout think he needed a quick bathroom break, but that wasn't what he had in mind. Once everyone departed, he closed his eyes and sent his *scythen* toward the holler.

Hello, Harlan.

Hi, Mister Fergus.

Is everything okay there?

Yes, for now. Mama and Mister Ray and Miss Dani and Mister Sam are here now. So are six Murdocks.

Oh dear.

It's okay. They're on our side now. They defecated.

I think you mean defected.

Yes! Willa is better with words than me. But I don't mind because there's a lot of stuff I can do that she can't.

Indeed. Like what you're doing right now.

Right!

These Murdocks ... your mama is sure they're not lying?

Yes. I touched Colton to test for honesty. When he said he hated the Murdocks and had been planning to leave with his friends this summer, he was telling the truth. He thinks defecting to the Whitakers is an even better idea.

All six of these Murdocks feel the same way?

Well, there were nine to start. Colton killed the other three because they were loyal to the Murdocks.

Ah, I see. An effective demonstration of his veracity.

That's a word Willa uses sometimes.

I bet she does. Very well, Harlan. I think I have a clear picture of what's happening there. Please let your mother know more Murdocks are coming your way, and so are the Scouts.

Yes, we know. I just saw the blips, and I told Mama. Get here as fast as you can. It's going to be close.

Chapter 35

Willadean

"I wish we could be on the front lines," Willa said in disgust.

She and Harlan and the other kids had been forced to relocate to a safe place two miles from the village. Mama had tricked her by asking where she and Harlan liked to go when they were hiding from evil fairies in the woods. When she'd stupidly described the location, Mama rounded up everyone twelve and under and sent them to the clearing with the triangle logs.

The small area, nestled in a thickly wooded part of the forest, was one of Willa's favorite places. Something about the location felt … *tingly*. Like magic permeated the ground and soaked into the rocks and trees. She'd read about ley lines and believed magnetic energy channels converged right in the middle of the triangle of fallen trees. Maybe that's why it was so easy to get a fire going in the center of those logs; the flames got an energy boost from earth's magnetic field.

Thelma had filled clean pillowcases with yesterday's leftovers, some cold bacon and dried peaches. A chilly mountain stream flowed nearby, so they were in good shape in terms of water. The kids had been told to bring sleeping bags and all the warm clothes they could carry; they might have to spend the night since nobody was sure when the Murdocks would attack.

If the Murdocks won, they'd be staying away much longer than just a night.

"The front lines? You have a death wish, cherry bomb?" Kenny said. Based on age, the fourteen-year-old shouldn't be here, but Miss Dani had said he should go with the other kids to the safe place. In fact, she'd demanded he be put in charge of the group. But now that they were here, he'd wordlessly relinquished command to Willa.

Maybe there was something to that 'smartest kid in the world' claim.

"No, I don't have a death wish. But we could be a big help. I'm an excellent shot, and Harlan's pretty good, too. We should have every single person that can pull a trigger holding off the Murdocks. Especially if they arrive before the Scouts."

Kenny gave her an odd look. About a dozen children sat in a tight group nearby. They looked scared and miserable, but holler kids weren't crybabies, and they followed orders quickly and quietly. They'd done everything Willa had told them since leaving the village, without so much as a single complaint.

The impromptu adventure would have been fun except for the mountain of worry Willa carried. *What if the Scouts don't arrive in time ...*

"What if the Murdocks prevail?" Kenny said, mirroring her own thoughts. "Who's going to take care of these kids? Your mama made the right call. And since I'm a lover, not a fighter, we're both exactly where we should be, for a million different reasons."

"I guess you're right. It's still frustrating."

"Think we should get a fire going?" Harlan asked with a meaningful glance at the huddling children. "It might help make everyone feel better."

"No. We don't want to advertise our location. If we absolutely have to make a fire to keep from freezing, we will. But we're not freezing yet. We can gather firewood, though, and start working on some temporary shelters since not everyone has a tent and we might have to spend the night. Let's get moving, people! We're going to build some lean-tos."

Harlan and Kenny exchanged a grin, probably at Willa's expense.

Well, she didn't care. She may not get to kill any Murdocks today, but she could damn sure keep these kids comfortable and safe. While the weight of the Winchester in her hand felt reassuring, the pressure of the seven-inch fixed-blade Bowie against her ankle felt *dangerous*. Not the knife itself, but the way she felt while wearing it.

No Murdocks would threaten any of the kids under her care and live to tell the tale.

Chapter 36

Ray

"Did Dani put me here so I could keep you safe or the other way around?" Ray said.

"Maybe a bit of both," Serena Jo replied, squinting through the scope of her Mossberg Patriot, a rifle left behind by her father. His farewell letter was stuffed in her pocket. She told Ray in no uncertain terms that she was not interested in having a conversation about it. Not yet. And if the battle went badly, that conversation may never happen.

It was a good thing Ray didn't suffer from claustrophobia. The crawl space beneath Serena Jo's cabin provided excellent cover from which to kill invading Murdocks, but it was a tight squeeze. He was beginning to wonder if the Murdocks would ever show up. They'd been in the dank space for hours, lying on the cold soil.

After the children had left, Dani directed the remaining Whitakers to concealed positions throughout the village, positions that would also provide optimal vantage points for killing the enemy. The new Murdock recruits were staged out in the open at locations where they could be easily seen. The logic behind that was twofold: Seeing their comrades would imply the village had been secured, thus prompting the invaders to lower their guard. Conversely, in the event of a full-scale attack, the Murdock defectors would be first in the line of fire. It was a win-win strategy, according to Dani.

"What do you think our odds are?" Ray said, suddenly overcome with emotion as he gazed at Serena Jo's lovely profile. She had been through hell recently: first the Lizzy madness, then getting shot in the leg, now leading her small village against a ruthless barbarian horde.

"Roughly fifty-fifty. Maybe sixty-forty."

Ray impulsively reached for her hand and pressed his lips against the palm. "You're the most extraordinary woman I've ever met. I want to spend the rest of my life with you."

She smiled, but didn't turn to face him. "You realize the rest of your life may be down to minutes, right?"

"I do, and I'm at peace with it. If my life ends here and now, I don't care. As long as it ends by your side."

She sighed. "I'm not the romantic type, Ray. And I don't want to go out in a blaze of glory. I just want to live through this day. My children need their mother."

"Of course. But if that happens ... if we both survive ... will you marry me?"

She gifted him with an appraising glance before returning to her rifle scope. Seconds passed in silence. He began to get an unpleasant sensation in his stomach. *Please don't leave me hanging ...*

Finally she said, "I won't marry you. I've never been married and prefer it that way. But I will *partner* with you. Basically, we get all the perks of being married minus the patriarchal structure of a traditional marriage."

Ray laughed. "I accept your terms. Let's make it official. Serena Jo, do you take me as your partner? Do you promise to love me forever, tolerate my annoying habits, and laugh at my lame jokes for the rest of your days?"

This time when she looked at him it lasted for a full half-minute. She smiled, then refocused on the dirt road beyond. "I accept. Now please stop talking and aim your rifle, pointy end toward the bad guys."

He did. And just in time.

The first contingent of Murdocks had arrived.

A band of hardened men and women approached one of the Murdock deserters from the northeast end of the village. Ray didn't know all their names, but he thought this one was Colton. The kid couldn't be more than eighteen, but he carried himself with the confidence of someone twice his age. He lifted his hand in greeting but remained planted in the middle of the dirt road that ran through the village. Dani made him swear an oath that he wouldn't budge, no matter how many bullets started flying.

He honored that oath now. The invaders appeared wary but not especially tense. They weren't expecting a show of force from the Whitakers, the bulk of whom they believed to be miles away. And it boded well that one of their own stood brazenly in the middle of the village.

Ray strained to hear the conversation once the group stopped a few feet from the Murdock youth.

"Where the fuck you been, boy?" one man said. He seemed to be in charge, but he couldn't be Wyatt. This man was neither handsome nor cultured. He looked like an extra from some old spaghetti western, the grimy bandit who gets shot off his horse during the movie's dramatic climax.

"Hey, Hank. I've been right here. I figured instead of grabbing just one kid for a bargaining chip, why not all of them?"

"Is that right? Where are they? And where's the rest of your team?"

"They're around. The kids are stashed in the school building. Appropriate, huh?" Colton's laughter sounded completely natural.

"So why didn't you bring 'em to Wyatt. He's fucking pissed. We been waiting for hours."

"We thought we'd do a little shopping. You know, house-to-house, seeing what these Whitaker pussies might have that's worth a fuck. We were just about to round everyone up and head your way, but this is better. Lot more comfortable here than out there in the woods."

Hank nodded. "True."

"Where's everyone else?" Colton said, flicking a casual glance at the group behind Hank.

"Still back at camp. Wyatt sent a few of us to find out what the fuck happened to you."

He's lying, Ray thought instantly.

Serena Jo whispered, "He's lying. I think the whole damn clan is nearby." She chambered a round in the Mossberg. Ray's rifle was already locked and loaded.

Colton had made the same quick determination. Instead of answering, he flung himself on the ground as he withdrew a handgun from its holster. Without hesitating, he shot Hank in the throat. Hank returned fire before he hit the ground, striking Colton in the shoulder. Then the older man went still.

The next moment, all hell broke loose.

The remaining Murdocks scattered as bullets rained down on them from seemingly hundreds of directions; in actuality, they came from a little more than a dozen. Dani had spread out her small infantry specifically to give the impression of greater numbers, a shock-and-awe strategy that seemed to be working. But it wouldn't last. The villagers didn't have access to unlimited ammunition, and most of what they did have had gone with the Scouts.

Sam dashed into the street, grabbed Colton's boot, and dragged the boy into a nearby house. It didn't seem possible that he could move so quickly, nor that he didn't get shot himself in the process. But they both made it safely inside a nearby cabin.

Gunfire continued for a few more moments. Three additional Murdocks fell. But much too soon, the cacophony ended.

Serena Jo looked at Ray expectantly. All he could do was shrug and whisper, "I'm out too."

"Is that all ya got?" someone yelled from the edge of a nearby tree line.

Dani's acerbic voice came from close by, right outside Serena Jo's cabin, it seemed. "You're not man enough to handle all I've got, you backwoods jackass! Did your cross-eyed mama teach you how to shoot?"

"I'll show you. Come on out, bitch!" the man called.

A rustling sound came from the outside wall. Dani's face appeared in the crawl space opening.

"Insulting someone's mama riles them up every time," Dani said. "Cover me. Whichever of you is the best shot." She tossed something under the house, then her face disappeared.

Ray silently offered the Beretta to Serena Jo; her two-handed police-style grip looked rock-solid.

A blur of movement appeared to the right of their field of vision. Serena Jo began firing, quickly but methodically, in the direction of the voice in the trees. As Dani zig-zagged across the road, she fired an identical gun into the tree line.

Anguished screams emanated from the woods.

"Dumb fucks!" she hollered from the direction of Sam's retreat cabin.

"She's fast," Ray said.

"Freakishly so. Her boyfriend, too."

"What now?"

"That depends on the next few minutes. If help doesn't arrive, I'm going out there to work out a deal." She withdrew a white dish towel from the pocket of her jacket.

"What? No! You said yourself there's no civilized deals to be made with Murdocks."

"I know what I said. But it could buy some time for everyone else. Look, I know what Wyatt wants."

Ray swallowed hard. "What?"

"Me."

Chapter 37

Fergus

"I hear gunfire," Fergus said, struggling for the oxygen necessary to speak while running. The shots echoing from the village kicked up the Scouts double-time race to a triple-time sprint. Under normal circumstances, Fergus would have had no trouble keeping up. But just prior to their accelerated pace returning to the village, he'd completed a similar journey from Idlewild to the Scout camp.

He reached deep into his energy reserves, hoping there would still be enough to lift his firearm when they arrived. If more than a handful of Murdocks needed killing by his hand, he might be in trouble.

As they approached the village, the Scouts divided into three groups: Gray Wolf would approach from the east and Night Owl from the west. The few remaining Black Bears would hang back, ensuring the Scouts didn't get outflanked. They hoped to push the Murdocks into a tighter group within the village proper. And with any luck, they'd shoot them all at once like so many redneck fish in a barrel. Fergus approved of the plan, but he wouldn't participate. He had his own strategy, one that required stealth, keeping a low profile, and the use of Skeeter's ghillie suit.

He donned the suit now as the Scouts melted away into the landscape. By the time he was in position on the outskirts of the village, the gunfire had ceased, leaving a sulfurous mist in its wake.

Dani's voice echoed from somewhere within the village. "What a bunch of pansy-asses! Come out and fight like you weren't raised by kittens!"

Fergus snorted beneath his camouflage.

Minutes passed with no Murdock response. He checked the cylinder of his revolver, a gift from Ray during the Lizzy business, and the 12-round clip of the Smith & Wesson he'd filched from Jackson's armory two days earlier. Everything was in order. It wasn't much, so he must make every bullet count.

Movement through the netting caught his attention: a blur of blond hair and a white fluttering above it.

No ... no ... no!

Serena Jo strode toward the tree line north of the village, waving a piece of white cloth in the air. Surely she was too smart to expect Murdocks to honor a formal surrender. She must be desperate, not realizing the Scouts were surrounding the invaders even now.

Fergus drew a bead on the tree line, waiting for any kind of movement from within. Several heartbeats later, he saw a rustling of branches and began the steady pull of the Smith & Wesson's trigger when Serena Jo was twenty yards from the trees.

Before he could fire the shot, another blur charged into his range of vision.

Damn it, Ray!

His bean-counting bureaucrat friend dashed toward Serena Jo, tackling her just as bullets whizzed from the trees. Ray was no Baryshnikov, but he got the job done. Neither of them appeared injured.

Dani and Sam ran from their cabin, laying down cover fire while Ray dragged a pissed-off Serena Jo toward a dry gully next to the road. As Dani and Sam began their retreat, a piece of Dani's sleeve tore apart. She'd been hit, but she didn't stop until she and Sam reached cover.

At that moment, the Murdocks charged. Dozens of them poured into the village from every direction. Several made a beeline for the gully.

Fergus took careful aim, desperate to make every bullet count. He killed three of them before the Smith & Wesson jammed.

Fuck! Should have started with the revolver! He tossed the gun aside and drew the Ruger. Five bullets.

More Murdocks streamed out of the surrounding forest. They seemed to be everywhere at once. Fergus focused his attention on the ones heading toward the gully.

He drew a breath, exhaled half of it and started firing.

Four more Murdocks went down. Just as he was taking aim with his final bullet, knowing he couldn't get all the attackers before they reached the gully, a sharp whistle pierced the air.

Everyone seemed to pause in mid-action, as if a divine puppet master had hit some celestial pause button.

Fergus broke the spell, firing his last round into the invader closest to the gully.

The Murdocks scrambled off like cockroaches in a kitchen when the ceiling light flickers on. They recognized the Scout whistle, and they knew what it meant.

The cavalry had arrived.

The fighting became frenzied, fierce, and bloody, but it was over quicker than an armed skirmish between a large group and a small group had any right to be. The Scouts should have been overwhelmed by the horde, but their intense training paid off. Despite their humble clothing and hodgepodge weaponry, they performed like a Marine platoon.

Murdocks fell by the dozens, brought down by the relentless, methodical gunfire of the Scouts. The carnage was uncomfortable to watch, but still, Fergus did, and not without a twinge of elation. Once he managed to get his gun unjammed, he even joined in, casting off the ghillie suit as well as the oath he'd sworn in *Cthor-Vangt*.

Today he was harming humans, and not just in self-defense.

Eight more Murdocks fell by his hand. More than a hundred more were killed by the Scouts. When the fog cleared minutes later, bodies littered the village. Some didn't move, while others cried out in agony.

The job of putting down those Murdocks who were beyond help fell to Colton, the Murdock deserter. The youth believed it was his responsibility and also his cross to bear. Dani, her bicep bound in a makeshift bandage, followed close behind. Under her direction, none of the Murdocks' wounds were deemed survivable.

Once a honey badger, always a honey badger.

Eleven Scouts had also been killed and five more sustained life-threatening injuries. They were being carried to a make-shift hospital in the schoolhouse.

"I don't see Wyatt," Serena Jo yelled as Fergus approached.

"Are you sure?" Ray asked with a frown.

"Yes, I'm sure," she snapped. "Colton!" she called.

The teenager jogged over, his face splattered with blood and his injured shoulder in a makeshift sling. "Did you find Wyatt?" she asked him.

"No ma'am."

She raised her voice. "Has anyone found Wyatt's body? Luke, have you seen him?"

"No ma'am. And I've stared into the face of every dead Murdock. He ain't here."

When the golden eyes landed upon Fergus, he could see terror in their depths.

"To the children! *Now!*"

Chapter 38

Willadean

Willa was certain she heard the faint sound of gunfire, although two miles would be quite a distance for noise to carry if it came from the village. She didn't need to hear it with her own ears, though, to know a battle raged there. She had Harlan.

He sat on one of the triangle logs with his eyes screwed shut, trying to explain what he was able to pick up with his weird telepathy. All the children gathered around to listen, so Harlan was careful to use language that wouldn't be upsetting.

"There's a lot going on. All the blips have come together, but I think our blips are winning."

"The Whitakers are beating the Murdocks?" Willa demanded.

"I think so, but it's kind of hard to tell. Give me a few minutes, Willa. This isn't like watching a breaking news story on TV."

"Geez, okay."

Kenny reached for her hand and gave it a reassuring squeeze. When he released her fingers, a warm tingling sensation remained, unlike any she'd ever felt. She glanced into his eyes and saw he was staring at her. He'd felt it, too.

Harlan's musical voice interrupted the shared reverie. "We're winning. No doubt about it. And Willa, Mama is okay. Her blip is steady and strong, although it does seem a bit ..."

"A bit what?

"I'm trying to think of the word. Not all of us are writers, you know."

She bit her lip and waited.

"*Agitated*. That's the word. I think everything is okay. I need to disconnect. My brain hurts."

"Whew! Good job, Harlan. We still may have to spend the night here, kids. Let's get a fire going. You think that's okay?"

Harlan nodded slowly. "I think so. I'm a little tired after all that."

"Take a nap. Kenny and I will handle this."

"Okay," Harlan said with a yawn. The next minute he was curled up in his sleeping bag.

"Guess that psychic business takes a toll," Kenny said.

"It must. Speaking of, things have gotten too weird around here. Now that all the drama seems to be coming to a close, I have a lot of questions." She poked his skinny chest. "And some of them involve you."

"Me? I'm not the least bit weird. I'm delightful." He tossed a log onto Willa's barely smoking campfire.

"No! It's too early for a big log. Good grief. Has nobody taught you how to build a fire?"

"No, but I reckon I'm fixin' to learn."

"You have to start with dried moss or dead grass. Once you have small flames, you keep adding more until you get larger flames. Next is kindling, like twigs and small branches. Once you have a vigorous fire going, you add small logs. You don't start out with a tree trunk, city boy."

"Do tell."

She blinked at him. "You knew all this about fire. You were just distracting me from my questions."

"I don't care what everyone says, I think you're quite bright."

She punched his shoulder.

"Well, isn't this an interesting scene. It's something between *Children of the Corn* and *Friday the 13th*." A high-pitched masculine voice called from the woods just before the man stepped into view. Except for the creepy grin, he would have been handsome. He pointed a gun at Harlan's sleeping bag.

"Don't move or I won't hesitate to kill your brother, Willadean. The last time I saw you, you were tied up in a clearing. I'm still quite angry that someone killed my friend in order to save you. I bet I can convince you to tell me who that person was. I'm Wyatt, by the way. Oh my, you are a beauty. A real chip off the old block, or in your case, a chip off the old ice block."

Wyatt sauntered toward the campfire, keeping the gun trained on Harlan.

Willa's mind raced. She had set the Winchester against one of the logs before starting to build the fire. There was no way she could get to it in time. Jackson had issued Kenny a revolver, but it was next to her rifle. They'd both believed they were out of danger.

Two of the smartest people in the world should have known better.

"I can see you're struggling to find a solution to this dangerous situation. Let me be clear: There isn't one. All you can do is mitigate the bloodshed."

"What do you mean?" Her fingers itched to pull out the ankle knife, but the time wasn't right. She must be patient and draw Wyatt closer.

"Come with me without a fuss and I won't kill all these kids, including your fragile-looking brother and your skinny black boyfriend." He made a *tsking* sound with his tongue. "Does your mama know about this fledgling relationship? I can't imagine she does. Serena Jo may have gone off to college and gotten herself a high-brow education, but her roots are in the holler. Mountain folk don't take kindly to their offspring gallivanting with negroes."

Much to Willa's dismay, Kenny found his voice. "And negroes don't take kindly to gallivanting with inbred, bucktoothed, cracker barrel peckerwoods like you."

Wyatt shot Kenny in the leg. As the boy fell to the ground, the hatred emanating from his brown eyes was frightening. Hatred like that made a person reckless, and Willa knew Kenny needed his wits about him.

"Kenny, shut up," she said. "I mean it. This is no time for gallantry."

"Gallantry? I doubt it. She's right, though, *Kenny*. One more word from you and the next bullet will hit just below that nappy hairline."

Kenny opened his mouth to reply, but Willa stopped him. "He won't say another word. If he does, I'll never forgive him. You got that, Kenny?" She meant it, too. If they were going to be best friends, or perhaps more when they got older, he'd better not get himself killed.

Kenny's gaze shifted from Wyatt to her. Her hand suddenly tingled where he'd touched it.

He gave her the barest hint of a nod.

"Excellent. Now, Willadean, come with me. I suspect by now your mama has realized I'm still alive. She'll come here looking for me, and she will find the two of us together. Oh, what a party *that* will be. She'll do anything I ask to spare the life of her precious child. Maybe just for the fun of it, I'll let you watch. What do you think, Willadean? Wouldn't that be fun?" His eyes glittered, and the setting sun glinted off his shark-smile.

She realized at that moment that her would-be captor was insane.

She also realized Wyatt had no intention of letting any of the kids out of this situation alive, no matter how willingly she went to him now.

Well, she wouldn't go out with a whimper. She'd go out fighting——scratching and biting and clawing——and with any luck, at least one good stabbing.

"Drop dead!" she yelled.

Then she screeched like a berserker and launched herself at Wyatt.

Her actions took him by surprise. His mouth dropped open, though his gun remained pointed at Harlan. That was stupid of him. She'd placed herself directly between the gun and all the kids, including her brother.

The only person he could shoot now was her, and that's what he did.

Chapter 39

Harlan

Harlan woke up to the sight of Willa screaming like crazy and running toward a creepy man with a gun.

"Willa!" he tried to yell, but nothing came out. His newly found voice failed him. As he scrambled out of his sleeping bag, he focused on Willa running straight toward that gun.

I'm about to watch my sister die.

Her death was an inevitable outcome of the horrific scene playing out before him. There would be no last-second superhero coming to her rescue. Spiderman wouldn't descend from the trees. Wolverine wouldn't leap from the bushes, slicing away with razor claws. Superman wouldn't swoosh down from the heavens and block the bullet meant for his sister.

None of those things would ever happen, *could* ever happen. Nor did they.

Instead, a bald figure darted from the woods and leapt between the crazy man and Willadean. The bullet meant for Willa struck him in the chest.

As Pops hit the ground, he raised his beloved Josie, the ancient shotgun that had been on this earth far longer than Harlan himself, and unleashed her deadly beauty upon Willa's assailant. The shiny teeth within Wyatt's ghoulish grin exploded first. The second pump of the shotgun took off the top of his head.

When Harlan saw the blood, he reached toward the smallest child sitting nearby and placed a hand over her eyes.

***

"Can you save him?" Kenny asked. "Like you did for me?"

"Harlan!" Willa pleaded. "Snap out of it! Pops is dying! Do something!"

Harlan shook his head. He couldn't explain how he knew; he just did. The Shift confirmed there was no hope. His grandfather was gone.

"It's too late, Willa. And even if I could do something, he wouldn't want me to. He knew this was how it would end for him. Remember his letter? Everything he ever did was for his family. This was his final and bravest act of love."

He reached out and pulled her into a gentle hug.

Harlan was dog-tired, but he needed to do this for Willa. He found a pool of calm from somewhere within himself——his chest or maybe his brain; he really didn't know where exactly——and directed it into his sister.

Her reaction was instantaneous, although not the one he'd hoped for. She stopped screaming and switched to tears.

Chapter 40

Ray

"I may never get used to this stuff." Ray raised the mug to his lips and slurped a bit of liquid fire. "But I'll keep trying."

Fergus chuckled. "That's what I like about you, Ray. You're a tenacious bastard."

After enduring unimaginable stress these past few days and being pushed to the limit of his physical endurance, he'd earned this peaceful reprieve with his new friend. Everyone else had gone to bed early——deservedly so.

However, when he built a small campfire at the edge of the village and invited Fergus to join him for a late-night drink, he did have ulterior motives.

"Here," Ray said, handing a flask to Fergus. "It's the last of the Four Roses. Sadly, the rest of my bourbon was blown up."

Fergus took a sip. "Ahhh. Now that's what proper whiskey should taste like. Cheers!" He took a second gulp, then offered the flask back to Ray.

"Finish it," Ray said. "The Old Smoky is my future now, along with a lot of other rather dramatic changes."

"Indeed. So, she agreed to keep you around, did she?"

"I can't imagine why, but she did. And for that, I'm eternally grateful."

"I know why. You're a good man, Ray. One of the best I've met in all my travels." Fergus tipped the flask again, then gazed up at the star-filled sky. "Serena Jo sensed a diamond in the rough with you. She'll cut and polish your facets in no time, and just to her liking."

Ray laughed. "She's smart enough to know exactly how far she can push me, which is apparently pretty damn far. But there are things I won't do, even for her. She seems to instinctively know what they are. I think we'll make a great team."

"I agree, as long as you don't forget who's in charge." Fergus smiled.

"No fear of that."

"It's interesting. Since the pandemic, I've encountered several fledgling communities, and in almost each case, females were in charge. They're frequently smarter than us. If the women had always been in charge, perhaps we wouldn't be in the mess we're in now."

Ray's eyes narrowed. "That's good in theory, but as you told me recently, this whole thing——the pandemic, those who survived as part of some inexplicable natural selection——wasn't natural at all. You claimed it was orchestrated by ancient humans who live below the surface of the planet."

"Oh, right. I figured we'd have to circle back to that at some point. In hindsight, it wasn't even necessary to pull back the wizard's curtain. Dani convinced Serena Jo to accept her help without a pressure campaign from you."

"Yet you *did* pull back the curtain, and now I need you to clarify a few things."

"Like what?" Fergus took another long pull on the flask, then burped happily. He wasn't drunk, but he was homing in on tipsy.

"How much of that was bullshit? That thing Hannah did with the knife. Was it a trick? How did she pull it off? You must have been in on it."

The blue eyes twinkled. The beard twitched. But Fergus remained silent.

"Don't hold out on me. We've been through too much together. You owe me, Fergus."

"I beg to differ, Ray. I don't owe you anything. Actually, you have me to thank for your current romantic bliss. You're welcome."

"You said you broke an oath by telling me all that stuff. What oath? And to whom?"

Fergus blew out a long breath, burped again, then turned to face Ray.

"I'm going to explain a few things for one reason only: You're alive today because of Hannah. Because she *literally* brought you back from death, and every day you live on this earth should be seen as her gift to you."

"So the oath was to her?"

"No. The oath I took was to those ancient beings I described. They do exist, and the dwelling they built exists. It's located a few hundred feet below the surface of an unremarkable wheat field in the center of an unremarkable state. What abides beneath that wheat field is anything but unremarkable. When I was harvested more than ten thousand years ago ...”

"*What?* You're telling me you're ten thousand years old?”

Fergus placed a finger against his lips. "Don't interrupt a storyteller as he's hitting his groove. As I was saying, they brought me to that place. I was a wild-eyed, blue-faced barbarian back then, but the *Cthor* recruiter recognized that I was special. As, indeed, we all are." He made a sweeping motion with his hand. "They explained how everything worked and then they made me an offer I couldn't refuse: virtual immortality in exchange for a smidgen of my DNA and occasional forays above-ground to harvest more subjects in the years to come." He sighed and took another sip of the bourbon, then he placed his hand on Ray's shoulder.

A jolt of energy discharged from that hand into Ray's consciousness. With it came a tsunami of images and information and concepts, many of which Ray couldn't begin to grasp.

But two final insights came through which he could: Fergus wasn't tipsy at all, and he wasn't lying about any of this. With every fiber of his being, Ray realized this incredible, farfetched, *insane* story was utterly true.

"Holy shit."

"Right. I'm tired. It was easier doing that than trying to sweet talk you."

Ray fell back in his chair, speechless.

"I had actually decided to leave you in the dark and sneak away before you could verbally pummel the truth out of me with intoxicating lubricants and persuasive speeches. But something happened that changed that."

"What?"

"This one," Fergus jerked a thumb toward the gloom behind him. "He's the other reason I decided to enlighten you about life's mysteries."

Harlan glided into the firelight. "Hi, Mister Fergus. Hi, Mister Ray."

"Aren't you supposed to be in bed?" Ray somehow managed a semi-normal tone. His thoughts were still a whirlwind.

"I'm leaving with Mister Fergus," Harlan said. "He's taking me with him to the underground place."

Ray jumped out of his chair. "Oh no he's not! What the hell, Fergus?"

"He wants to go, and he belongs there. His gifts are the rarest I've ever seen. More importantly, he won't feel like a freak there. The place is filled with people just like him."

"I won't allow it!"

"It's not even remotely your decision."

"Does Serena Jo know about this? She couldn't possibly. She'd never allow her child to be taken from her."

"She'll know soon. And in the kindest way possible."

Ray ignored Fergus and knelt in front of the child. The boy's unusual eyes gleamed like gilded marbles in the firelight.

"Your mother will be devastated, Harlan. You can't believe this is a good decision."

Harlan smiled, then wrapped his arms around Ray's neck. "It's the best decision ever."

Chapter 41

Fergus

"We're walking the entire way?" Harlan asked.

"No, I expect the bus to appear at any moment," Fergus replied as they traipsed along the faded blacktop of westbound Interstate I70. "Ah, there it is now."

The engine of an F150 diesel rumbled from behind. The pickup rolled to a stop beside them, and the driver's window glided down.

"Hop in, my dudes," Dani said with a wolfish grin. She truly was in her element out here in the metaphorical Wild West. Perhaps killing a few dozen bad guys would quell her primal urges for a while.

"It's just going to be the boy," Fergus said, taking Harlan's small hands into his own.

Harlan closed his eyes. "Ah, okay," he said a few seconds later. "Will you tell Amelia thank you from me? She sure gave me a lot of good advice over the years."

"Now there will be others just like her who can give you more good advice in the years to come."

Harlan glanced at Dani and Sam in the truck, then whispered to Fergus, "Am I really going to live forever?"

"Only if that is your wish."

"That's not your wish?"

"Not any longer. This is the right path for you, son. Don't doubt it for a second."

"Oh, I don't. I'm excited about not being a weirdo anymore."

Fergus smiled. "You were never a weirdo. You were always incredibly special."

"What is this I'm hearing?" Dani cut in. "You're not coming? I'm not running a damn daycare, Lucky Charms."

Fergus snorted. "It'll just be for the ride to Liberty. Harlan will be collected there."

"Collected? What the hell, Fergus?"

Harlan gave Fergus a wink, then reached his arms toward Dani. After a few seconds of Harlan's impulsive hug, she calmed down.

"Get your butt in here, kid. I'll take you to Kansas, but if at any point you ask me if we're there yet, I'll strap you to the tailgate."

Harlan smiled and clambered into the back seat. As they drove away, Harlan's voice wafted through the window.

"By the way, Mister Sam, congratulations!"

***

"About time, you sexy beast," said Amelia, who wore nothing but a smile.

A bit more silver threaded her dark braids now, but she looked as beautiful as ever. A glass-smooth turquoise sea and pastel sunset provided the perfect backdrop for his beloved. He took a full five minutes to breathe it all in.

She gazed at him affectionately while he indulged himself. His brand new, vastly shortened life was getting off to a delightful start. What better way to launch into the beginning of the end than with an energetic romp on the beach?

Fergus growled in a way he hadn't since living on the rocky coastline of a wet, chilly land somewhere well beyond the tranquil ocean that lay before him.

He swept Amelia into his arms and made himself a promise he hoped he could keep:

I will never leave her side again.

Chapter 42

Willadean

"Please don't cry, Mama. You'll see him again. He promised me he'd be back for regular visits. And look," she pointed to a paragraph in Harlan's letter. "He said it may be as early as summer. That's just a few months from now."

Mama looked at her like she'd lost her ever-loving mind. Willa sighed, then glanced at Mister Ray, who gave her a terse head-shake. The two had agreed that Mama could never know Mister Ray had known anything about Harlan's decision to go live with the Cave People.

They weren't really cave people, but because they lived in some bizarre underground cavern, that's the name Willa gave them in her head. Even if she had qualified to go, she would not have chosen to. There was too much of Hannah in her blood to willingly live under the conditions Harlan described.

"I'm going after him," Mama said, jumping from the kitchen chair so suddenly she knocked it over. Her tear-streaked face was a picture of agony.

"There's something else I need to tell you, Mama," Willa said. "Please, sit down and let me give you a hug first."

Willa took several deep breaths and concentrated on the calming technique Harlan had taught her. She'd practiced on Mister Ray before giving Mama the letter. Mister Ray fell asleep within a few seconds, so she figured she was already pretty good at it.

Just as she was pretty damn good at everything she set her mind to.

Since Kenny had decided to stay in the village, he would be her next project. If he planned on being her boyfriend someday, there were a few rough edges she'd need to polish first.

Chapter 43

Willadean

"Do you think the Whitakers will ever accept the new folks?" Ray asked as they were getting ready for bed.

Serena Jo had declared the word "Murdock" off limits, just like swear words. When the Idlewild survivors were absorbed into the village, resentment had bubbled up on both sides. But the survivors didn't have a choice other than to join their ranks. They would have starved to death before spring without their kinfolk to provide for them. All that remained of the Murdock clan consisted of half-starved kids, traumatized females, and the six teenage boys who'd had the sense to desert when they saw an opportunity.

"Yes, I do. But it won't happen overnight. Everyone will just have to suck it up."

"Thelma seems to appreciate the extra help in the kitchen house. Don't tell her, but I think Louise's cornbread is better than hers."

"We'll keep that to ourselves. I don't want the new folks to feel like second-class citizens, but in some ways, they are. They don't have the skill sets we Whitakers have. There were a lot of reasons why we looked down on them. Eventually, they'll have to prove themselves, just like everyone else did."

Ray nodded, crawling into bed beside her. On Saturdays and Wednesdays, Serena Jo spent the night with him in his newly decked-out cabin: he was now the proud owner of a 50s-era kitchen table, a half-cord of firewood he'd chopped himself, and a lovely tea set. Serena Jo provided the coffee.

"Was Willadean terrorizing the babysitter when you left?" Ray asked with a smile.

"Oh, yes. I had to pay the poor girl with my last bottle of lavender body wash. Hope you don't mind cedar and soapwort."

"You could roll around in bear scat and I'd still want you."

Serena Jo laughed.

"It's been a while since I've heard that sound."

She stopped smiling suddenly, and her eyes turned misty.

Stupid, Ray!

She sighed. "I can't explain it, but I know Harlan's okay. I can feel him out there. I know Willa can, too; she has the twin connection. But what I feel goes beyond that. I swear, it's like I receive thoughts in my head that are coming directly from him."

Ray kept his face impassive. "What does he tell you?"

"He says he's happy. That he's learning all kinds of wonderful things. That he's made new friends who are just like him. He promises me he'll come for a visit in June. That's what I cling to. That's what keeps me from losing my mind, although I'm sure you think that ship has sailed."

"I believe every word."

"You're just saying that to get into my pants." She gave him a shaky smile.

"Did it work?"

"It would have if I were wearing any," she whispered, then blew out the lantern.

Epilogue

"Gah, this hurts!" Dani said through clenched teeth.

Sam gently swabbed her face with a cool cloth. "You're a tough cream puff. You can handle it."

"I can't believe I let you talk me into this!"

"I didn't. You decided all by yourself. I just happened to be in the right place at the time."

"Hey, you got it right!"

"Got what right?"

"Never mind. Another contraction is building. If I say something horrible in the next couple of minutes, don't take it personally."

Sam looked into her ravaged face with more love than she'd ever seen. Yes, he'd always loved her with all his heart. But now that heart would expand to make room for two.

"I never take anything you say personally. It's a survival mechanism."

Dani barked a laugh that turned into a growl of pain.

"You're gonna owe me big time," she said when the contraction passed. The pains were getting closer. The ankle-biter would arrive right on schedule.

"I already owe you, Dani. I love you so much sometimes my chest hurts. I owe you for that love, and I owe you for this new one, too. I guess I'll always be a deadbeat since I can never repay you for any of it."

She reached for his hand and kissed it just as another contraction began.

"You can bite my hand if you need to. I heal fast, so bite away."

She didn't bite, but she considered it.

When he saw the pain had faded, he leaned in and whispered in her ear, "*Be comforted. The world is very old. And generations pass, as they have passed, a troop of shadows moving with the sun. Thousands of times has the old tale been told. The world belongs to those who come the last. They will find hope and strength as we have done."*

"Where did you hear that? Oh, I know. Pablo!"

Sam nodded. "Our family, our *generation,* our *troop of shadows* ... we're all going to be just fine. I promise."

The End

Excerpt from Demon Chase

If you enjoyed the Troop of Shadows Chronicles, you will probably like my latest series, A Monstrous Dread. Here's an excerpt from book one in the series, *Demon Chase*.

Ida Grove, Nebraska

Jillian realized she was down to minutes now, but precisely how many? Eluding malevolent supernatural beings wasn't an exact science and never would be, no matter how meticulously she planned or how carefully she lived her life.

She crammed socks, toothpaste, a grimoire, and a silver crucifix into a duffel, then slammed the motel door behind her. She slid behind Prudence's steering wheel and fired up the beast of an engine. A few seconds later she was squealing out of the parking lot, eyes glued to the no-frills motel reflected in the rearview mirror. She floored the gas pedal the moment rubber treads connected with highway asphalt.

One Mississippi...two Mississippi...three Mississippi...

The orange metal door of Chambre 12 at the La Parisienne Motor Inn blew off its hinges and into the former parking space of the fleeing Taurus. Chunks of moulding and tarnished brass hardware littered a future crime scene. The local sheriff's department would classify the destruction as a potential terrorist attack, but at least they wouldn't have to call an ambulance or a coroner's wagon.

"Too damn close," she muttered to the mirror.

Flying westbound along NE-2 at Prudence's top speed of 137 mph, Jillian was thankful for the early hour. At six o'clock on a Sunday morning, she had the road all to herself—lucky for her, but luckier for fellow motorists. Monitoring the ribbon of asphalt unfurling through the windshield, she reached for the glove box. Fingers slid across the Glock 19, then latched onto one of the burner phones.

"Hey, Stan, do me a favor and pass your phone to my brother."

"No can do, Ms. Beaufort. You know the rules."

Damn it. She pulled up her t-shirt, keeping one hand mostly on the wheel, then snapped a pic of her boobs. The plain Jane bra covered the nips, thus conserving a modicum of her self-respect. Or maybe a smidgen. Possibly a crumb.

"Just sent it. Will you please give him the phone now?"

"I guess, but next time I want something in black with a bit of lace."

"Fuck off, Stan."

"Fucking off now, Jill. Here's your brother."

"Don't call me tha—" she started to say, but Stan was already gone. She winced at the loud thuds of the phone traveling through Jackson's food tray opening.

"Hello, Jillian." Her twin's voice felt like a whiskey shot tastes, warm and soothing with the suggestion of danger.

"How's it going, Jackson?"

"Can't complain."

"You never do. I'm not sure I would be as stoic in your situation."

"I'm where I need to be."

"I don't agree." She knew from experience he would now change the subject.

"That business at the motel was too close for comfort."

"No shit."

A frustrated grunt huffed through the speaker. "Maybe don't let it get down to the wire like that."

"Maybe mind your own business." As soon as the words tumbled out, she wanted to claw them back and cram them down her stupid pie hole. "Sorry."

"Forget it. You're heading north, like we talked about?"

Her palms tingled, a weirdo version of standing neck hairs. Other than Stan, was there someone or something in Jackson's proximity tripping her internal warning system? Or had she merely cruised through the lingering spirit of someone killed on this lonely stretch of highway? 'Tingling palms' weren't terribly precise in predicting danger that could come from multiple directions.

"Yeah, just like we talked about," she said. "You still think it's a good option?"

"For now."

"Roger that. I'll check back when I can."

She rolled down the passenger window and heaved the phone into the fringe of a fallow wheatfield. Farmer Brown wouldn't find that phone until spring. And with luck, neither would the things that chased her.

Continue reading Demon Chase here.

Your Opinion?

What did you think of *Those Who Come the Last*?

If you didn't like the book, please tell me... if you did like the book, please tell everyone. My email address is: nicki@nickihuntsmansmith.com.

If you liked the book, please leave a review. Studies have shown that most readers say reviews (both the number of reviews as well as the rating) are an important factor in their buying decision. Please take 2-3 minutes to leave a review.

Here's a link to Amazons review page for *Those Who Come the Last*.
    https://www.amazon.com/review/create-review?&asin=B09V489WLN

You can follow me on Facebook at:
    https://www.facebook.com/AuthorNickiHuntsmanSmith/

You can signup for my newsletter at:
    https://nickihuntsmansmith.com/webs. My subscribers are the first to know of a new release.

I look forward to hearing from you!
Nicki Huntsman Smith

All Nicki Huntsman Smith Books

All my books are enrolled in the Amazon Kindle Unlimited program. So if you are a Kindle Unlimited member, like me, you can read all my books for free.

DEMON CHASE- Book 1 in A Monstrous Dread SeriesA nail-biting, supernatural suspense horror series begins with DEMON CHASE.

TROUBLED SPIRITS – Book 2 in A Monstrous Dread Series – The thrills continue in Wyoming

A DIFFERENT KIND OF MONSTER – Book 3 in A Monstrous Dread Series – Not all monsters are demons...(Estimated publication date is February, 2024)

SUBLIME SEVEN Time Travel with a Transcendent TwistFollow the evolution of a soul as told through seven incarnations on earth and beyond.

TROOP OF SHADOWS – Book 1 in the Troop of Shadows ChroniclesA riveting, multi-character post-apocalyptic journey starts here with Book One.

BEAUTY AND DREAD – Book 2 in the Troop of Shadows SeriesThe second installment in the Troop of Shadows Chronicles follows the characters you loved (and hated) in Book One.

MOVING WITH THE SUN – Book 3 in the Troop of Shadows Chronicles SeriesThe third installment in the series takes place in Florida and introduces a new cast of characters, along with some old favorites.

WHAT BEFALLS THE CHILDREN – Book 4 in the Troop of Shadows Chronicles SeriesThe fourth installment in the series takes place in Appalachia and introduces new characters to love and hate, along with an old favorite.

THOSE WHO COME THE LAST – Book 5 in the Troop of Shadows

Chronicles SeriesThe fifth book in the series returns to Whitaker Holler where two adversarial clans finally determine the fate of their people once and for all.

DEAD LEAVES, DARK CORNERS – A collection of short storiesAn eclectic assortment of nail-biting short stories and one spine-tingling novelette.

SECRETS UNDER THE MESAA pinch of "X-Files" and a dash of "Stranger Things.

Report Typos and Errors Here

Thank you for helping make my books error free. I have tried to make it a s simple as possible to report any type of error you might have found.

If you click on the link below, you will be taken to my website where I have a form specifically designed to capture the error information.

If you are on on a Kindle or any other type of ereader you can just click on the link. If you are reading a paperback, you will need to type in the URL.

Report all errors here:
https://nickihuntsmansmith.com/errata

Made in United States
Orlando, FL
14 January 2024